THE CASE OF THE FICKLE MERMAID

A BROTHERS GRIMM MYSTERY

P. J. BRACKSTON

PEGASUS CRIME

NEW YORK LONDON

For my dear friend Maddy Westlake,
because to think of her is to smile.

THE CASE OF THE FICKLE MERMAID

Pegasus Crime is an Imprint of
Pegasus Books LLC
80 Broad Street, 5th Floor
New York, NY 10004

Copyright © 2016 by P. J. Brackston

First Pegasus Books cloth edition January 2016

Interior design by Maria Fernandez

Library of Congress Cataloging-in-Publication Data is available.

ISBN: 978-1-60598-946-4

10 9 8 7 6 5 4 3 2 1

Printed in the United States of America
Distributed by W. W. Norton & Company

ONE

The ship certainly was impressive. Gretel was aware that docked vessels were apt to appear large, as one was more accustomed to seeing them on a distant horizon. Even allowing for this, however, the four-masted cruise ship that now towered above her was still magnificent. A shiver of excitement rattled up her spine, causing the stays of her corset to creak, as if they were emitting faint, ghostly cries to warn their brethren of the likely fate of whalebone in these parts. In her idle moments—which some might say were many, but which she considered all too scarce—she had often dreamed of taking a cruise. At such times her beloved tapestry daybed had become a sumptuous cot in a spacious stateroom, lilting gently with the swell of the summer ocean, the sound of lapping waves and crying seabirds her lullaby, and the smell of expertly prepared seafood at once both calming and stimulating. She had drifted into most pleasing fantasies of sunsets reflected on the balmy sea; of promenading on deck in her very best gowns; of dining on fine food in the company of an equally fine captain; of evenings of erudite and glamorous entertainment. Which meant that the decision to take on the case at hand had not been a difficult one. When the messenger gull, sent by the captain himself, had arrived at her home in Gesternstadt with a request for her services as a private detective, she had known at once that she would accept.

"I say, sister mine, these trunks are exceedingly heavy. What on earth have you got in here?"

Alas, Gretel's vision of her elegant and sophisticated cruise had not included the very broad, very Bavarian, and, in her opinion, very irksome presence of her brother.

"Stop whining, Hans. I told you to fetch a porter."

"There are none to be had. All snapped up by the regular cruise-goers who know what they are about."

As if to underline his point, an expensively turned-out couple swooshed by in a cloud of powder and perfume, followed by designer trunks and cases stacked high on trolleys pushed by panting porters. Gretel sighed. It would have been so much easier, so much cheaper, and so much all-around nicer without Hans to cramp her style. How could she hope to be accepted into the upper circles of high society while accompanied by a brother who practically had "Provincial and Proud of It" stamped in India ink on his forehead? Each time work required her to travel, Gretel promised herself she would not allow Hans to tag along, and yet each and every time, she found herself traveling *à deux*. Hans always contrived some reason, some mitigating circumstance, some bargaining chip with which to plead his case. On this occasion he had insisted that she could not possibly make the dauntingly long journey from Gesternstadt through the greater part of Germany to the port of Bremerhaven alone. It was too far and too dangerous. Gretel had maintained that his being there would do nothing to make the journey any shorter, and that she had rescued *him* from danger on many more occasions than he had ever come close to rescuing her. Hans had countered that she would be journeying farther afield than ever before, no doubt encountering all manner of nefarious ruffians, villains, and nincompoops. She declared that she failed to see how adding to their number by taking him along would help. His response to this had been two days of pouting and petulance, during which time not a door in the house remained unslammed. At last she had capitulated, in part to save them from a hefty carpentry bill, but mostly because, though it pained her to admit it even to herself, he had a point. A woman traveling alone was prey to all manner of unwanted attention. This was a business trip, and time and the tide at Bremerhaven waited for no man, woman, or private detective. If she was to be on board the *Arabella* when she set sail for her second cruise of the summer season, she could not afford to be delayed or hindered en route. Hans, using nothing other than his size, might just deter bothersome opportunists.

Whether or not he was the reason she had been able to make her journey unmolested she would never know for certain, but the desired result was all that really mattered, and the pair had arrived at Bremerhaven in good time.

"Come along, Hans, don't dawdle."

"Dash it all, Gretel, I'm doing my best. Why a person has to travel with so much in the way of luggage I can't fathom."

"Fortunately, you are not required to understand. Ah, here we are." They reached the gangway leading from the dockside up onto the ship. A smartly uniformed young sailor clutching a scroll of names stepped forward.

"Your name, please, fraulein?" he asked.

"I am Gretel of Gesternstadt. Yes, *that* Gretel," she added, to fend off the inevitable question. "I am here at the request of the captain of this good ship, who is expecting me, so I should be grateful if I might board swiftly. I assume there is someone who will show us to our quarters?"

But the youth was shaking his head. "Forgive me, fraulein, but you are not listed here."

"What? Not?"

"Not?" echoed Hans wearily from behind the trunks.

"I'm afraid not." The sailor paled at the darkening expression on Gretel's face.

"There must be some mistake. Kindly check again. Gretel of Gesternstadt, a two-berth cabin reserved on the *Arabella* departing this very day."

"The *Arabella*? But, fraulein, this is not the *Arabella*."

"Not?"

"Not?" puffed Hans, beginning to teeter beneath the weight of the luggage.

"This is the *Fair Fortune*, flagship of the Thorsten Sommer fleet. The *Arabella* is moored over there."

Gretel turned to follow the direction in which the young man pointed. She lifted the silver lorgnettes from where they rested upon her sturdy bosom and put them to her eyes. She knew she should not be surprised. This was, after all, the way of things. Something splendid and beautiful and thrilling was dangled in front of her, only to be whipped away and replaced by something altogether plainer and more mundane. The *Arabella* was not, in truth, a poor ship. She looked sound enough, and solid enough, and big enough. But she was not elegant. She was not stylish. She was not the sort of ship that had sailed so serenely through the silky waters of Gretel's fantasies. Where the *Fair Fortune* had burnished mahogany masts with shiny brass fitments and finials, the *Arabella* had a workaday, tarry look to her. Where the *Fair Fortune* sported a high-end finish to her flags and bunting, her ropes and tackle, her balustrades and handrails and gleaming portholes, the *Arabella* opted for a no-nonsense, no-frills, handsome-is-as-handsome-does decor. Indeed, each ship could be summed up by its figurehead. On the prow of the *Fair Fortune* rode an exquisitely carved Botticelli-like beauty, with a refined brow, gentle gaze, and decorously positioned robe. The *Arabella* would apparently be led out to sea by a woman with the dress sense of a harlot, the muscular arms of a stevedore, and a hard look in her eye to match. Gretel wondered that she did not have a pipe clenched between her teeth.

After trudging a short way farther along the quay and wobbling up the alarmingly narrow gangplank to board the correct vessel, Gretel directed Hans to find his way to their cabin and install himself and the luggage there.

"Oh?" Hans paused to lean heavily against the largest trunk, dabbing at his sweat-beaded brow with a gray handkerchief. "And what will you be doing while I am carting your entire wardrobe hither and yon?"

"I shall find the captain and introduce myself."

"Can't I just leave everything here for now? I mean to say, a man needs his refreshment, after so much traveling, and such like . . ." He trailed off under Gretel's glare.

"Hans, do I need to remind you that this is a business trip? That I am here to do work, for which I hope to be paid? And that if I am not able to concentrate on the task in hand I might not prove effective, and so that payment might not be forthcoming . . . have you considered the consequences of such an outcome for yourself?"

"Not too many evenings at the inn, I should imagine."

"Not for a very long time. Now, do as I ask. You shall get to the bar soon enough, I promise."

The main deck of the *Arabella* did nothing to alter Gretel's view of the ship. For the most part it was concerned with matters entirely to do with sailing, rather than the needs of those aboard in the capacity of cruisers. Such concessions as had been made to comfort were scant. There were, here and there, seats on which to sit and take in the sea views, some wooden and fixed, others of the stripy-cloth-reclining variety. A worn and incomplete set of deck quoits took up an unimportant corner. Nothing more was offered. Sailors clambered up rigging and over bollards and so forth in large numbers. The crew did not wear uniforms but a muddled mix of rustic sailor's garb and working clothes, giving no indication as to the rank or function of the wearer. This troubled Gretel. How was she expected to know whom to ask for a plate of sandwiches, and whom to address as "Captain"? A grubby fellow in baggy trousers and a short-sleeved shirt—the better to display his bulging muscles and bold tattoos, no doubt—raised his head from his job of coiling rope to stare at her. Gretel tried her brightest smile.

"Would you be so kind as to tell me where I might find the captain?" she asked.

The sailor straightened slowly, his eyes narrowing in suspicion.

"Thar'll find he aft," he growled. "Him's cabin lies 'neath the poop," he continued in the manner of one addressing a simpleton. "To the stern, woman. To the stern!" He jerked his head in the direction of the back of the ship before returning his full attention to the rope.

Gretel was still attempting to unravel the mouthful of seemingly unrelated and incomprehensible words when a loud, commanding voice nearly blasted her off her feet.

"Gretel of Gesternstadt! Here you are, and a sight for sore eyes, if I may say so."

She turned to find, standing some way off, his hand on the wheel of the ship, Captain Tobias Ziegler. He cut a fine figure, with a scarlet coat, tight-fitting and silver-braided, and a feathered tricorn of French navy, which seemed splendidly appropriate. From where she stood Gretel could make out an abundant beard; fine, strong features; and dark, dark eyes capable of a powerful gaze. The captain descended from what she would later learn was the poop deck, dropping down the stairs, a hand on either rail, his feet not once touching the polished wooden steps. In an instant he was by her side, the hat whisked from his head to reveal an impressive head of glossy black ringlets, which were loosely secured at the nape. He bowed low, making an unnecessary show of the whole business. Despite her inclination to dislike such showmanship, Gretel found herself snatching her fan from her skirt pocket and working it beneath her chin.

"Captain Ziegler." She nodded.

"You are welcome, fraulein. Welcome aboard the good ship *Arabella*."

"I am pleased to be here, and ready to offer my assistance in the mysterious matter of the mermaids."

At this the captain's demeanor altered at once. All courtesies abandoned, he stepped forward and grabbed Gretel by the elbow, roughly steering her to a less populated area of the deck.

"Have a care, fraulein!" he hissed. "My men are spooked enough as things are. It will not go well with them to know I have required assistance in searching out the truth of these sightings. They must not know what you are about. I entreat you, be discreet in your work."

Gretel pulled her arm free and took up her lorgnettes to better inspect her new client. At such close range and with the aid of her glasses, she saw an altogether different fellow. His lean physique remained, but the red coat was clearly military issue of some sort, and had a disturbing patch over the heart, the size and shape of a hole one might imagine a musket ball would produce. The feathers of the hat were not glamorous plumes; rather they appeared to have been plucked directly from a variety of passing seabirds and farmyard fowl. The beard, while manly, was worryingly unkempt, and she suspected that the gloss on the captain's ringlets was not the result of good health and vitality, but of oil of some kind. Or possibly grease. Human or otherwise.

"I assure you, sir, I am the very embodiment of discretion. My inquiries will be thorough, diligent, and successful, but not, I stress, via slipshod methods. I must assume it was my reputation that prompted you to engage my services. That reputation is dearer to me than my own brother, and I would do nothing to dent it."

"That is good to hear indeed." The captain relaxed sufficiently to treat Gretel to a broad smile. The instant he did so, she was assaulted by a jolt of memory. The sight of his white but unusual teeth, two of which crossed slightly, in his brown face, with those deep-set eyes, combined to stir some long-forgotten knowledge. Stir it, as a creature on the sea floor might stir the fine sand, sending up a cloud of confusion and murk. What that memory was would not reveal itself to her completely. Not yet. She made a mental note to return to sift through those swirling sands in the next available quiet moment.

The captain went on, "May I suggest you let it be thought you are here for a recreational cruise, nothing more?"

"In which case you must resist using my name loudly when we may be heard lest someone recognize it," she warned him. "As to the notion of recreation, I am already breathless with anticipation of the delights and comforts that sailing on the *Arabella* might offer me."

If Captain Ziegler detected any mockery in her words, he chose not to show it. Lowering his voice once more, he said, "This voyage must be a success, fraulein. Word has spread of the disappearance of my two crewmembers, and there are whispers of mermaids even now. It don't take much to put off paying customers, that's the truth of it. And my lads are getting windy. Mermaids are bad luck for sailors, and some will likely jump ship if there are more reports of the fishy little maidens singing in these waters."

"I sense you do not share their fear of the . . . creatures?"

"I do not. There's not a thing alive has scales that ever frighted Tobias Ziegler. There is room aplenty in the ocean for us all, don't you think?"

"Admirable sentiments, captain. Though for myself, I prefer the idea of *on* rather than *in* the ocean."

A commotion concerning the loading of supplies took away the captain's attention. "I must tend to my ship, fraulein. Pray excuse me, we will talk more anon."

"One more thing before you go . . . you do not believe that the missing crewmembers were scared away by the notion of the mermaids? You suspect something other will explain their disappearance?"

"I do. And I am prepared to pay handsomely to discover what that something may be. My very livelihood depends upon it."

"Be at peace, Captain Ziegler, you have come to the right person for help." She watched him stride away to give commands to his crew. He was a man of some presence, some appeal even, though his charms were, to Gretel's eye, a smidge too rough around the edges, lacking in refinement. It was clear, as she watched him go about his mastering of the ship, however, that he had the respect and even the affection of his crew. She noticed also her fellow passengers drifting somewhat restlessly, no doubt as impatient as she was to set sail and be off. There was a small man alone, in sensible clothing, who gazed intently out to sea; a young couple, so enraptured by each other that they might as well have been in a cave for all the interest they took in their surroundings; and a trio of women of a certain age at the far end of the ship, busily working their fans and twirling their parasols in a manner altogether too coquettish for their years. What other cruise-goers there were remained belowdecks, and Gretel suspected some might take a day or two to find their sea legs.

All at once, she found that the strains of such a long journey and many days traveling had caught up with her. She needed a little lie-down and a reviving glass of something before changing for dinner. She was on the point of moving, when something on the very periphery of her vision snagged her attention. She turned, not certain what she had seen or what she expected to find, but knowing there had been something. Yet when she searched the rigging and sails she could see nothing that fitted the glimpse of movement, the fleeting flash of color she had noticed. She peered upward through her lorgnettes, but still there was nothing. With a sigh she decided fatigue was adversely affecting her eyesight. She selected the cleanest-looking crewmember within reach and tapped him on the shoulder with her silver glasses.

"Be so good as to take me to my cabin, would you? A two-berth. Gretel of Gesternstadt. See if you can't find out where I am to be billeted."

The youth had a pleasant face and cheery manner that would surely fade in proportion to the passing years, particularly if he was to serve them on board a ship of such base company, Gretel felt.

"Of course, fraulein. This way, if you please," he said, scampering ahead.

"You are in possession of a list of guests and their allocated cabins?" Gretel had to hurry to keep up as the boy dashed down a flight of stairs so steep they could better have been called a ladder.

"No, fraulein," he talked over his shoulder as he led her along increasingly narrow corridors and down yet more steps, "and it would do me no good if I were, for I cannot read a word. But I know where the passengers are berthed. Follow me, if you please."

They dropped down still another deck, so that Gretel feared they would soon be in the hold.

"Are you sure this is correct? If we descend any farther we must surely find ourselves below the waterline."

The boy laughed at this. "Oh, no, fraulein! However could the cannons have been fired if they were not above the water?"

"The cannons?"

The boy had come to a halt in a passageway so narrow that even his slender frame nearly filled it. Gretel was uncomfortably aware of the walls pressing in on her.

"Yes, fraulein. When the ship was converted, the deck that used to house the cannons was given over for passenger berths so that the holes they once fired through could be fixed up as portholes. And very good ones they make, too. I am certain you will be pleased."

Before Gretel had time to process this information, he ducked into a cupboard and gestured that she should pass.

"Everyone else is aboard and has taken their cabins. There is one left for you at the end of the passage."

A glance showed her a stack of luggage filling the corridor and she recognized it as her own.

"Thank you," she said to the boy, pressing a coin into his palm. "Give me your name, in case I have need of you again."

"It is Will, fraulein. Thank you very much, fraulein!" So saying, he darted back the way he had come, carried swiftly up the stairs by his springy young legs and boyish enthusiasm for life.

Gretel squeezed herself onward until she was forced to stop by her own trunks.

"Hans!" she called out. "Where the devil are you?"

The narrow door opened. Hans's bulk entirely filled the frame. "You took your time. Thirsty work being an unpaid porter, you know."

"Why is the luggage still out here?"

He raised his arms as far as space would allow—which is to say barely at all—in a gesture of helplessness.

"It's it or us. We won't all fit."

"What? Nonsense. Let me see. Stand aside."

"There is no side."

"Hans, for pity's sake, don't be so difficult. Let me in!"

There followed a moment of squeezing and squashing during which Gretel was forced into a proximity with her sibling she had never been compelled to endure before, and would walk a very long way to avoid having to do ever again. At last, with a gasp and a popping sound, she gained entry into the cabin. "Small" was too big a word for it. She tried thinking of it as *bijou* in the hope that it might sound a little bigger and a little more sophisticated. It didn't work. She realized now that what she had taken for a cupboard when Will had stepped out of her path must have been another berth of similarly skimpy dimensions. There were two bunk beds, which ran the length of the space. The gap between the lower and the upper looked generous only when compared to the gap between the upper and the ceiling, which had evidently been designed to accommodate a person with neither bosom nor belly. Which ruled both her and Hans out. A tiny table was fixed into one corner, and beneath it sat a tiny stool, its silk cushion fooling no one as to its rustic provenance. On the far wall—where "far" is taken to mean the distance a person could easily spit should they feel so inclined (which Gretel did)—was the promised porthole. Its brass fitments were pleasant enough, and daylight did fall through it onto the threadbare rug. Sadly, the fact that it was at ankle height rendered it useless for viewing the outside world. Which was already beginning to feel like a distant memory. The cabin was, naturally, constructed entirely of wood, worn and polished by use over many years, so that Gretel had the impression she was standing inside a much-traveled packing crate. Or possibly a coffin. She gave a shiver. All thoughts of languishing on her bed while sipping a little brandy vanished.

Hans put a cigar in his mouth and took from his pocket his new silver lighter. He had purchased the modern device especially for the voyage, reasoning that sea breezes might extinguish a match too easily. He flicked at the flint striker with his thumb.

"Hans, if you start puffing cigar smoke about the place, the air in here will be used up entirely in a matter of moments."

"Oh? Now I am to be denied the smallest of pleasures?"

Gretel pushed him through the door. "Come along," she said, following him out. "We are in urgent need of three things. Air, ale, and an upgrade!"

TWO

The saloon bar on board the *Arabella* was a low-ceilinged room that had all the charm and appeal of a forgotten roadside tavern.

"Ah!" declared Hans. "This is more like it. Just what a fellow needs. My good man," he addressed the barman, "some of your finest ale, if you please." He slid onto a barstool with a nimbleness that belied his size. Gretel cautiously took up her perch opposite. The stools were sufficiently high that, once mounted, they raised the sitter uncomfortably close to the ceiling. Gretel decided this was not a room in which she would be wearing her fabulous new wig. The glorious object, a present to herself after her recent testing work in Nuremberg, sat snugly in its

14

box in her cabin, awaiting its moment to debut. It demanded altogether more glamorous surroundings than the ship had so far revealed, such that Gretel began to fear that she might not have the opportunity to wear it, nor some of the more elaborate new gowns she had purchased for the cruise.

"Here you are, sir, and for you, madam." The barman placed two tall glasses of beer in front of them. He was a slender man, presentable, well groomed, and attentive. The perfect combination for a barman.

Gretel raised her glass to him. "Your good health," she said before downing half her drink in thirsty swallows. She dabbed foam from her lips with a lace handkerchief. "Your accent . . . I could not help but notice . . . is it English, perhaps?"

"Madam has a keen ear! I hail from a small coastal town named Brighton, though I have not seen the shores of old England for many years now."

Hans drained his glass and banged it down on the bar. "Ah! Most acceptable. Another, barkeep!" he demanded, adding a loud belch as punctuation.

Gretel frowned. "Forgive my brother. We have had a long and dusty journey. His manners are a little frayed."

"Madam, think nothing of it. My sensibilities have gained a hardy veneer, I assure you." He leaned close, glancing around the half-empty room before confiding, "When first I took up my post as steward on the *Arabella*, I confess I was shocked. Oh!" He rolled his eyes heavenward. "You would not believe the uncouthness and obscenities I endured!"

"Ah, from the crew, no doubt."

"Crew, passengers, captain." He flicked his bar towel expressively. "I had never heard the like. I swear it is as if being on a ship puts it into a person's head that he may let slip the observance of the niceties and refinements that make this rough and ready life through which we must pass tolerable. Ooh, my word, my goodness, I cannot begin to tell you," he said, shaking his head and picking up a glass to polish it with vigor.

"Indeed." Gretel nodded. "I have heard it said that those traveling abroad for recreational purposes often omit to pack among their luggage their Usual Standards and Dignity."

"Madam, it is true! Or if they bring them with them, I see no evidence of it. Dignity? Upon my word!"

Gretel and Hans both stole a glance at the company in the bar. All seemed entirely respectable and subdued.

Guessing their thoughts, the barman added, "Oh, they can all show a little restraint in port. You wait till we set sail." He polished on, the glass in his hand gleaming. "Ooh, yes. Once we are at sea, that's when people show their true colors."

"How interesting." She leaned forward, hoping to draw him into further confidences. "Tell me, Steward, are there any better cabins than the ones on the lower deck? We seem to have been allocated somewhat inadequate accommodation."

"Ooh, well, madam, there is only the captain's cabin. Far as I know there's nothing more. We crew must make do with hammocks in the hold." Here he tutted and rolled his eyes again. "Such bedfellows!"

Gretel nodded sympathetically. "You seem to me like a man who knows what's what, knows what's going on. I heard that the ship's company is reduced by two. Did you know the crewmembers who are . . . no longer here?"

The steward's eyes flashed. "I did not, madam, as I am recently come to this ship, but I heard tell. One was a fine steward of many years' experience, the other a lookout boy of tender age. No explanation was given for their leaving. It is as if they simply vanished!"

"That must have been most distressing for the rest of the crew."

"There is unrest among them, madam, I would not be truthful if I told you otherwise."

"There must have been rumors . . ." She sipped more of her ale, allowing the barman time to consider how much to tell her. In her years as a detective, she had learned to spot those who lived to talk; who thrived on gossip; who never forgot an overheard word or a glimpse of odd behavior. Such a man could prove most useful in her investigations. At that moment, however, a stout figure entered the bar. He had about him an unmissable air of authority and a stern visage, the full force of which he turned upon the steward, silencing him instantly. Gretel did not allow irritation to take hold. There would be time enough to visit the bar again.

"Gentlemen, ladies," the imposing man addressed the small gathering. His clothes were particularly fine, Gretel noted, boasting excellent tailoring and expensive cloth. He wore a large watch on a heavy gold chain, which he took from his pocket, checking the time before snapping it shut again. "I am pleased to inform you that the *Arabella* is about to set sail." He looked around the room, his gaze taking in every person present, as if he were committing their faces to memory. Gretel felt a shiver as his eyes studied her, albeit briefly. He gave a stiff bow and continued on his way.

This information was greeted by a murmur of excitement. People got up to leave, heading for the upper decks from which they could view the casting-off and wave farewell to any who had come to see them off on their voyage.

"Come along, Hans, we must join the fray, show willing, play the part of enthusiastic cruisers."

"Must we? I rather like it here," he said, leaning happily against the bar, reaching for his freshly filled glass. Gretel had not the energy to cajole him.

"Have it your way. Once we are at sea I shall take myself back down to the priest hole that passes for our cabin and dress for dinner. I would appreciate your absence while I do so."

"If it means I can remain ensconced where I sit, I am happy to oblige."

Up on the main deck Gretel took a position at the railings overlooking the quayside. The gathering of well-wishers was pitifully small, and there were no streamers nor any band to send them on their way. Farther along the quay she noticed an altogether more colorful and elegant crowd amassing next the splendid *Fair Fortune*. With a sigh she turned and refocused her attention onto the activity on deck. She caught sight of the cabin boy.

"Will!"

He scampered over when beckoned.

"Tell me, who is that strutting fellow in the smart waistc't?"

"That is Herr Hoffman, the quartermaster, fraulein."

"He is an important person?"

"Oh, yes, fraulein. He is second only to the captain himself."

"Thank you, Will." She let him scurry off about his business, which was much and hectic, as setting sail appeared to involve just about every man aboard. Men swung about in the rigging overhead, or hauled on this rope or that lever. She watched Captain Ziegler, still resplendent in red, standing at the wheel issuing orders, while Herr Hoffman strode about, hands clasped behind his back, doling out an admonishment here and a rebuke there. Where one was swagger and show, the other was quiet determination and an ever-watchful eye. Where the first was glamor and charm, the second was stealth and sharpness. It struck her that the two men were each powerful in their own ways, and that such large personalities rarely sat comfortably at the same table. She wondered there was room enough for them both on board the *Arabella*.

Ropes and jiggers were untied from the quayside and thrown on deck to be swiftly coiled and stashed away. The anchor was weighed. A sail or two unfurled. Throughout it all, Captain

Ziegler's voice sang out clear as the ship's bell, though similarly showing signs of weather. The quartermaster moved among the crew, prodding and berating where necessary. Lesser men issued orders that were, to Gretel's landlubbing ear, composed of incomprehensible sailor-speak, but which resulted in one vital seafaring action or another. In no time at all, she felt the ship give a single mighty lurch before settling into a more stately movement away from the quayside, past the harbor wall, and swiftly and silently, without so much as a whistle blown, out to the open sea. She could not help feeling a smidgen of disappointment. A bit of bunting. A cheer or two. Maybe the odd handful of colored rice thrown. Any of the above would have been welcome. Would have gone some way to making her believe that she was actually setting sail on a cruise ship for the journey of a lifetime. Instead she had the feeling she might be on a vessel loaded to the gunwales, slinking out of port stealthily in the hope of avoiding the customs officers.

Still, she reminded herself, she was not a paying passenger. She was here to work. And work she would. She would find out what had befallen the two missing crewmembers. She would ascertain whether or not a mermaid did indeed live in these dark, icy waters. She would give her flamboyant and outlandish client answers, and he would give her money. That was the way of things. This thought made her feel altogether more cheerful, so that she found herself ready to face the cramped confines of her cabin in order to wash off the dust of the journey and dress for dinner.

※

Given the constraints of space, it took a good deal of puffing and struggling to extract a gown from her trunk, extract herself from her traveling clothes, bathe in the three inches of tepid water provided, and then fight her way into her chosen garment. By the end of it, her hair, according to the looking glass she had had the good sense to bring with her, was a fright. Muttering curses along the lines of how much easier it would have been had the occasion been sufficiently grand to warrant wearing her beloved, as-yet-untried, wig, Gretel battled her increasingly frizzing locks into some semblance of order. She applied powder liberally, followed by an extravagant spritzing of perfume, and then went out along the passage. Sideways, as the cut of her gown was too full for forward movement. A person less enamored of fashion, less wedded to the challenge of keeping up with the very newest of new when it came to *haute couture*, might have opted for one or two simpler garments for daytime sailing. But Gretel was not such a person. So it was that she made crablike progress the length of the ship. During this ungainly journey, she had the curious sense that she was being followed, and yet whenever she looked behind her, the passageway was empty. She squeezed on, her path involving strenuous effort when ascending the near-vertical stairs, so that she arrived in the dining room more than a little short of breath, temper, and love of her fellow mankind.

The room itself offered nothing likely to restore her to good humor. It was capacious, but this was to its detriment, as the quantity of diners was small. Each party sat at some remove from the next, so that the tables appeared as life rafts adrift on some unknown sea. An attempt had been made with the decor—to wit, swags of silk at the windows, silk cushions on the hardwood chairs, and no shortage of lamps—but the overall effect remained somewhat desultory. And brown. Very brown. The same brown as the wood that was both skin and skeleton of the ship herself. As if everything had received a coat of treacly varnish. Even the scruffy assortment of waiting staff, some of whom she recognized as crewmembers who not many hours past had been occupied in the business of sailing the ship. They had cleaner clothes on, but nothing could hide their salt-weathered skin and callused hands as they held chairs for the ladies and fetched drinks hither and thither. She was pleased to see the steward from the bar among them. At least he had the look of someone who could be trusted to serve food.

As was the case in the bar, the ceiling was unpleasantly low. In such a large room this had the effect of suggesting it was actually, if imperceptibly, pressing downward. Gretel saw at least three passengers stooping or crouching as they walked. She was baffled by this curious construction. The *Arabella* seemed to have been designed with no thought as to the appeal of its interior spaces—or comfort thereof—in regard to its clientele. She recalled Will telling her that the ship had been converted for cruising, leading her to ponder exactly what its previous incarnation had been. Particularly given that it necessitated cannons.

"Gretel! Over here!" Hans's cheery voice reached her through the general hubbub. As she approached him, the reason for his good cheer became evident. His cheeks had about them a particular glow, his eyes a particular twinkle, such that only quality ale and plenty of it could bring about. "You are not a moment too soon," he told her. "Dinner is about to be served and I am assured we are in for a feast of some quality and flair!"

"I find that hard to believe," she told him, taking the seat next to him. Their table was set for six, with all their fellow diners save one already seated. She exchanged nods and politenesses with them as she wrestled her skirts into place on the less than generous chair provided. She was on the point of inspecting the silverware as Hans hailed the ubiquitous steward to request wine, when there arose from the assembled company a burst of glove-muffled applause heralding the arrival of Captain Ziegler.

"Hrmph," said Hans through the unlit cigar jammed between his teeth, "not very good form, is it? The captain being late. Mean to say, if the rest of us can get here on time . . ."

"His tardiness is not born of disorganization, Hans. It is calculated. This is a man who likes to make an entrance."

"You think so?"

As they watched, Captain Ziegler gave a low bow in thanks for his warm reception. He acknowledged the room with a sweep of his feathered tricorn before returning his hat to his head. As he made his way to his table he paused to kiss a hand here, to playfully punch a shoulder there, to bestow a lingering look now and again, to wink lasciviously where called for. There was about his gait a confidence and a swagger that was at once both ridiculously narcissistic and enormously appealing. His spell fell over all present like a soft, warm wave lapping a tropical shore. Even Hans was won over.

"He's coming this way!" he piped. "Look! Look, Gretel, he is to dine with us. We are at the captain's table!"

"Calm down, Hans, before you swallow that vile cigar."

"Ahh, Fraulein Gretel!" The captain bowed again, taking her hand and pressing it to his lips.

Now, Gretel had had her hand kissed before. Many times. There were kisses she would rather forget and kisses she would always remember. Sadly, more of the former than the latter, but that was the way of things. Etiquette, tradition, good manners, all were designed to encourage this liberty-taking. On good days it made her feel like a queen. Or a pope, possibly. On others it made her skin crawl. At the periphery of her vision she became aware of jealous glances from women not so blessed as to be enjoying the full force of Captain Ziegler's attention. She noted one or two men among them. She was aware of Hans beaming in a that's-my-sister-don't-cha-know kind of way. But beyond that, nothing. No violins. No celestial choirs. No desire to swoon. No desire at all, in fact. For all the captain's many charms, he could not reach her. Gretel knew that, since she was already in a detective/client relationship with the man, this was a Very Good Thing and boded well for a working partnership that would remain just that. She was also conscious of the fact that this lack of attraction brought to mind an Other. A man who, contrarily, *was* able to move her. A man whose company she missed. A man she wished very much right at that minute was the one whose teeth were grazing her palm. But he was long ago and far away. She must deal with the matter in hand. On hand. Literally.

"Save your appetite for the meal, captain," she insisted, withdrawing her hand. "I hear it is to be worth the wait."

"Oh, it will be," he assured her. "Our cook was schooled in Paris, no less." He held her gaze. "I'm certain you will not be disappointed."

"I'm certain too!" chirruped Hans.

"I am hard to impress," Gretel warned.

"I will make it my personal duty to see that you are," the captain said.

"I will be! I'm easily impressed," Hans insisted, puppylike in his enthusiasm but still failing to attract Captain Ziegler's attention.

"Let us hope that Cook is equally committed to his work," said Gretel, summoning the steward for more wine in an effort to defuse the moment. She knew what the captain was about. What better way to convince all who cared to think about it that she was here for recreation, rather than in her capacity as detective, than to have her seen flirting with the master of the ship? It was not a ruse she felt inclined to encourage, however.

At last Captain Ziegler took his seat. At a neighboring table, Gretel noticed Herr Hoffman looking bored and checking his pocket watch. As more wine was poured and the first of many courses appeared, she scrutinized the passengers at her table. Across from her sat a young couple who revealed without being asked that they were on their honeymoon. Certainly Rudie and Lena Schmidt wore the inescapable glow of love, lust, and lots of money recently spent on showing it off. Next to them sat the lone middle-aged man she had also seen up on deck. His name was Dr. Becker, retired, and he told them he was a keen watcher of birds, and hoped to see many rare species on visits to the famously wild islands that dotted the Schleswig-Holstein coastline.

Hans had eyes for nothing but the food.

"I say, sister mine. This is most excellent. Puffin eggs, lightly poached, on a nest of crispy kelp. Quite delightful." He tucked in, failing to register the manner in which Dr. Becker blanched and pushed his plate away. "Mmmm! Delicious. A triumph. What luck, to have such cuisine on board, eh?" He elbowed Gretel happily, and she marveled at how quickly his breathless interest in the captain could be diverted by a small plate of food. Hans continued, "If the rest of the repast is as fine as this, well! We are truly in for a rare treat."

Whether this was to prove true or not, they would have to wait to discover, for at that moment Will the cabin boy came screeching into the dining room.

"A mermaid! A mermaid! A mermaid!" he cried, pointing backward and upward, his eyes bright, his whole body trembling. "There is a mermaid singing!"

THREE

Up on deck, everyone peered into the darkness. The diners had shown a surprising turn of speed in the scramble from their tables, so that by the time Gretel reached the upper level she had to fight her way through the throng of passengers and crew. There was a great deal of excitement, a heady mix of wonder and fear. Some of the crewmembers were muttering prayers. Others had faces glum as doom and shook their heads solemnly.

"Where is it?" asked Rudi Schmidt cheerfully enough, he and his bride evidently considering mythical sea creatures as all part of the fun of a cruise. Gretel could see they were protected by a bubble of young love that could not be dented.

Will pointed into the gloom. "The singing came from over there. I heard it! We all did, clear as day."

The crew began to argue about who had and who had not caught the sound of mermaid song until Herr Hoffman had to hush them to a tense silence. Captain Ziegler leaned on the rail, holding a lantern aloft, scouring the dark horizon.

All listened, breath held.

There was no wind to disturb the quiet. The night sky was black as ship's tar, devoid of moon or stars.

The only sounds in that moment of suspense were the slow, rhythmic creaking of the ship and the wheezing breath of one of the older sailors.

And then, there it was, an unmistakable, ethereal melody that could only be formed by a mer-creature. The song was high and pure and sharp, so that it cut to the very soul of any who heard it. The beauty of the sound moved some to tears. Others appeared enraptured, transported to a distant, secret place. Gretel observed these effects with interest. The captain, who remained inscrutable, was right when he said many of his men feared the mermaid. To them it augured storms, pestilence, madness, or shipwreck. It was disconcerting to see such anguish on the faces of strong men. Even the quartermaster, who was doing his utmost to remain unmoved, gave himself away by a small muscle twitching in his jaw.

At that moment there came a break in the cloud, allowing through a little moonlight. People strained their eyes anew, leaning forward, scanning the now-gleaming surface of the sea. The water was calm but still the moonbeams danced and flickered, playing tricks upon the vision of those who looked upon it. The *Arabella* had left the port of Bremerhaven far behind, so there was nothing but empty sea on all sides. The singing continued.

"It is growing louder!" Will declared.

One of the crew, fear in his voice, said, "We ought be sailing *from* it, not *t'ward* it!"

"There!" cried Hans. "On that rock, look!"

Sure enough, there was a cluster of rocks, a miniature island of sorts, where by rights there should not be. And on it was a shape, a silhouette that was hard to make out. Gretel cursed herself for not wearing her lorgnettes. Captain Ziegler called in vain for his telescope. There were gasps, and entreaties to various deities for protection. There followed a sudden movement, and it was gone. Slipped into the sea. Vanished. For a moment Gretel wondered if the captain would lower a boat and give chase, but he clearly gauged the mood of his men carefully, and she suspected he did not wish to risk a blatant refusal by the crew in the face of an order. Slowly, the intensity of the moment began to lessen. There was nervous laughter. Feeble jokes were cracked. People drifted away from the rail of the ship, some returning to the dining room, others going about their seafaring tasks. Gretel watched them all, taking care to note who was scared, who was enchanted, and who, most curiously of all, remained utterly impassive.

❖

The following morning Gretel awoke with the sensation that she had been trussed like a game bird ready for the oven. Her arms were squashed tight to her sides, her shoulders pressed up against something unyielding, and she had lost all sensation in her feet. It took a moment or two to recall that she was in fact wedged into the narrow cot that was her bed. That she had slept comfortably through her first night at sea had nothing to do with her billet, and everything to do with a large meal and several generous brandies. The memory of the fine food cheered her enough to open her eyes. Staring up at the underside of the upper bunk, she deduced by the gray light that it must be close to dawn. A rumbling noise to her left alerted her to her brother's presence. Stiffly, she propped herself up on one elbow. Hans, fully clothed, was flat on his back on the rug, filling entirely the floorspace of the cabin, an extinguished cigar stub stuck to his bottom lip.

"Hans!" Gretel barked. "Hans, wake up, for pity's sake."

"What? What? Twist! I'll raise you five! Banker pays all! Oh, good morning, sister."

"Long night of card playing, was it?"

"I rather think it was," he said, attempting to sit up and then quickly thinking better of it and reclining again, his hand over his eyes.

"I daresay there was no shortage of players happy to part you from your money. Or rather, *my* money."

Without opening his eyes, Hans replied, "You surely know me better than that."

"Oh? How much did you win?"

He dug in his pockets and pulled out a fistful of notes and coins. "This much," he said, waving it blindly at her.

"Time well spent, then. And at least your absence allowed me room to *faire ma toilette* before retiring. We simply must find a larger cabin . . ." she puffed, struggling to swing her legs over the side of the bunk. They came to rest on Hans's ample stomach. "Why aren't you in your bunk?"

"Too stormy. Didn't want to risk it. Ship rolling all over the place."

"We have encountered not so much as a stiff breeze since setting sail. Any instability you experienced was due to ale and brandy, not oceanic conditions."

"If you say so, though you might say it a smidge more softly. No need to shout in a room of this size, one would think."

"What you need is breakfast. Which means you will have to stir your stumps."

"Breakfast. First sensible thing you've said." Hans risked opening his eyes, blinking energetically to clear the blur from his vision. "Matter of fact it should be something well worth getting up for. Every bit as scrumptious as our meal last evening. I met our cook in the saloon bar. Splendid fellow. Good card player, too, though fortunately not as good as me. Name of Frenchie."

"He is French?"

"No, but he's been to France. He is a man who speaks my language."

"Gibberish?"

"Food." Panting and grunting, he righted himself, hauling on the uprights of the bunks, which creaked alarmingly but did not give way. "I'll go ahead, let you do whatever it is you do to get from . . ." He paused, gesturing at her weakly. ". . . that, to . . . well, how you eventually look."

"Hans, leave now while you still can."

An hour later they were both seated in the dining room. The tables were laid out less formally than on the previous evening, inasmuch as there were no place cards, so that the passengers were able to follow their own preferences as to company or solitude. Hans had already made the choice of a seat by the low window by the time Gretel arrived. A combination of him waving cheerily and Gretel glaring served to deter any who thought they might join them. Not surprisingly, the honeymooners were nowhere to be seen. Dr. Becker had almost finished his breakfast and had his nose deep in a volume on ornithology. The captain was no doubt busy captaining. They were spared the stern presence of Herr Hoffman. The number of empty tables suggested their fellow cruisers were either late risers or poor sailors. Or possibly both.

The barman appeared in his capacity as steward once more, arriving on swift, silent feet to place before them jugs of aromatic coffee and hot milk.

"Good morning, madam, sir. Will you be wanting continental or a full cooked breakfast?"

"Yes!" said Hans.

"What's on offer?" Gretel asked.

The steward stood, tea towel draped over his cocked arm, eyes raised upward as he listed, "We've calf's liver, lamb's liver, kippers, grilled gammon—"

"Yes!" Hans interrupted.

"—warm rolls, croissants, brioche, soda bread. Oh, and black bread, just in case you're feeling homesick," he added with a shrug.

"Yes!" said Hans.

"I'm sure Cook can select the perfect platter for us," Gretel suggested. "Tell me, steward, before you go, what is your opinion of the curious occurrence last evening?"

"The mermaid, d'you mean, madam?"

"Are you a believer or a skeptic?"

"Oh, my word, it's not the strangest thing I've ever encountered. Not by a very long chalk, I don't mind telling you." He leaned close to whisper, "I've seen things out at sea would make a singing girl with a fishy tail look commonplace."

"So you are apt to believe that such a thing was out there, in the dark, serenading us?"

"Why not?"

"Were you not afraid, as many of your shipmates were? Such a singular thing . . . ?"

"I'm from England, madam, a very singular nation." So saying, he left to fetch their food.

Gretel took advantage of the hiatus to consider the facts so far. She had been summoned because there were reports of mermaid sightings and two crewmembers had disappeared. Whether these two facts were connected remained, as yet, unproven. According to both Captain Ziegler's brief and the testimony of the steward, both men were natural sailors, unlikely to have simply fallen overboard. They were not, other than serving aboard the same ship, connected to each other, so their vanishing was unlikely to have been a planned thing between the two of them. They had given no indication that they intended leaving, they had simply and mysteriously disappeared a short while after the mermaid had been heard singing. The captain feared he might lose more men, and that rumors of bad omens, not to mention vanishing men, might adversely affect his business. This was only his second season operating a cruise ship. He had informed her that his life savings were invested in its success. The appearance of the singing mermaid of the previous evening had been interesting, but far from conclusive evidence. Was the thing a mermaid? If not, what, or who, was it? And why had it taken it upon itself to perch on a chilly rock in the middle of the night? If its aim was to frighten sailors, then had it lured away the missing men, like a North Sea Lorelei? Or was it harmless, and the matters unconnected? There was much to discover, indeed. Gretel resolved that directly after breaking her fast, she would inspect the ship closely and engage as many crewmembers in conversation as was possible without arousing their suspicion as to her motives for being on board in the first place.

She opened her mouth to ask her brother to pass the coffeepot but the look of him stopped her. Hans gaped, blanched, winced, grimaced, and generally looked for all the world as if someone had just tipped a bucket of iced eels down the back of his shirt. Gretel turned to follow the line of his appalled stare to see what could have transformed him thus. Had she not turned, the nasal whine of the voice that assailed her that second would have been horribly sufficient for the purposes of identification.

"Hansel! Oh, *liebling*, my gracious, my goodness. Is it really you? It is! It is my darling Hansel!" cried the red-haired banshee swooping on them from the far end of the dining room.

Birgit Lange. It could be no other. Though many years had passed since Gretel had last been forced to endure the woman's company, the memory of certain people simply refused to fade. In that instant, as Birgit continued to coo and shriek in equal measure, Gretel was transported back in time as if by some cruel magic. Back to the one and only occasion in his life when Hans had fallen in love. It had not been a gentle tumbling into a state of joyful bliss; rather a headlong plunge, a panic-inducing descent, into the passionate arms of Fraulein Lange. Gretel could have told him it would all end in tears. In fact, she did tell him. Several times. Often quite loudly. But he would not listen. He was a man enthralled, and the object of his breathless affection dug her claws in deep. From the beginning, Gretel had been baffled as to the woman's motive. After all, fond as Gretel was of her sibling, his charms were few, his qualifications as a potential husband fewer. True, he could cook and could play a fair hand of any game of cards ever invented, but there his talents ended. He was a creature who responded to firm but gentle bullying with a willingness to please, so long as what was being asked of him did not require anything much in the way of effort, skill, or wits. Braise a haunch of mutton, certainly; dig the garden, certainly not. Set down stores of kirsch-soaked black cherries for winter, happily; put up a set of shelves, sadly, no. Pickle a barrel of cabbages, simple; provide a stable income and comfortable home for wife and family, simply out of the question. Gretel had tried to see him as another woman might, but he remained an overrisen, undercooked doughboy. He was not square of jaw, he was not in possession of a twinkling eye, nor a shapely calf. Indeed there was not one inch of him that could be described as athletic or handsome.

Two baffling months had passed, during which time she had suffered interminable hours of Birgit's company, and had to put up with Hans floating about the house wearing a rose in his buttonhole and a silly grin on his face, spouting appalling poems, before something his paramour had said to Gretel in an unguarded moment had made all clear. Somehow, Birgit had got hold of the idea that Hans had a vast horde of money made from his brief moment of fame when they were children. That he lived in a small house in an unremarkable town with his sister seemed not to alert the woman to the unlikeliness of this being the case. She had convinced herself that he had made a minor fortune trading on his experiences in the woods and his escape from the witch, telling his story, receiving a generous payment from King Julian, no doubt publishing his memoirs and having a sausage named after him, and that this money had been sensibly and successfully invested. Clearly, Birgit had not taken the trouble to know Hans at all.

Not surprisingly, she eventually learned the truth. Not surprisingly because Gretel told it to her. It had been clear that her brother would be dumped the second his ghastly girlfriend discovered that his entire fortune consisted of a souvenir jubilee coin, a gold pocket watch (won in a poker game), and a handful of loose change. Gretel saw no advantage to spinning the thing out. Why prolong the agony? Particularly her own. Better to bring the doomed affair to a swift end. Her assessment of the lack of regard Birgit truly had for Hans had been accurate. It was one of the few times Gretel regretted being right. She could not have foreseen the gnashing of teeth and the rending of cloth, the wailing and sighing and sobbing and crying and generally horrendous behavior Hans was to take up. The months of Hans in Love paled into insignificance when compared to Hans with a Broken Heart. He moped about, relentlessly lachrymose and moribund. He even, for one whole hungry week, refused to cook. And he never again let anyone ever, no not ever, at all, no sir thank you very much, call him Hansel.

"Hansel! My goodness! How marvelous that I find you here. And unchanged, after all this long, long time."

Hans offered nothing by way of reply save for a squeak of protest as Birgit settled herself, uninvited, upon the chair next to him.

"And sweet sister Gretel! Also unaltered by the many years since we have seen each other."

"Birgit, I assure you it feels as if it were only yesterday," Gretel responded through clenched teeth. "Are you here with your husband, perhaps?"

It was a forlorn hope.

"Alas, you see before you a bereft widow," she explained, looking anything but as she fluttered fan and eyelashes at Hans. "Poor, dear Albert fell victim to the dropsy last summer. I miss him still, but life must go on."

Hans was giving every impression of a person whose life might not go on very much longer. The ability to speak seemed to have left him. His mouth opened and shut in the manner of a landed tuna that had given up all hope of returning to the water. His bulging eyes suggested that merely drawing breath might soon prove beyond him.

"So you are here accompanied by . . ." Gretel clung to the notion that there must be somebody responsible for the dreadful woman.

"Two dear friends, Elsbeth and Sonja." She pointed toward the far side of the dining room without for one second taking her eyes off Hans.

Gretel picked up her lorgnettes to peer into the distance. Inspection of Birgit's traveling companions confirmed her worst suspicions. She got quickly to her feet, taking hold of Hans's arm and hauling him up with her. "If you'll forgive us, Fraulein Lange, my brother is feeling unwell."

"Oh! Nothing serious, I hope? He does not suffer failing health in general? No terrible ailments that might shorten his life?"

"Merely a case of *mal de mer*. He needs to lie down," Gretel explained, wheeling Hans about and propelling him away from the table.

"Until later, then!" Birgit called after them.

But Gretel did not take Hans to their cabin. She knew her brother well, and she knew when nothing but strong alcohol would do. Despite the early hour, she dragged him to the saloon bar. It was, unsurprisingly, empty. Propping Hans up on a stool, she rang the bell. When no one came to their aid, she took it upon herself to step behind the bar and fetch a bottle of brandy and two glasses. Hans downed the first shot, then the second, after which his eyes at least lost their disturbing stare.

"That's the way," Gretel told him. "One or two more of those and you will be ready to try a little bite to eat, I feel certain of it." She needed him to come to his senses so that she could talk frankly to him about the danger he was in. Birgit's mission aboard the *Arabella* was plain as the plain nose on her plain face. The appearance of the other women with her confirmed it. Gretel knew a hunting party when she saw one. Widows. On the prowl. Looking for new husbands, preferably with frail constitutions and healthy bank balances. Hans's best defense was his continued lack of wealth, and they must do their utmost to make his financial ineligibility clear to Birgit. But first he must regain what wits he possessed. "Come along."

Gretel patted his hand—she was not given to demonstrations of affection with her brother, but the situation called for extreme measures. "Drink up and we'll see if we can't get that fine sounding breakfast brought in here. I think this is a safe enough place to hole up at this hour."

But Hans shook his head, and the words he uttered next were proof, if proof were needed, that they were in deep trouble.

"You know," he said, his voice faltering, "I do believe my appetite has fled."

FOUR

L eaving Hans in the bar, Gretel went up on deck, feeling
more than a little out of sorts. Having Birgit Lange on
board was going to be a constant source of irritation
and distraction, not to mention emotional torture for Hans.
Nothing and no one else had ever put him off his food. Gretel
was here to work, and the last things she needed were the
screeching presence of Hans's ex and her brother maudlin
and needy. What was more, she had missed breakfast. The
medicinal brandy she had shared with Hans lurched around
unpleasantly in her otherwise empty stomach. She had done
little to progress the case she had been summoned to solve,
and was unlikely to make much headway unless she was

properly fed. There were men to be questioned and the ship to be examined. While she knew clues were scant, she must search for them, and quickly, if the captain was to believe his investment in her to be money well spent. She took several large gulps of fresh sea air, but they did nothing to fill her up. The day was bright and the sea calm, so she spent some time gazing upon it in the hope that the blue of the sky and the sparkle of the water would have beneficial and restorative effects on her. Whether it was the brightness of the sunshine or the unaccustomed movement of the ship, she could not be sure, but something suddenly gave Gretel the impression that a figure had just swung through the rigging. Not a person, but someone smaller. Or something. She put her hand to her eyes to shade them and squinted upward, expecting to find, perhaps, a monkey. She had heard of sailors who acquired such exotic pets on their far-flung travels. Now she glimpsed whatever it was, a silhouette against the sun. It scampered along a boom, its tiny feet seeming to scarcely touch the slippery wood. And then it was gone, vanished among the sails before she could obtain a clear view.

Blinking, she rubbed her eyes and her mind at once returned to the irritation that was Birgit. It was too bad, having to suffer her company on board, but she knew that she must not let this irksome development hinder her investigations, and she resolved to start interviewing the crew forthwith. Given her gnawing hunger, she decided that the ship's cook might be a good person to start with.

The galley was a place of heat, steam, noise, and raised voices. It looked to Gretel's eye woefully small, given the size of the ship and number of mouths to be fed. She sidled through the entrance and wedged herself between a tallboy and a stack of barrels so as to be out of the way. Breakfast over, it was evident preparations were already under way for the next meal. The sight of slabs of chocolate being melted, the sound of something sizzling in a pan, and the aroma of freshly baked bread combined to render Gretel quite faint with desire. So much so that as a tray of warm brioche flashed past her, held aloft by a red-faced boy, she snatched one up for herself and stuffed the thing whole into her mouth. The sweetness of the new dough, its glorious buttery texture, the delicate flakiness of it as it melted on her tongue nearly caused her to swoon. She felt instantly better, and pondered the fact that healthy lungfuls of ocean air could not compete with a tummy full of sugar and fat when it came to giving one a boost.

"What are you doing in my kitchen!" yelled a small, round-faced man dressed in the whites of a chef and sporting a black bandanna and a sparse goatee. He held a fearsome knife with a curved blade and bone handle, which he seemed to be in the habit of gesticulating with as he spoke. The effect was unnerving.

"Forgive the intrusion," Gretel began. "I was called away during breakfast, and—"

"Passengers are not allowed in the kitchen!" he barked.

"Of course, I have no wish to interrupt your excellent work—"

"If you want something to eat, ask the steward. You cannot come in here!"

Gretel remained steadily impervious to the man's blustering and played what she believed to be her trump card. "Sadly, my brother, Hans, is indisposed. He mentioned what an exceptional poker player and a thoroughly helpful fellow you are . . . Herr Frenchie, if I have it right?"

"Hans?" The little man's face twisted through a variety of expressions, touching on puzzled and passing through surprised before arriving at delighted. "Ah, Hans! My good friend! He is unwell? Why didn't you say so? Do not tell me the sea has unsettled his digestion, no! I refuse to believe this. Hans is a man of substance."

"Few would argue with that."

"A man of iron will!"

"Iron stomach, certainly."

"If he is ailing, he must eat. I will prepare him a fish broth." He waved his knife and snapped orders at his sweating minions. "I am famous for my bouillabaisse," he explained, gathering handfuls of ingredients. "I trained in Paris under the great Alphonse Dubois. There is no other living who has this recipe." As he talked he chopped, sliced, and diced with alarming speed and impressive dexterity.

"I am certain if anything can restore Hans to good health, it will be your cooking," said Gretel, her mouth watering as the fumes of garlic simmering in white wine reached her nostrils. She struggled to stay focused. "Might I ask, how long have you been cook aboard the *Arabella*?"

"Since first she started her life as a cruise ship. That is to say, this will be my second summer serving under Captain Ziegler."

"And you find him a fair master to serve?"

"Not the shallots, you imbecile!" Frenchie yelled, causing Gretel to jump, a sous chef to whimper, and the lower lip of the galley boy to tremble. "If I say spring onions I mean spring onions! Yes, fraulein." His voice returned to a softer level as he addressed Gretel without missing a beat. "He is new to the business, but not to captaincy. He runs his ship sound enough. Does this look like fennel to you, boy?!" he demanded of a passing lad, cuffing him about the ears with the offending bunch of celery.

"I cannot help observing that I did not see you on deck when the mermaid was sighted. Have you no interest in such things?"

"Little interest and less time. I never leave my post during service!"

"Of course. And yet others felt compelled to do so. I understand there are some who are greatly disturbed by the notion of these fishy females."

But Frenchie was no longer listening. He was in the throes of creation, and nothing would penetrate his consciousness until the fabled seafood soup was completed. Gretel watched him as he worked on, her stomach groaning forlornly all the while, though the noise was drowned out by the cacophonous music of the kitchen. At last the dish was finished. The cook became suddenly still, all around him hushed for this moment, as he lifted the ladle to his lips for the final tasting. Nobody spoke, nobody moved. The galley boy ceased breathing, judging by the color of him. Frenchie slurped. He savored. He swallowed. He smiled! All present applauded before scurrying back to their multifarious tasks. A generous bowl of the precious concoction was whisked away to Hans. The cook called for glasses and took a heavy bottle of brandy from the shelf beneath his workbench. He poured two measures of the darkly tempting drink and handed one to Gretel.

She would, truth be told, sooner have had the soup, but the choice was not hers to make. She tipped her head back, thinking to down the shot swiftly lest her stomach have time to rebel, but the quality of the brandy as it entered her mouth made her pause. She sipped, enjoying the warm, aromatic flavors and detecting nothing of the customary harshness she had come to expect from the ship's alcohol. "My, my," she said, "I must congratulate you on the quality of your cellar, Herr Frenchie. This is most excellent."

The cook shrugged, tapped the side of his nose, and mumbled something about any chef being only as good as his ingredients. It was evident to Gretel she would get no more from him on this matter now, but would certainly question him further at another time.

Once back up on deck, Gretel located the captain. There was an air of busy calm among the crew as they went about their arcane tasks to keep the ship on course and on speed. On such a balmy day, the open water offered few challenges. As she approached him, Gretel saw that the master of the ship had his spyglass to his eye. Following the direction of his gaze, she was able to make out another ship some way off. Even at such a distance she was reasonably sure that it was the same vessel she had seen alongside the quay at Bremerhaven.

"Keeping a keen eye on the competition, captain?" she asked, attempting to look at the ship through her lorgnettes, but finding them of no help.

"Good morning, fraulein," he replied, passing the telescope to her so that she might take a closer look herself. "The *Fair Fortune* has the advantage in sail, sailors, and spending. Seems I must always be trailing in her wake," he added with not a small measure of rancor in his voice.

Gretel squinted through the eyeglass. It took a moment for her to adjust the device to suit her own vision, but at last the *Fair Fortune* sprang into crisp focus. She was even more impressive with her sails set than she had been at anchor. Her lines were graceful and curvaceous, her proportions ample but never heavy. She handed the scope back to its owner. "She is very fine, it is true," she said, "but the *Arabella* has her own charms. There are sure to be those who would prefer a more . . . *authentic* cruising experience." Even as she said it Gretel feared, glancing at the captain's threadbare coat and the ragtag crew behind him, that the experience might prove a bit too authentic for some. Herself included.

"I must trust the preferences of paying passengers, then. I am new to this game, as you know, fraulein. Where I cannot compete on scale and coin, I must offer something other to win their custom."

"Are there more ships plying their trade in these waters?" she asked, pleased with her own grasp of the sailing lexicon.

The captain gestured at the distant vessel. "She has a sister ship, the *Pretty Penny.*"

"Sailing under the same flag?" she asked, warming to the theme.

"Aye, both owned by one Thorsten Sommer, damn his eyes. The man could not be more slippery had he been fathered by an eel."

This was such a disconcerting notion that Gretel quite lost her stride regarding seafaring terminology. She simply put the question, "Might it not be within the reach of reason to suggest that Herr Sommer is not happy to see a new cruise ship in what he possibly considers to be his territory? And that it might be to his advantage were your enterprise to fail?"

"He would like nothing better! But I shall not give him that satisfaction. It would take more than a lard-bellied Norseman, fat with his family money and from dining with royalty, no less, to turn me from my chosen course!" So saying, he faced Gretel, his eyes flashing, a determined grin lighting up his craggy features. Thus animated, he was quite transformed, his gaze disarmingly charismatic. And familiar, somehow. Gretel once again had the strongest sense that she had seen this devilishly handsome face before, but still she could not say where nor when. Attempting to return her energies to the case she was charged to solve, she filed away the facts she had gleaned so far. Thorsten Sommer had surely to go atop her list of suspects regarding the missing crewmembers, with or without the assistance of what might or might not be a mermaid.

At that moment, the quartermaster descended from the poop deck wearing his habitually solemn expression. Gretel noted the minute alterations in Captain Ziegler's stance, as if he were slightly bracing himself for an attack, or at least readying himself for a difficult exchange. In the event, the two traded nothing more than curt nods and Herr Hoffman continued on his way. Gretel seized the moment.

"A dour fellow, your quartermaster, captain." When this observation failed to draw him out, she continued. "Such a demeanor cannot be conducive to a pleasant partnership, one would have thought."

"I look for no pleasantries from Hoffman, nor him any from me. 'Tis not required of us that we be friends. He knows his job."

"Which is why you engaged him, no doubt?"

"It is. That and . . . well . . ." He fell silent, apparently deciding against sharing the completed thought with Gretel.

"Come, come, captain. There can be no secrets between you and me. If I am to assist you, to do what it is I do best, it is necessary that you inform me fully and frankly of the setup of this ship, of the workings of your business, and of the salient facts regarding your crewmembers. Do not be coy."

The captain nodded. "Very well. I do not like the man. He sets himself above me, or would do, were such a thing not to smack of mutiny and likely get him hanged. He covets my ship and position both. He carries a grievance not against me, but against the world, that these things are not his. This has soured him, and his only happiness is to share that sourness."

"So why then employ him? There must be others can muster a crew and fill his shoes?"

"He brought with him something I could not have else. In a word, reputation. In another, respectability. Both crucial for the cruising business. Passengers must have confidence, must be reassured, d'you see?"

Gretel was not at all sure that she did, but any chance she had of questioning him further on the matter was stamped beneath the kitten heels of Birgit Lange as she tottered across the foredeck toward them, waving a lace handkerchief and shrieking effusive greetings.

"I will take my leave, fraulein," said the captain, striding for his cabin before Gretel could persuade him otherwise.

"Gretel! Oh, Gretel, how delightful. Here you are! Now, tell me, where has that simply wonderful brother of yours got to?"

With a deep sigh, and a growling stomach, Gretel realized that the woman was going to prove harder to shake off than a Baltic barnacle.

FIVE

Over the following day and night, Gretel's time was taken up in unreasonable quantities by Hans and the avoidance of That Woman, as he had insisted she be named. Attempting to flee from someone while sharing a ship was not an easy task. The narrowness of all corridors and passages and the broadness of Hans, and indeed herself (though she preferred to think this was at least in part to do with the current fashion for exaggerating the hips, even where no exaggeration was called for) did not aid them in their need to be stealthy and swift. Far and away the worst aspect of this unasked-for game of hide-and-seek was the disruption to meals. Brandy seemed easy enough to come by, as the bar was not a place a lady (lady!) could modestly frequent in the morning, and later in the day a hip flask in the cabin provided fortifying swigs. Food was more problematic. No sooner would Gretel wedge Hans into a dining room chair or have him recline on deck on a stripy lounger, hastily summoning the steward to take their order for a seafood platter or cheese omelette, or even a bite of cold meats and bread, than That Woman would heave into view, uttering her terrifying "tally-ho," and they would be forced to their feet again, retreating with decreasingly plausible mumbled excuses. Hans claimed not to care. His appetite had jumped ship, and he saw little chance of it ever being found. Gretel was beginning to fear her newly acquired gowns would soon hang loose on her withering frame if she did not gain sustenance somehow, somewhere.

On the third afternoon, the *Arabella* put into the small harbor at Friedrichskoog. The stop was scheduled in order to take on fresh supplies, but passengers who felt so inclined were permitted to go ashore for an hour or two. Hans protested that he did not feel in the least inclined. Gretel insisted that the change of scene and possibly a new bar to enjoy might do him good. Hans declared that the ale and brandy were as good on board as any he was likely to find in such a humble harbor. Gretel pointed out that he might find a little *weisswurst* and mustard to go with the ale. Hans sighed and said that even a sausage could not tempt him now, such that he must surely be beyond saving. At which point Gretel bared her teeth, grasped him by the collar, and explained that the only way she would get five minutes' peace in which to sit and dine uninterrupted was if he were safely out of the reach of That Woman, which meant getting him off the ship, and that being the case, Gretel could either send him ashore or tip him over the side. Either was good for her. Hans sulkily opted for a quayside inn.

Gretel bustled him onto the gangway before hurrying to find Birgit. It went against her every instinct to actually seek her out, but she needed to buy her brother a little time to ensure he was not followed. As luck would have it, she found his ex-paramour in a flutter of excitement as she and her companions were being escorted by the captain on an impromptu excursion to Schloss Winzig, the town's one architectural feature of any merit.

Gretel raised an eyebrow. "Captain Ziegler, I would not have singled you out as a lover of historic buildings."

He leaned close to whisper, "Needs must, fraulein. We cannot be seen to be lacking in cultural activities on our cruises."

Birgit pounced on Gretel. "But are you and your brother not planning to accompany us?" she asked, her face an equal mix of hope, disappointment, and rouge.

"Alas, no. My brother is indisposed. I am on my way to plead with Cook for another bowl of his superior fish broth."

"Oh, poor Hansel! Might he be well enough to receive a cheering visitor later on, d'you think?"

"I very much doubt it," Gretel replied, making a brief bow and backing away, the thought of her first decent meal in days lending wings to her heels. She went straight to the steward, who was polishing glasses in the bar. "Just the man," she told him, hoisting herself up onto a stool. "Would you be so good as to take my compliments to the chef, apologize for disturbing him, and tell him I am in dire need of a proper feed."

"You do look a little peaky, madam, if you'll forgive my saying so."

"I have traveled beyond peaky, young man, I am drifting into the dark waters of sickly, and am in danger of washing up on the rocks of unwell. I require good food and plenty of it."

"If I may venture to suggest madam's hair might also benefit from a little attention?"

"You may and it might. All this gritty sea air and my per-spiration-inducing cabin do nothing for it. But who is there to help me?"

"Allow me to be of assistance."

"You?" Gretel eyed up his worn bar towel, unconvinced.

The steward nodded. "At the risk of sounding vain, madam, I will say I have a talent for such things. Before coming to work on the *Arabella*, I was in service as footman and valet in more than one fine home. Upon my word, such glamor! On each occasion, it was not long before the lady of the house recog-nized my gift for improving her coiffure and this became a regular part of my duties. I had even begun to consider finding premises from which to offer my skills to a wider clientele. But alas, life has a habit of pushing us in the most unexpected of directions."

"So you find yourself here. A jealous husband, perhaps?" Gretel suggested.

At this the steward gave a soft laugh. "Yes, madam, jealous of his wife."

"Ah," said Gretel. "And your choice of a position aboard a cruiser . . . ?"

"The *Arabella* was the first ship sailing out of the nearest port to the scene of my . . . situation. I was fortunate the crew was light one steward."

"Indeed, one of two crewmembers to have recently, er, left." She paused, allowing the young barman to offer what he knew of their unexplained disappearance. She already had him marked down as a keen sharer of gossip, so when none was forthcoming, she surmised that he had none to give. "Well, then, until the occasion allows me to don my exceedingly splendid wig, I should be grateful for any assistance you can offer regarding the styling of my hair, Herr . . . ?"

"Everard, madam. Just call me Everard," he insisted.

"As you please. But first, I must have food."

They arranged for Everard to visit Gretel's cabin with quantities of hot water later that day, before he was dispatched to the galley to plead with Frenchie to save Gretel from starvation. The ship's cook did not disappoint. Gretel spent a happy hour in the saloon bar, which was blissfully empty save for herself and Everard's gentle presence. She began her feast with a bowl of the renowned bouillabaisse—which was every bit as exquisite as its reputation suggested—accompanied by warm French bread with which to scoop up tender prawns and mop and dip at will. Next came an expertly steamed sole, drizzled with butter and lemon. This was followed by melt-in-the-mouth *boeuf en croute* garnished with baby vegetables and a robust red-wine *jus*. Between courses, tiny sorbets and savory mousses were served as *amuse-bouche*, and Gretel would happily attest later to anyone who might ask that her *bouche* was indeed highly amused. She was offered a selection of desserts so delectable and delightful that she considered it would be churlish to refuse any of them, so that she enjoyed first a *galette roulade* with raspberries, chased down by a particularly creamy *crème brulée*, and settled into place by a hefty helping of profiteroles. After such a symphony of flavors and a veritable opera of tastes and textures, Gretel asked herself whether or not she might have preferred more familiar fare: the odd *weisswurst*, perhaps, a spoonful of cabbage here or there, a few steamed potatoes, a slice or two of black forest gâteau, possibly? When the answer came to her clearly "no," she experienced a fleeting flash of guilt, but it passed soon enough when Everard returned with a board of French cheeses. She ate on, the glorious food fueling her spirits, her body, and her mind, so that soon she was certain she was once again in tip-top condition to do her very best work. After a short nap, obviously. She took herself up on deck and selected a chair with a helpful recline and a footstool. The weather was pleasantly warm, with a gentle breeze causing the ship's flag to flutter in an appealing manner. She was on the starboard side of the vessel, so that the noises of the quayside would not disturb her, and she was certain she would be able to rest well. However, as she half closed her eyes, she became aware of both a movement and a presence close to her left shoulder. Her limited vision allowed her only a partial view of her new company, but she sensed at once that whoever it was—whatever it was—was not entirely human. Her first thought was the monkey she fancied she had seen swinging through the rigging, but that did not seem to fit. Keeping very still, she asked softly, "If you wish to speak to me, there is no need for shyness. We are quite alone. Why don't you show yourself?" She opened her eyes fully once more and watched as the small, dark shape slipped silently from its perch behind her and came to rest on the edge of the ship's rail in front instead. What a curious creature it was! No taller than a decent-sized wig, it had the slender form of a tiny person, but was covered entirely—even its sweet face—in velvety purple fur. On its back were two pairs of silvery wings. Its eyes were golden and attractively almond-shaped, and its miniature hands and feet had dainty fingers and toes, also purple-furred, with silver nails.

"Well, I'll be . . . A sea sprite!" Gretel murmured.

The sprite smiled, showing disconcertingly sharp, pointy white teeth. "You're supposed to say, 'There's no such thing as a sea sprite!' aren't you?" it teased.

"And spit loudly to the left, I believe. Yes, I am aware of that unsavory custom."

"Aren't you going to do it, then?"

"There seems little point, when the evidence before me is so very . . . convincing." As she watched, the nimble creature walked happily up and down along the narrow rail, its wings quivering lightly to give it perfect balance. "Do you live aboard the *Arabella*?" Gretel asked it, playing for time while she searched her mind for what she knew of the things. Should she be on her guard, or were they harmless? She couldn't bring the necessary facts to mind. All she could summon was the knowledge that they were neither male nor female, which did not feel like a useful detail at all, and that they were playful. Or was it mischievous? Or dangerous? It appeared friendly enough, but those teeth looked as if they could deliver a nasty bite.

"Oh, yes, this is my ship," the sprite replied. "I've been here longer than anyone. Right from before ever the *Arabella* was a cruise ship. Longer even than Captain Ziegler." It frowned as it spoke, folding its tiny arms tightly across its plush chest, but Gretel detected a slight softening of its features at the mention of the captain.

"And what trade did this vessel ply before it was converted to accommodate cruising passengers, can you tell me that?"

The sprite chose not to answer. Instead it suddenly flitted through the air. It was more a fluttering jump than actual flight, but conveyed it quickly from the rail to Gretel's chest, where it crouched, examining her lorgnettes.

"I say!" said Gretel. "Would you mind alighting elsewhere?"

"These are nice," said the sprite, ignoring her remark. "Will you give them to me?"

"Alas, I have need of them. Besides, they are too big for you."

"Oh, I don't want to wear them, silly. You are a bit silly, aren't you?" The thing leaned forward until its face, and therefore its teeth, were uncomfortably close to Gretel's own. "I'll see if you are. I'll give you a puzzle, and if you can't solve it, then you must be silly."

Without waiting for her to protest, the sprite jumped up, wings a blur, and resettled on the empty deck chair beside her. It thought for a moment, cleared its throat, and then spoke again. "Look once, look twice, look again at the tooth; first the coat, then the badge, then the mouth for the truth!" And with that, it sprang aloft once more, disappearing among the rigging.

Gretel pondered its strange rhyme, rather wishing it hadn't involved making her think about teeth. There might be some information to be gained from the creature, that much was plain. What was also clear was Gretel's own need for some rest after her feast. She was too dozy and too well fed to solve puzzles. She would return to the matter a little later when she was refreshed from slumber. Once she was certain the sprite was not about to leap onto her chest again, she risked closing her eyes. The sun was still warm, and her belly still full, so that she was soon able to drift quickly into a happy, restorative sleep.

She was awoken an hour later by some unknown person apparently washing her face with a rough flannel. Gretel squawked, struggling to sit up and put an end to the unasked-for lavation. "Stop it, I say! What the devil do you think you're doing?" She opened her eyes expecting to see a madman with a fetish for cleanliness, but instead found, looming over her, an enormous hairy brindled hound, its slobbering tongue still straining to lick her further, the stench of its foul breath all but knocking her senseless. As she cried out and fought to push the thing away, she noticed it had a collar with a rope attached to it, and that on the other end of that rope stood her brother.

"Hans! What in the name of all that is sensible are you doing with this monstrous dog?"

He hauled on the fraying leash, dragging the panting beast backward the best he could. "Not a dog, sister mine, a mer-hund!"

"A what?" Gretel stood up, still groggy from sleep and somewhat shaken from the manner in which she had been woken. Looking about her, she saw that they were once more at sea. So deep had her slumber been that she had not even been aware of their setting sail, but the port of Friedrichskoog was now beyond one of the apparently identical blue-gray horizons that currently surrounded them.

"A mer-hund," Hans insisted on explaining. "Here, look at his paws—webbed, see? For swimming both on top of and beneath the surface. And his fur, incredible stuff, practically impervious to water."

"It certainly smells as if that were the case," said Gretel, quelling an uncharacteristic wave of nausea as the creature's body odor assailed her.

"He's just back from hunting. Drew a blank this time, but he'll find your mermaid, you mark my words. Bred for the job. Been used for generations to find the fishy little things."

"How much did you pay for him?"

"Have you any idea how hard these are to come by this far north?"

"How. Much?"

"I used my winnings from the other night."

"And?"

"And the spending money I brought with me."

"You mean the spending money I furnished you with which was to last the entire trip, not a measly couple of days."

"Dash it all, Gretel, have a little faith. He'll make it back for you and more besides. When he finds the mermaid and solves the case, well, how will you like him then, eh?"

At that moment the hound quivered, pointed with nose and paw, and then flung itself over the side and into the sea.

A cry came from atop the rigging. "Mer-hund overboard!"

"There goes our money," Gretel muttered wearily.

"No, he's working. He's on to something! Look at him go!" cried Hans excitedly. He commenced dashing up and down the deck, calling encouragement to his stinking—and at that moment sinking—investment. Gretel allowed herself a single deep sigh, but then her flagging spirits were lifted a tad when she thought what a cheering effect the hound was having on Hans, and what an effective Birgit deterrent such an animal might prove to be.

"A curious creature," came the softly spoken comment to her left. Turning, she found Dr. Becker.

"Are you referring to the hound or my brother?" she asked, and then, upon seeing the consternation on the gentleman's face, added, "As a matter of fact, I think them a well-matched pair."

The doctor relaxed, clearly relieved he had not inadvertently caused offense. "He will need to be a strong swimmer," he observed, nodding at the ocean. "There is a wind getting up and the water is becoming quite choppy. I have noticed the way the gulls behave when the weather is about to change. It is almost as if they have some inbuilt sense, some barometer of their own creation, which allows them to know what lies ahead and seek shelter when necessary. Quite fascinating."

"Quite," Gretel agreed.

"Did you know," he went on, his features aglow with love of his subject, "that the black beaked gull, after fledging and leaving the nest, will not set foot on land for nearly two years?"

"I confess I did not," she replied, thinking to herself that she had not felt the lack of this knowledge but that evidently it was a source of great joy to the mild-mannered doctor.

"Or that the albatross will stay aloft or on water for five years?"

"Alas, I was ignorant of that fact too, until now. Thank you for enlightening me."

"They mate for life, most birds, you know. Astonishing, given the perilous lives they lead. We could learn so much from them, if only we took the time."

"Indeed," said Gretel, rather thinking that time was in fact taking her, and in the general direction of her cabin.

Dr. Becker lifted an outlandish eyeglass to his spectacled eyes. Gretel had not seen its like before. The device was larger and much more cumbersome than her own lorgnettes, and yet had two lenses, rather than a single one, such as the captain's telescope had. She watched as the doctor swept the darkening waters with his gaze thus freakishly extended. She peered into the nothingness of the ocean surface, but could see neither flesh, fish, nor fowl.

"You have found something, with your . . . glasses?" she asked him at last. "A bird of some rarity, perhaps?"

"Sadly, no," he replied, lowering the heavy things, "not a bird. But I can see a ship."

"Really?" Gretel lifted her lorgnettes and tried with, without, with, without, but she could see no ships.

"Please." The doctor took the leather loop from around his own neck and smiled at her. "Try my binoculars. They work on the same principle as your glasses, but their forte is power, rather than decoration." He helped her put them to her eyes and turn the small wheel that helped adjust them to her eyes. At first she saw nothing but gray-blue-blur, but then, there it was, so close it made her take a step back.

"Good lord! A ship where seconds before there was none. Astounding! Such detail. I can read the name . . . yes, it is the *Fair Fortune*. I can even see the people on deck." She continued to watch the ship as it changed its course fractionally, bringing it a little nearer. Soon she was able to make out the elegance of the gowns worn by the ladies promenading on board, and could see the string quartet playing for them, and the silver trays of champagne held high by white-gloved flunkies. Everything looked so grand and gracious and glittering and in no way whatsoever resembled the grittiness on offer aboard the *Arabella*.

"I can see you are impressed by my glasses, fraulein. I find them invaluable in my pursuit of shy and wild birds."

Gretel was aware that the doctor was speaking, but his words fell on deaf ears. Two things had captured her attention and held it in an iron grip. Two things, or, rather, two people. For the ship had glided sufficiently close for her to be able to discern their features clearly enough to identify them. The first, with her unmistakeable beakish nose, sharp expression, and angular physique, could be none other than Baroness Schleswig-Holstein. A distant cousin of King Julian the Mighty, she had the distinctive bearing of the Findleberg family. Gretel recalled the last time they had met, during a testing case of art theft in Nuremberg. If memory served, she had not made a good impression on the aged royal. Neither woman would consider it a blow should their paths diverge permanently. No, it was not the baroness herself who interested Gretel, it was the tall, broad-shouldered figure who stood at her side. Who must be there acting as her personal bodyguard, lent out by King Julian whether he willed it or no. Even at such a distance the sight of him had the power to reach parts of Gretel that had lain hitherto undisturbed, at least since the last time she had been in his company. She experienced the now-familiar combination of conflicting emotions. There was joy at seeing him again, hand in hand with pique that he had not sought her out while they were both back in Gesternstadt. Here was the hot flame of excitement brought about by his manly form, dampened down by the wet blanket of disappointment that he was enjoying a glamorous cruise without her. Uber General Ferdinand von Ferdinand. The man who had saved her from a lion. The man who had seen to it that she was not, after all, tortured or executed, when others would have had it so. The man who had sent her the Swedish wolf-fur cape. The man who, damn his dark, smiling eyes, his flowing salt-and-pepper hair, his well-turned ankles, his handsome frame in his handsome uniform . . . was currently steadying the scrawny arm of a blue-blooded shrew on a stingingly desirable ship instead of being where he should be, doing what he should be doing. On the wretched *Arabella*. With Gretel.

"Bastard!" she snapped.

"Bustard? Where?" the good doctor wanted to know, taking his glasses from her to scour the horizon.

While he was happily engaged in his search, Gretel was able to slip away to her cabin.

SIX

Upon my word, my goodness," Everard could not help himself declaring on taking a closer look at Gretel's hair. "My gracious," he added, somewhat unnecessarily, Gretel thought.

"I have realistic expectations," she told him. "We are at sea, the wind is increasing, the ceilings are low, the accommodation cramped and airless. These are not, I recognize, conditions conducive to hair at its best. I ask that you do the best you can to render it kempt, stylish, and secure." She had removed her dress and petticoats, as the width of its birdcage would have made it impossible for the steward to get anywhere near her otherwise. She found she was not uncomfortable in this condition of *deshabille*, not in Everard's presence.

He sucked air through his teeth, shook his head, and tutted. "I don't know whose salon you attend when you are home in . . . where was it again?" he asked, removing quantities of pins as he spoke.

"Gesternstadt. A small town in Bavaria. You won't have heard of it. Nobody has. Unless, of course, they are looking for—" She stopped herself just in time, recalling she was supposed to be traveling without giving away the real reason for being on the *Arabella*. "—oh, I don't know, all things quaintly Bavarian . . ." Everard gave her a look that told her clearly how little appeal such things, whatever they might be, held for him. "But it does boast a reasonable establishment run by Madame Renoir. She is better than one might hope to find in such a backwater."

Everard arched his neatly plucked brows. He picked up a bristle brush and began applying it to Gretel's frizzing locks. She clenched her teeth but would not complain. She had always known she must suffer to present herself to the world in the way in which she wanted to be seen.

"It must be washed," he decided, "and I will apply a coating of coconut oil to restore luster."

"Luster, you say?"

"I will then commence ridding you of tangles and . . . passengers . . ."

"What? Hell's teeth!"

"Just a few lice, madam. Unpleasant but harmless. A common complaint among sailors."

"Sailors! I am no Jack Tar! I have been aboard this dismal ship for a matter of days and you tell me I have an infestation passed on to me by the crew?"

"Madam, calm yourself." Everard helped her lean back on the stool so that her hair could be submerged in the bowl of hot water on the tiny table. "I will soon have you free of them, and I promise you will be happy with the end result of my labors."

She was about to rant further on the indignity of catching vermin from burly seamen, but the heat of the water, the perfume of the soap, the fragrant steam, and Everard's expert fingers soon soothed her. Within moments, everything seemed long ago and far away and not really all that important at all. She had thought to quiz him further on his fellow shipmates, but now she felt so blissfully quieted she simply could not bring her mind to bear on business. It was at times such as these that the harshness of her own day-to-day existence was brought home to her. Not for Gretel the pampered life of an adored wife, a woman with no worry beyond what to wear for which glittering social occasion. Not for her the comfort of a sizable inheritance to cushion her from the world and its woes. No, since the day she had rescued her brother from the witch, she had known that everything was Up To Her. Food on the table? Up To Her. Fire in the hearth? Up To Her. House in which to have a hearth? Up To Her. It was true, King Julian had provided a donation when their story first broke, sending them both to fine schools, with a little left over to aid the purchase of their home in Gesternstadt. But any such funds had run out many years ago. She viewed Hans as an expensive fixture in her life, and did her best to count the benefits he brought with him (which were few and almost entirely food-based) and not dwell on his attendant irritations (which were many). The plain fact was, no one was going to see to it that Gretel enjoyed the standard of living she knew she would thrive in. It was Up To Her to secure it, even if that meant hard and often dangerous work. Therefore, to enjoy a few peaceful moments in the care of the gentle and talented Everard seemed a small and just reward for all that she had achieved so far.

Into this pleasant reverie burst Hans, red-faced and full of his own rather more basic concerns.

"I say, Gretel, you'll never guess . . . oh!" He was brought up short by the sight of the steward rhythmically working his fingers through Gretel's hair. A shocked glance took in his sister's state of semi-undress and the enraptured expression on her face, and embarrassment overcame him. He retreated, backward—there being no space for him to turn around—muttering apologies and pulling the door firmly shut behind him.

Gretel sighed. She was aware that the only jumping her brother ever did was to conclusions, usually the wrong ones. She would set him right later. For now she was determined to enjoy the rest of Everard's ministrations. He combed, he brushed, he curled, he tonged, he spritzed, he pinned and powdered until at last he held up the hand mirror so that she might see the finished 'do.

"Is madam pleased?" he asked.

"Madam is *delighted*," she assured him. Her hair stood high and bouffant, secure, yet a little daring in style, and had indeed acquired a charming luster. "Everard, you are wasted as a steward, if I may say so, but I am exceedingly glad you are here for my voyage." She plucked a lacy shawl from the bed and a folded note from her corset. "Here, with my thanks," she told him. "By the way, during your time on this ship, have you ever encountered a sea sprite?"

"There's no such thing as a sea sprite, madam," he said quickly, lobbing a dry little spit into the washbowl while holding it to his left.

"No, of course there isn't. Well, thank you again," she said as he left. "And if you should see my brother on your way out, I should be grateful if you would send him to me. He rarely does anything with any speed, but he is surprisingly swift when it comes to spreading rumors."

When Hans arrived, he brought the mer-hund with him. The thing was horribly wet from its swim, so that the cabin was instantly filled with the pungent pong of damp dog. Damp, fishy dog.

"You can't bring that in here," Gretel protested, fending it off with her fan as it attempted to climb onto her lap and lick her face once more. "For pity's sake, get it away from me!"

Hans hauled on the rope and issued commands that had no effect on the creature's ebullience whatsoever. "I can't leave him outside, he might get lost, or start barking for me. He doesn't like being left on his own. Anyway, there's no need to make a fuss. He's only being friendly," he insisted.

"I prefer an acquaintance of longer standing before any such intimacies!"

"So I noticed earlier," said Hans, finally succeeding in dragging the mer-hund to sit at, or rather on, his feet.

"And what is that supposed to mean?"

"Well, dash it all, a fellow expects to be able to return to his cabin without finding another fellow already in it."

"Everard kindly agreed to attend to my coiffure."

"Oh, really? All part of a steward's duties nowadays, I suppose?"

"Don't pretend you know anything about who does what on a ship, Hans."

"I know what I saw, and I know who I saw doing it, and to whom, and it was most definitely on a ship at the time. Though could have been anywhere, I suppose. Mean to say, not confined to onboard, that sort of behavior, far as I've heard . . ."

"Hans, stop. Please. Believe me when I tell you Everard's interest in me arises from a purely professional arrangement."

"He's a gigolo?! Gretel, I am shocked!"

"He's a hairdresser! Now for pity's sake bring your attention to the matter of that . . . animal."

"This animal, as you rather harshly call him, has spent the past two hours working diligently on your behalf, matter of fact."

"I find that hard to believe."

"Kept sending down a man on a rope to help him back aboard, but no sooner had he set paws on deck than . . . hup! Over the side and off he'd go again. Didn't want to give up. Highly tenacious. It's bred into them, you know."

"Fascinating. And did he find anything?"

"Well, one time he did come back with a fish. Not just any old fish, mind you, no. It was thought to be a blue-nosed rib fish, which are known to be found only in close proximity to mermaids. Sometimes called mermaid fish, in point of fact."

"And was it?" Gretel asked, her interest finally piqued.

"Alas, it was not. It was later identified as a red herring."

Gretel narrowed her eyes at both man and hound. "I fear, brother mine, that you have been sold a pig in a poke."

❧

Later that night, with the three of them packed into the cabin like salted fish in a jar, sleep proved as elusive as the mermaid. Hans had, with some difficulty and much complaining, clambered into the top bunk, Gretel was once again wedged into the bottom one, and the mer-hund lay on the floor, just about filling all remaining space. The amount of air that had to be shared between them was pitifully inadequate, a fact not helped by the fishy farts the dog emitted at irregular intervals as the hours passed. Only the thought that the revolting animal had so successfully pulled Hans from his slough of despond over Birgit stopped her shoving the animal out into the passageway. Meanwhile, her brother's every second breath was a rumbling snore, as was his habit. The wind outside had strengthened, causing the ship to pitch and roll with increasing severity. At times its movements were so violent, Gretel would certainly have been tipped out had there been sufficient space. Yet again, she promised herself that something would have to be done about the size of their quarters. She thanked the heavens that she, and indeed Hans, had been blessed with staunch stomachs that remained unperturbed by the bucking and leaping of the *Arabella* as the weather worsened. She found her mind straying into the equally turbulent waters of her feelings for Ferdinand. What was he doing at that very moment, she wondered. She was reasonably certain that whatever it was, it was a good deal more pleasant than her own current cruising experience. Here she lay, wide awake, no sensible notions regarding the case entering her head, her beautiful hairdo unnoticed and unappreciated, suffering a jarring lullaby of wind (both inside and outside the cabin), her brother's juddering snores, and the arthritic creaking of the ship. She could stand it no longer. A few deep breaths of sea air and a turn around the deck might prove restorative.

She wriggled from her cot. As there was scant floorspace on which to put her feet, the business of extracting herself from her bed and changing from horizontal to vertical was a struggle. The mer-hund was sleeping so deeply it barely stirred as she stumbled over it. She pulled her shawl over her head and took her coat off the peg on the back of the door and slipped it over her peignoir, reasoning there would be few about to witness her curious attire. Most of her luggage was still stacked outside the door, so that she had to squeeze her way past it all, slowing her progress sufficiently to hear plaintive wails and cries coming from other cabins along the passage. Clearly not everybody was as sanguine regarding the choppiness of the sea and the unsettling motion of the ship.

Once up on deck, it became clear to Gretel that this was indeed weather of some significance. Men scurried about in all directions, tying this to that, hauling on ropes, wrestling with sails, and generally giving the impression that there was much to be done, and done with all haste. She wondered if she should be alarmed, but noticed that the captain himself was not to be seen, and convinced herself that an emergency would surely rouse him from his bed. Herr Hoffman, though he was aloft in charge of the wheel, stood at the epicenter of all action, barking orders, growling at the crew, but evidently not in a state of agitation or vexation. The *Arabella* answered the urging of the sailors, turning into the wind, prow first to the enormous waves that had got up seemingly out of nowhere. The night was dark, the sky heavy with clouds that now began to rain onto the deck. The noise of the breakers, the shouting men, the raging wind, and the cracking and groaning of the ship were near overwhelming.

"Get those sails down, boys!" bellowed Hoffman. "Trim the mainsail, Bo'sun Brandt, if you please! This is no time to let her have her head. Hold her steady and she'll take us safely through."

The ship lurched and leapt so that Gretel had to clutch hold of the nearest solid object if she were not to fall over. She thought of the passengers below, clinging to their bunks, seasick, no doubt, but unaware of the terrifying wildness of what was going on outside. She pulled her coat tighter around her and knotted the shawl at her chin. A part of her—a considerably ample part—wanted very much to scuttle back to her own fetid cabin, put a pillow over her head, and pray persuasively to anyone she could think of. But another part, the part that knew a rare thrilling moment when it came along, wanted to stay. Wanted to witness man pitted against the fury of the ocean. Wanted to watch those brave, strong, more than a little heroic men heave on a rope or climb up a ladder or swing through the tilting rigging. The thickset man she knew from Will to be the boatswain, or bo'sun, as it was known, loomed at her out of the jumping lamplight.

"Tha'll get a drenching, squatting yon like a booby in a flurry!"

"I beg your pardon?" Despite the cacophony, she could actually hear Bo'sun Brandt quite well, but could not find the sense in his words.

"When she takes a dip, tha'll be wetter'n a squilgee!" he yelled.

"Indeed." Gretel continued to hold on to the bollard, hoping the man would go away and leave her alone, but he seemed to expect something of her. "Am I in the way?" she asked. "I merely sought a little fresh air, though I confess, this is somewhat fresher than I had anticipated."

He rolled his eyes and shook his head. "Get yersen below, woman! We need no deadwood cluttering the deck, waiting to get washed o'erboard!"

As if to underline his point, a vast wave, suggested only by a darker darkness than the surrounding night, reared up above them. It glimmered in the light of the ship's lamps as the wave stayed suspended for the briefest of moments. There were shouts. Voices were raised in warning or alarm. Gretel recognized one of them—easily the shrillest—to be her own. And then the wave descended, breaking over the stoic figurehead on the prow, sending such a weight of water onto all who were on deck that the force of it tore the shawl from her head and threatened to sweep her over the side. She held tight, and the pressure subsided. Spitting water, she looked about her to see the crew pick themselves up as if nothing had happened and go about their business. Herr Hoffman admonished them for taking any opportunity for a break, cursed them for landlubbers, and demanded they see to their duties. Bo'sun Brandt nodded at Gretel in a manner that could only mean "I told you so," which quite possibly he had. Her clothes heavy with salt water, her hair ruined, her body bruised, Gretel mustered her damp dignity the best she could and wobbled her way toward the stairs. As she was about to descend, she turned and noticed that the quartermaster was no longer at the wheel; that position had been taken up by another crewmember. She spied him, instead, attending to one of the lifeboats. For a second she feared they were in real peril and would all be called to abandon ship, but no, he was not launching the thing. He was joined by none other than Bo'sun Brandt, and for a long moment the two busied themselves lashing the ropes that held the canvas cover in place. Naturally, it was important that the lifeboats remain secure, and it was entirely possible that the freakish wave had loosened the ropes that held them in place. But there was something about the way in which the two men bent their heads together. Something about the furtive glance Hoffman gave over his shoulder. Hoffman, a man whose every movement and every word was considered and clear, deliberate and plain for all to understand. Why should he, of all people, have cause to be furtive, Gretel wondered.

SEVEN

The following morning, Gretel awoke to find that the storm had abated, and the *Arabella* once again floated gently upon a calm sea. Hans, having slept through the tempest, declared himself famished and ready to brave the dining room. As this was the first time he had shown any interest in food since Birgit's appearance, Gretel was keen to seize the moment. She suspected That Woman was quite possibly neither an early riser nor a good sailor, so the sooner they were seated at their table the better. They wasted precious minutes in an argument about whether or not the mer-hund would be permitted to enter the dining room. Gretel was certain it would not be, and that even if it managed to slink in unseen, its stink would soon give it away. In the end she was made to promise Hans could visit Frenchie directly after they had broken their fast in order to find food for his new pet. They dressed hurriedly (Hans doing so in the passage behind a screen of trunks, his doting hound watching him all the while) and then moved past the other cabins as silently as they were able. Gretel had high hopes of finding the dining room empty at such an hour. Her mind was already racing ahead of her, imagining the melt-in-the-mouth butteriness of the cook's croissants, the sweet, salty tang of the maple-cured bacon, the rich golden glow of eggs fried in the very finest olive oil. Such a breakfast could set one up to face just about anything.

Alas, there was no breakfast.

This was because there was no cook.

Frenchie had disappeared.

The place was in uproar. Crewmembers had gathered to hear the news and looked anxiously about them, as if the chef might be discovered sleeping beneath a table or curled up in a window seat. Gretel noticed Will and Everard and even Bo'sun Brandt among them looking sorrowful. Captain Ziegler, with a face like thunder, strode up and down the room, his rage filling the space, his furious expletives ricocheting off the low ceiling, causing people to scramble for cover. "Why cannot I sleep without my ship falling to chaos?!" he roared. "What manner of crew have I that they let such things happen?"

Herr Hoffman, still gelid of eye, but for once looking as if his composure might fracture, attempted to placate his master. "The man was ungovernable, captain. Maybe he was on deck in the storm, drunk, and was swept overboard."

"Frenchie could hold his drink as well as the next man." The captain shook his head. "And he had more sense than to take himself wandering when the sea was up. Damn and blast your eyes, Hoffman! You had the watch. Did you see nothing?"

"We were about our business with the ship. The night was black. 'Twas all we could do to see those who wanted to be seen, never mind a person keeping himself hidden," he insisted.

The captain rounded on him, eyes ablaze. "And who's to say it was Frenchie's choice to leave his beloved galley, tell me that? The man lived for his art. For his kitchen. I say he would not leave it. Not but he was dragged!"

An uneasy quiet descended. Gretel felt the captain, in his anger, had made a serious error of judgment. Whatever he believed might have happened to his chef, to baldly state in front of his already jittery crew that some dark deed had befallen him was to risk dangerous unrest among the men. He had told her that they were on edge after the earlier disappearances, and since then there had been a further sighting of the mermaid. How much more sensible it might have been to go along with the quartermaster's theory of a drunken accident, if only temporarily. If he had done so he could have bought them—could have bought her—a little more time to get to the bottom of things without spooking the crew further.

It was at this point that Captain Ziegler noticed Gretel. "And you!" he cried, utterly forgetting the subterfuge they had agreed upon, and before she had a chance to stop him. "What is the point of you being here, fraulein? I am not paying you to be at your leisure! Is Gretel of Gesternstadt no more than a reputation and a deal of talk?"

A collective expression of bafflement visited the faces of his crew. They were, after all, simple souls, and for all their traveling had clearly been nowhere near Bavaria. Unsurprisingly, it being a region locked by land. Nevertheless, Gretel could not help feeling a tad niggled that her name meant nothing to them.

Herr Hoffman then did the only thing that ever made him remotely likeable in her view by asking, "You mean, *that* Gretel?"

Clearly the cat was out of the bag, brightly striped, bushy-tailed, scampering about the room, lively as could be and impossible to ignore. Gretel drew herself up, put to the very back of her mind the knowledge that her hair looked as if it had been through a storm, because it had, and stepped forward to take control of the situation.

"Captain," she said calmly, "I am, of course, saddened, as we all are, to hear that our wonderful cook is missing."

"Frenchie!" breathed Hans, tearfully.

"It may be," she continued, "that some tragic mishap befell him. It may be that the truth behind his absence is revealed to be more sinister."

"Frenchie!" Hans sobbed.

Gretel ignored him and pressed on. "Whatever the circumstances of his disappearance, rest assured I will discover them. And yes, Herr Hoffman, to answer your inquiry, I am indeed *that* Gretel, here in my capacity as private detective." She paused to let the assembled company have their gasps and murmurs. The captain appeared to be on the point of raging again, but she held up a hand and went on. "It is no secret, I believe, that the disappearance of two crewmembers during the *Arabella*'s previous voyage has not been explained. Your captain cares for his men, and for the good name of his ship," she said, turning to address this statement to as many as she could, trying to ignore the despairing way Everard was looking at her hair. "It is this conscientiousness, this integrity, that led him to engage my services. I promise you, this case can and will be solved."

The crew muttered and shuffled their feet, regarding her warily, none of them quite daring to mention the elephant in the room. The slender, fishy-tailed elephant.

It was Will the cabin boy who finally summoned the courage to whisper the words, "But what about the mermaid?"

The mutterings grew quickly louder until there were shouts and curses and even a bit of fist waving. The captain would stay silent no longer.

"Damn your cowardly eyes! Be ye afraid of such nonsense? Have you had your wits addled, all of you? What care I if there be a singing maid on a rock? Tobias Ziegler fears nothing that lives in, on, or under the sea, and I'll suffer no lily-livered curs aboard my ship!"

Gretel hastened to quieten him before he did any more damage.

"If I might suggest, captain, that you and I retire to your cabin to further discuss the matter . . . ?" She placed a steadying hand on his arm and was surprised to find it trembling. For all his swagger and bravado, the man was disturbed by something. Before he could reply, there came a shrill wailing from the doorway. Birgit and her cronies fluttered into the dining room in a flurry of fans, frills, and flirtatious glances.

"Is it true?" she demanded, all but flinging herself at the captain. "They say the cook has been murdered, his throat slit, the galley running with blood, before his body was tipped into the cruel ocean!" she shrieked. Her companions cried out. One of them swooned quite expertly. Unfortunately for her, she had chosen to rely on the gallantry of Herr Hoffman, who merely stepped aside, allowing her to fall instead into the burly embrace of Bo'sun Brandt.

"Frenchie!" moaned Hans. Even the arrival of That Woman could not shake him from the shock of losing his new friend in such an apparently gruesome way.

The level of noise and unrest was increasing by the second. Gretel placed herself firmly between Birgit and the captain, leaning in close, so that her words were heard only by him.

"If I might further suggest, captain . . . nothing fuels disquiet like hunger, and there is little that quells it better than a good feed."

"Fraulein, have you lost your mind?" he hissed. "We have no cook, woman."

"You have not Frenchie, but, fortunately, you do have my brother. He is, as luck would have it, the most excellent chef, and would gladly step into the breach."

Captain Ziegler regarded the tearful Hans skeptically. "You are certain he is up to the task?"

"I am. He is. Leave it to me. Send your crew about their work with the promise of extra rations in an hour, then go to your cabin. I will meet you there. Hurry now, the mood hereabouts turns uglier with every passing moment."

He did as he was told, accepting his instructions with uncharacteristic meekness. Gretel hurried to her brother's side and shook him roughly.

"Hans, snap out of it. We have need of your services. Get yourself down to the galley, find an apron, and do what you were born to do."

"Play cards?" he asked, blinking.

"Cook, for pity's sake."

"But Frenchie . . . ?"

". . . would not have wanted these people to go unfed, now, would he?"

Hans looked around the room as if seeing all the strained, angry, or hysterical faces for the first time. He was evidently already coming around to the idea of saving them all from starvation when he spotted Birgit, heading toward him. She was the deciding factor.

"I'll do it," he declared, turning on his plump heel. "For Frenchie!" he called back as he disappeared down the nearest flight of stairs.

Gretel ignored Birgit's stream of questions and entreaties and made her way quickly across the main deck, up the still-slippery stairs to the poop deck, past the wheel, and knocked on the door of the captain's cabin.

"This is a disaster!" Captain Ziegler wrenched his hat from his head and flung it down on his desk. Gretel was about to begin her complicated work of calming him down, extracting useful information from him, and ensuring that he favorably reviewed his damning opinion of her progress so far, when she was struck dumb by the loveliness of the captain's quarters. The cabin was as broad as the ship, with a wraparound mullioned window, making it a triple-aspect billet with deep, thickly cushioned window seats. The cot, if such it could be called, was a feather bed set into a cozy structure that would prevent the occupant from tipping out even in the roughest of seas. The soft furnishings were of the highest quality, damask and velvet and silk, and the lamps and candelabra were either gleaming brass or softly shimmering silver. Crystal glasses and decanters sat on the wide central table, and there was an imposing desk to one side, on which were laid charts and maritime navigational devices. It ran through Gretel's mind that she would give a fair sum, had she been in possession of one, to spend the voyage in such luxuriously appointed accommodation. Much as she would have liked to raise the matter of an upgrade of some sort, *any* sort, she had to acknowledge to herself that this was not the moment.

The captain gestured for Gretel to avail herself of one of the fine mahogany chairs at the table while he plucked the stopper from the nearest decanter and poured them both a measure of brandy. He sat heavily opposite her, his face still dark with anger. He leaned forward on the table, his expression one of challenge.

"Well, fraulein, let's have it. What is your plan? Your hour has come. Will you be found wanting?"

It was clear to Gretel that she was in the presence of a man who felt threatened by circumstances and would very likely look for someone to blame for his misfortune. She was determined that that someone would not be her. She took a sip of brandy, and was disappointed to find it decidedly inferior to that she had shared with Frenchie in the kitchen. While she knew a good cook prided himself on his ingredients, the liquor had been unnecessarily good for cooking purposes, and yet here was the captain drinking the same second-rate fare that was served in the bar. Grateful, in any case, for the reviving warmth it offered, as her empty stomach growled in protest, she brought her mind to bear on the matter at hand.

"In times such as these, Herr Captain, I find it best to return to the facts, and the facts as they present themselves to us thus far are these: two crewmembers disappeared on your previous voyage; mermaids were heard singing and seen sitting on both that voyage and this one; a fine and, I venture to say, dedicated chef has vanished. These occurrences may or may not be connected. Only time will tell."

"Time we do not have! Disappearing crew are apt to disturb their fellow sailors and paying passengers all the same. I cannot run my venture without the first, and there will be no point in my doing so without the second."

"Time, and diligent investigation. The former we must all bend to; the latter I am here to provide, and rest assured, captain, I will find the truth. I always do."

"Always, aye, maybe, but how many more souls must be lost before that truth is found?"

"Hopefully none."

"A sailor does not stay afloat long on hope."

"Nor does a detective solve a case solely upon it, but that does not mean we should not hold it to us as we work. For work we must. It is action that will save the situation now."

"What would you have me do?" he asked, spreading his arms wide in a gesture that suggested both desperation and a willingness to do whatever must be done.

"The immediate problem—that of having no cook—has been surmounted by the installation of my brother, Hans, in the galley."

"Aye, it is good of him to take on the task."

"Believe me when I tell you he is more than happy to do so," she said, recalling how swiftly he had moved when Birgit advanced upon him. "Though that is not to say he would not appreciate having his talents recognized. A cabin of his own, perhaps . . . ?" She let the idea hang. "Next, we must conduct a thorough search of the ship. I am sure your men have already been told to look for their fellow crewmember, but they must look again, and this time they must look for the slightest clue, the slightest trace, a kerchief, a knife, signs of a scuffle . . . whatever there may be."

"I shall put my best men on it."

"Excellent. I myself will question those who worked with Frenchie, as well as those who were on deck last night."

"That will be the greater part of the crew," Captain Ziegler warned her. "With such a sea up, most hands were on deck."

"Then most hands will be closely quizzed." She drained her glass and stood up once more.

"And what of me, Fraulein Gretel?" the captain demanded. "I cannot stand by while my crew is decimated and my business threatened with failure. What task shall I set myself to in order to save both?"

"Your work is of crucial importance," she told him. "You must set about diverting the passengers from this unsavory event. Hans will feed them; Mother Nature has blessed us with clear skies and calm seas today. You must see to it that their minds are occupied with happier thoughts than those that arise from dwelling on a possible murder, or kidnap, or being spirited away by mythical creatures from the deep. I recommend music. Dancing. Simple pleasures that soothe body, mind, and soul."

"Yes!" The captain sprang to his feet, a roguish smile transforming his countenance. "You have it right, fraulein. I will send a messenger gull at once. We are within reach of the port of Busum. I will summon musicians."

"Splendid! I recommend you move among your men and passengers now. Let them see you are unworried, that everything is in hand, and tell them of the wonderful entertainment that awaits them this evening. If there are any murmurings regarding poor taste, respect for the unfortunate cook, and so on, quell them with stories of Frenchie's good humor. Tell them how it would have pained him to see them so glum on his account. In short, Captain Ziegler, employ your not inconsiderable charm," she told him, noticing anew the singular manner in which his teeth crossed, giving his grin a mischievous allure. Again this stirred in her some long-forgotten memory, though it still would not reveal itself.

The *Arabella* became a place of intense activity. Crewmembers scoured the ship for any sign of their absent cook. The captain went about lavishing attention and charisma upon his passengers, promising them delights and entertainment, calming their fears, and generally playing down the matter of the missing man, even going so far as to suggest he might have jumped ship for the sake of a sweetheart in a nearby port. He worked his talent for leadership upon his men, too, pausing to pat a back or give a nod of encouragement in a convincing manner wherever he could. Soon the mood on board was quite altered.

Hans outdid himself. The minute he tied the apron strings around his ample form, he was a changed man, no longer lachrymose and woeful, but focused and determined. Frenchie was now someone he had to live up to and whose memory he must serve well. That Woman was not allowed entry to the galley, so that he was able to put her from his mind altogether while he worked. And work he did, falling with glee upon the well-stocked larder, issuing orders to the galley boy to chop this and slice that while he himself mixed and blended and seared and tossed, for all the world as if he were back in his own beloved kitchen in Gesternstadt.

Gretel set about questioning the crew. She was relieved to be able to cast off the disguise of a vacationing passenger and reveal her true identity and purpose. It felt right to be frankly and openly putting questions to people, taking notes, circling salient points, underlining anomalies, and generally considering possibilities and theories. She was in her element, and confident that the case would now progress swiftly. She would have preferred to go about her investigations without the assistance of the perpetually damp and malodorous mer-hund, but as it was not allowed in the galley and howled noisily if left for any time in the cabin, she was forced to keep it with her. After two hours of diligence, only one person remained to be quizzed. She found the quartermaster at the wheel, his cold eyes fixed on the distant horizon as he kept the ship on her course. The mer-hund, ever Gretel's shadow, padded around the poop deck behind them.

"Herr Hoffman, I trust my questions will not prove a dangerous distraction," she said, coming to stand beside him.

Hoffman kept tight hold of the worn wooden handles, minutely adjusting the wheel this way and that as required. He did not look at Gretel as he spoke. "I've been all my life at sea, fraulein. Taken on as a cabin boy when I had seen but eight summers, and the greater part of my years since have seen me aboard rather than on land. I've held the position of quartermaster these five years since. I am not to be distracted by a woman's chatter," he told her.

"Quite," said Gretel, refusing to rise to the bait.

"Ask what you will. I have nothing to hide."

"I sincerely hope that is the case," she replied, "but if it were not, I doubt any amount of interrogation on my part could unearth a secret you wished to keep."

This unexpected tack caused him at least to glance at her. He looked for a moment as if he might make a comment, but instead kept his mouth shut in a firm, hard line. Gretel pressed on.

"I noticed last night, when I was taking a little air . . ."

"You were ill advised to be out of your cabin and on deck in such weather, fraulein. There were waves of sufficient strength and size to sweep even you over the side."

Gretel chose to ignore the small but ungallant "even" in his remark. It would not do to lose her composure with such a man. ". . . I noticed that, while you had command of the ship, the captain was nowhere to be seen. Even when the storm was at its height. It is clear he trusts you utterly with his ship and his crew."

"Would be little point in having a quartermaster if that were not the case. A man does not keep a dog and bark himself."

Gretel could not help pausing to look at the mer-hund. She decided it was her turn to be provoking. "Surely, Herr Hoffman, you do not consider yourself your master's pet?"

There was an instant of silence, save for the brittle, scratchy sound of offense being taken, yet still Hoffman would not let his stony façade crumble. "It is as you said: the captain trusts me to do my job. And I do it. That is the beginning and end of our relationship."

"Indeed. And while you were doing your job so splendidly, you found it necessary at one point to give the wheel to a person of lower rank, so that you might attend to one of the lifeboats."

"What of it?"

"Forgive me, Herr Hoffman, I am a woman come late to the sailing party, but it seems to me more important that the man in charge should be steering the ship, rather than fiddling with rope and such like."

"The lifeboats must be secured. For the safety of crew and passengers."

"Quite so, but I understand that the maintenance of ship's equipment—rigging, sails, and the like—falls under the tender auspices of the boatswain. Is that not the case?"

"Ordinarily, it is. But Bo'sun Brandt was not at hand. There was much to be done, and scarce enough crew to do it. I saw that the lifeboat required lashing and chose to see to it myself, rather than have Brandt fetched," he explained, with impressive plausibility.

"I see," said Gretel. "Thank you so much for clearing the matter up for me."

"Have I then?"

"Oh, indeed you have," she told him. "I will trouble you no further." So saying, she took herself off, narrowly avoiding an undignified descent of the stairs as the mer-hund bounded past her. Hoffman had unwittingly given himself away. Gretel knew that, had she confronted him directly regarding his conversation with Brandt near the lifeboat during the storm, he would have invented some harmless explanation. By allowing him to choose to lie about Brandt's having been there with him, he had revealed this as something he wished to hide, and therefore as something significant. Quite what it signified she did not yet know, but she resolved to find out as quickly as she was able.

The calm sea allowed the summoned musicians from Busum to meet the *Arabella* at the given rendezvous point without difficulty. The promise of evening entertainment had done precisely what Gretel had assured Captain Ziegler it would do; the passengers could think of nothing else. They had enjoyed Frenchie's cuisine; they had, briefly, lamented his loss, but their fickle hearts had happily moved on to more joyful pursuits. Men and women alike disappeared to their cabins to ready themselves for a few hours of fun and frivolity. Hans, of course, refused to leave his post, and so continued his work in the galley, promising a late feast for all the dance-goers. Gretel found herself caught up in the moment, not least because it would mean an opportunity, at long last, to wear her divine wig. Everard was fearfully busy with preparations for the evening, but still managed to slip away for ten minutes to assist Gretel.

"Fraulein, you look magnificent!" he declared, stepping back as best the confines of her quarters would allow, which necessitated him all but standing on Hans's hound. He had brushed and tamed her salt water–tangled hair until it was sufficiently malleable once again to force beneath a fine net. This allowed him to fit the wig in place and secure it with pins. It was undeniably a superb creation. As Gretel regarded her reflection in the looking glass, she congratulated herself on money well spent. A wig was not something to scrimp on. It was a statement of grandeur, a declaration of the wearer's love of style, and fashion, and all things elegant and refined. Everard had skillfully dressed the wig, teasing the piles of curls and twists of snowy white into perfect shape and condition. The tiny silver beads and bells that threaded through the creation sparkled attractively in the low light of the ship's lamp. He leaned forward and dabbed on a little more powder for the finishing touch.

"Exquisite!" He smiled.

Gretel smiled back. There was nothing like a bit of dressing up and showing off to give one a boost. It had been a long, hard day, which came on the heels of an uncomfortable, sleepless night. The drama of Frenchie's disappearance, and the hours of work that followed, had left her drained. Now she felt restored. Rejuvenated. She knew she looked particularly fine, and now she would drift about the dining hall—transformed for the evening into a mini ballroom—enjoying the admiring glances of the other passengers. She might even dance. True, this would not be as spectacular as a ball at the Summer Schloss, or a grand occasion on board the mighty *Fair Fortune*, and she would not have the opportunity to be waltzed or polka'd by Uber General Ferdinand von Ferdinand, but still . . . she was wearing her wig, and she intended to enjoy every minute of it. She thanked Everard, insisting he accept a generous tip before he hurried back to take up his position as steward once more. It was early, however, and she did not want to lessen the impact of her entrance by being among the first to arrive. A short turn about deck would be just the thing, she decided. Hans had sent down a juicy bone for the mer-hund, which Gretel now gave him so that she could leave without his kicking up a rumpus at being shut in without company. The last thing she needed was a pungent, hairy chaperone to color her enjoyment of the occasion.

Up top, the air was fresh but warm, the sky a slowly deepening blue, the sea flat as a silk bedsheet. Gretel leaned on the rail, enjoying the way the lightest of westerly breezes refreshed and soothed her at one and the same time. She knew she cut a striking figure. From the corner of her eye she was aware of the honeymooning couple turning to look at her. Birgit and her cohort craned their necks for a better view. Even Dr. Becker lowered his ever-present field glasses in order to take in her glamorous appearance.

Which, for the briefest of moments, was all so very harm-
lessly pleasant and lovely. Why was it, Gretel asked herself
later, that such joy could only ever be fleeting? Why was it
that such gentle pleasures that might, admittedly, be defenseless against accusations of pride, but which were otherwise
simple delights that caused no one any distress, had to be
paid for in such currencies as shame and humiliation? Would
it have been too much to hope for that the soft zephyr that
barely rippled the sails could stay as such, and not suddenly
develop a stiff gust? It seemed that it would. For such a gust
did indeed develop, whipped up from who knew where, to
hit Gretel with its full force. She teetered against the rail, but
was never in any danger of tipping over it. What was unable
to withstand the brisk blowing, however, was her beloved
wig. Or rather, the pins that secured it. The wind whisked
the towering confection from her head, suspended it for the
shortest of moments in the air above, and then swept it out to
sea, where it landed with a poignant splash before descending
to the depths.

From atop the rigging there came a shout.

"Wig overboard!"

Without a word, Gretel turned on her heel, hitched up her
skirts, held her hair-netted head high, and returned to her cabin
and the uncritical gaze of the mer-hund.

EIGHT

Two days after Frenchie's as-yet-unexplained disappearance saw warmer weather still, and an excursion was arranged to one of the tiny nearby islands so that the cruise-goers might indulge in some sea-bathing. The Schmidts cornered Gretel at breakfast and spent two courses extolling the benefits of saltwater swimming, listing among them glowing skin, increased vigor, healing of old wounds and scars, and a boosted appetite. Gretel assured them that her appetite needed no boosting, and that in her experience sea air could prove the ruination of a good complexion. However, she was pleased to share that she would in fact be taking advantage of the excursion, as she had never visited such a place before, might not be given the chance to do so again, and firmly believed in experiencing what life had to offer when such occasions presented themselves. The loving couple was not really interested in her reply, for they were still immersed in their love for each other, and indeed their love of that love. Long before Gretel had come to the end of her response, Herr and Frau Schmidt had turned their attention from her and back to themselves.

The truth was, Gretel had other reasons for booking her seat on the tender that was to take them to Amrum. Whatever the magical properties of seawater, she felt she had already seen, swallowed, and been doused in more than enough of the stuff. As for the notion of lowering herself, clad in a ridiculous bathing costume, into the briny surf for the purpose of floating about like so much flotsam, nothing could appeal to her less. However, Herr Hoffman was to accompany the passengers on the trip. She had overheard him insisting to Captain Ziegler that he should be in charge of the outing, remaining with the party throughout the day to ensure their safety. The captain had been happy to let him do so, clearly not relishing the prospect of having to play host himself. But why, Gretel wondered, was the quartermaster so keen to put himself forward for the duty? He was the least sociable man on board, and she could not, however hard she tried, picture him frolicking in the waves. There was something behind his action, some hidden motive, and if she was to stand any chance of discovering what it was, she must go to the wretched island herself. Fortunately, she had acquired a bathing suit for the cruise. She shuddered briefly at the memory of how she had looked wearing the thing in the privacy of her own bedroom. The thought of stepping out in public wearing nothing but the unflattering stripy horror was a depressing one. She clung tight—as a drowning woman to a barrel—to the fact that the island boasted bathing machines. She had been assured that one of these would provide total privacy for her sea-bathing.

The journey from the *Arabella* was pleasant enough. The ship's tender was both comfortable and seaworthy, and there was room aplenty for the brave band of passengers who had signed up for the excursion. There were the Schmidts, naturally; Birgit and her phalanx, no doubt lured by the promise of a miracle beauty treatment; and Dr. Becker, who told any who cared to listen and some who didn't of all the rare bird species he hoped to have sight of on Amrum. Aside from these, two elderly couples from Hamburg, a dry stick of a spinster and her matching sister, Gretel, two oarsmen, and Hoffman made up the party. Hans could now not be shifted from his kitchen, and would anyway never have put himself in such proximity to That Woman. He had assured Gretel that he would use the time to walk the mer-hund around decks so that he and it both might exercise.

The waters surrounding the chosen isle were shallow, so that the *Arabella* had been forced to anchor at some distance. When first Gretel had had Amrum pointed out to her, she had assumed that it was this distance that made it look so small. She was disappointed, then, to discover that it looked scarcely any larger when they were upon it. Hoffman and the seamen jumped out and hauled the boat onto the shore, wading through the water to do so. Everyone on board became quite childishly excited as they were required to disembark into the shallows themselves. Everyone except Gretel. Boots and shoes were removed first, and there was a deal of silly squealing and exclaiming as people splashed their way onto the beach. The temperature of the water came as a nasty shock. Given that it was summer, and the morning was already hot, it came as an unpleasant surprise to find that the sea itself evidently thought it was still winter. A chill shot through Gretel's feet, traveled up her entire body, finishing with a jarring pain in her teeth. By the time she came to stand on what passed for *terra firma*, she had lost all sensation in her toes. The sand, in contrast, had kept up with the changing seasons and was fearfully hot. A fact that revealed itself to Gretel as feeling returned to her lower extremities, causing her to hop from one foot to the other as if she were practicing some undignified rustic dance.

"Good grief!" she snapped. "Is one expected to enjoy such torture? Whatever next?"

"Oh, Gretel," giggled Birgit, "don't be a such a killjoy. We are here to have fun, are we not?"

"Fun? *Joy?*" Gretel did not trust herself to respond further. Looking about her, she surmised that Amrum offered an abundance of nothing. The beach stretched away in both directions, an uninterrupted expanse of nothingness. A little farther inland there were pale dunes, from which sprouted sparse, wiry grass, lonesome as the last hairs on the head of a balding man. There was not a bush, nor tree, nor building of any sort to give shade or shelter. To Gretel the place presented a perfect picture of desolation, so barren and bare it made her pine afresh for her own house and even the tweeness of Gesternstadt. At least her hometown was inhabited. Amrum was wilderness, which Gretel held meant a lack of anything one might actually wish for. Such as comfortable seating. Or a decent meal. Or something admirable by way of architecture, perhaps. Or society, indeed. What could the poor folk of Amrum do by way of cultural stimulation and refined living, she wondered.

"Is this place actually inhabited?" she asked of Herr Hoffman.

"There is a village further inland," he said, indicating somewhere beyond the dunes.

Dr. Becker smiled at her. "Fraulein, the beauty of this island is precisely the absence of man's heavy-handed presence. Here nature still rules. It is a paradise for seabirds."

"Indeed."

"Look!" he cried excitedly, pointed into the middle distance, his voice hoarse with emotion. "A lesser crested greater spotted egret, if I am not mistaken. Wonderful! And another. Must be a breeding pair." He had no need of his glasses now, only his hand to shield his eyes from the increasingly strong sun. Without waiting for anyone to comment on his find, he hurried off toward the dunes.

The quartermaster grunted. "It seems saltwater swimming holds no interest for the good doctor. This way, if you please," he called to the little group. "Allow me to show you to your bathing machine," he said, his tone uncharacteristically solicitous.

Gretel let him lead the way along the scorching sands. The others followed, laughing at the lopsided gait the shifting surface beneath their feet forced them into. The honeymooners took off their shoes, squealing at the heat of the sand. Birgit and her comrades followed suit. They blundered on for what felt like an age before the beach curved a little to the left, and behind some large dunes they found a row of curious, brightly painted wooden huts on wheels. Each had a pair of shafts, and a stout horse and its equally stout owner stood waiting to tow the devices out into the sea. Hoffman addressed the man with a string of curious-sounding words Gretel took to be Danish. The incomprehensible exchange seemed to result in terms being struck. Hoffman turned to the party.

"Ladies, gentlemen, please choose your bathing machine. You enter by the steps and door at the back. Inside you may change into your costumes, leaving your clothes on the shelf provided. When you are ready, sing out; the ostler will hitch up his horse and tow the carriage into the sea, turning so that you may exit down the steps and into the water for bathing."

Those present meekly did as they were bid. The steps were quite steep, and the doorway narrow, so that Gretel entered only with some effort and struggle. Inside was clean, but the space restrictive, so that by the time she had divested herself of her clothing and wriggled into her bathing attire she was unpleasantly hot and damp with perspiration. Gazing down at her body, she thought that she had never worn such an unflattering garment. The clingy nature of the fabric held every voluptuous mound and curve in a tight embrace, while the broad horizontal stripes she had been assured were *de rigueur* for such a thing had an unhelpful broadening effect. Comforting herself with the knowledge that no one else would be able to view her, as the bathing machine afforded her total privacy, she hollered for the horse to be brought. The animal's handler kept up a stream of unfathomable chatter as he backed the horse into the shafts, attached the straps and chains, and then led it forward. The deep, dry sand caused the contraption to lurch and sway alarmingly, but the pace was slow and steady, and they reached the sea without mishap. Gretel held on tight as the little house was turned and then backed into the surf. The final position was with the entrance door and steps in the sea, the rear, with the shafts and a small viewing window, facing back up the beach. The handler detached the horse and wound down two stabilizing feet from the bathing machine into the sand before heading off to move the next one into place. Gretel peered out through the little window. She could see Herr Hoffman seated among the dunes, leaning back on his elbow, relying on his hat for shade, taking out his pipe in the manner of one planning a lengthy stay. He did not look like a person about to do anything suspicious or interesting. The whole point of coming on the excursion had been to watch him, but there was nothing to watch.

With a sigh, Gretel decided she might as well experience what little the empty island had to offer and partake of the sea-bathing. She turned and opened the door on the seaward side.

She shuffled out and sat on the top step. To either side, panels protruded so that she could not see left or right, and no one could see the area of water into which the steps would lower her. The view directly out across the ocean was quite striking. The *Arabella* could be made out anchored at some distance, but other than that there was only an expanse of shimmering teal blue water, fading into pale blue sky at the horizon. Sunlight danced and sparkled on the gently ruffled surface. Somewhere high above, gulls called, their cries drifting away in a manner that was both plaintive and faintly soothing. Soft waves lapped at the bottom stair of Gretel's conveyance. She reached down and dipped a toe into the water. For all the heat of the day, it was shockingly cold. This was a disappointment, as Gretel always preferred her baths as hot as possible. However, she was so overheated by now that the coolness, and the refreshment it promised, was in fact quite appealing. Cautiously, she lowered herself down until she was seated on the bottommost step. She gasped as the water washed over her body, but held her nerve and her position, sighing as the invigorating salt water flowed over her. She settled so that she was submerged up to her waist, which felt both daring and yet reasonably safe. She had never learned to swim, and now was not the time to try. There was no necessity, she decided, to cast herself free of the safety of the bathing machine; here on the step, semi-immersed, she could surely enjoy all the benefits the sea had to offer without imperiling herself. She wriggled forward a little, so that she could comfortably lean back against the higher steps. Her eyes closed, her face shaded by the overhang of the roof, she felt blissfully relaxed.

In such a state she was able to consider the facts in a fresh light. Frenchie was still missing, his disappearance unexplained. Hoffman was hiding something. In this quiet moment, Gretel brought to mind the curious rhyme the sea sprite had given her as a puzzle. She had half hoped to encounter the little creature again. It seemed to her it was well placed to witness the goings-on aboard ship; perhaps it could shed some light on the case. Aside from this probability, something recent seemed to connect to it to other salient facts, though Gretel could not quite fathom how. She turned the words over in her mind, muttering them as she did so.

"'Look once, look twice, look again at the tooth'"—indeed, I should not like to look too closely at the sprite's own teeth. But it could not have been referring to itself, surely? No, another tooth, another mouth. "Ah-*ha!* I have it!" she cried, opening her eyes and sitting up a little. That smile, she had known there was something familiar about it—the crooked teeth. Captain Tobias Ziegler he might be now, but that man was and always would be none other than the Snaggle-Toothed Pirate! So famous that his likeness had been rendered in a thousand pamphlets and notices. How could it have taken her so long to see it? Granted, it had been a few years since his exploits were last reported, but even so, anyone in the southern half of Germany would have heard of him. The Mediterranean had been his favorite hunting ground, so that interest in his daring deeds was stronger there than in the north. Gretel reasoned that this could be the reason none of her fellow passengers had apparently recognized him. And the *Arabella's* former purpose was to sail the high seas in search of ships to plunder. That explained the nature of most of the crew. But not all of them. Not Hoffman. What was it the captain said? The reason he hired him . . . Gretel searched her mind for it. There was something he had brought with him that Ziegler could not do without. What, though? In an attempt to jog her memory, Gretel recited aloud the sea sprite's little rhyme.

"'First the coat, then the badge . . . . dum de dum de something-or-other . . . for the truth.' The coat? His pirate's booty taken from a conquered adversary, perhaps. The badge? A badge of honor? Of captaincy? That would fit. Hoffman is a professional sailor of some reputation. A *legitimate* reputation. Something a pirate would need to make the transformation from buccaneer to master of a cruise ship, one might imagine."

Pleased with her own insight, Gretel closed her eyes and settled into the water once again. She stifled a yawn. Several interrupted nights and patchy access to meals had taken their toll. Why should she not enjoy a little relaxation? As her body half floated, lifted and lowered by the ebb and flow of the waves, her mind too floated, further and further, until all thoughts became blurred and sounds muted, and sleep claimed her.

On waking, she had difficulty making sense of her situation. Her head felt hot, but the rest of her felt nothing at all. She was benumbed. Had she become a bodiless head somehow? What had happened to her, and where on God's earth was she? She attempted to sit up, but her limbs were reluctant to cooperate in their heavy, lifeless state. As she blinked sleep from her eyes, she recalled that she had fallen into slumber while sitting upon the steps of her bathing machine. How long ago must that have been? She was indeed, still on the steps, a point brought home to her with cruel insistence by the one sensation of which she was aware—that of the wooden steps digging into her back. The level of the water had risen so that she was now submerged up to her neck. Fighting mounting panic, she attempted to haul herself up the steps. Her costume had doubled in weight, now that it was saturated, and her chilled arms and legs moved only sluggishly and clumsily despite what she considered Herculean effort. She gasped in horror as she caught sight of her puffy, wrinkled fingers and palms. Once she had dragged herself out of the water and into the bathing machine proper, she could see that her feet were similarly transformed.

"How utterly revolting!" she told herself, her voice echoing flatly around the cramped space. She squinted out of the rear window. The sun had dropped to the inland horizon; the light was flat and dull. All the other bathing carriages had been returned to their original positions at the top of the beach, well above the waterline. There was not a living soul to be seen. No Hoffman. No Birgit et al. Not even the chunky cob and its master. No one. She had been abandoned. All of a sudden, the surf surged forward and upward. Gretel cried out as an unnervingly strong wave rushed into the wooden hut. As there was no way for it to get out, the level rose with alarming speed, so that even standing up she was doused to her bosom. As the wave receded, she cursed at the realization that all her clothes were now soaked, as the shelf on which she had so carefully placed them had been covered by the brief inundation. In any case, there was too much water and too little room for maneuver to allow her to change back into her petticoats and day dress. The awful truth presented itself to her, ugly side up. The tide was coming in. The level of the water inside the bathing machine was rising. If it was not to be all up for Gretel (yes, *that* Gretel) of Gesternstadt, she had to get out. Soon. And the only way out was down the steps and into the sea. It was hard to judge precisely how deep the water was that now surrounded the little wheeled hut, but going on the height of the floor, the size of the wheels, and the amount of water currently inside, the conclusion she came to was that she would be out of her depth. Which would mean swimming. Except that she could not.

How had she come to be in this predicament? It made no sense. All the other bathing machines were empty. The group from the *Arabella* gone. What would have made them leave her behind? The neat line the wooden carriages now presented did not suggest any haste or emergency. Why, then, had they not woken her and taken her with them?

Gretel had no answers for these questions. The only thing she was certain of was that Hoffman lay behind her situation. She had always suspected the man had something to hide. At last she had the motive that had driven him to play escort for the excursion. He had wanted to be rid of her. Her questions had evidently spooked him. He must have planned to maroon her in this way, and had clearly fabricated some story that convinced the rest of the party that she was no longer in her bathing machine when they left.

Fury began to form a cold, hard knot in Gretel's stomach. It was kept company by the colder, harder pain of indigestion, which reminded her that she had had nothing to eat or drink for several hours. With these twin goads lending her courage, she started her descent of the steps. She would not just sit about to meet a soggy end. She would walk on the seabed if necessary, scramble and claw among the seaweed and shells, hitch a ride on a passing turtle if she had to, but one way or another she would get out of her humiliating situation, save her own water-wrinkled skin, and return to the *Arabella* to deal with the murderous quartermaster.

There was a different coldness to the water now. Gone was the refreshing quality that had been so pleasant. Instead the water felt as if it might chill her to the very bone, or even stop her heart. Every fiber of her being cried out for her to stop, go back, stay out of those dark depths. But she knew she had no choice; she must go on. On tiptoe upon the bottom step the water was up to her chins. She leaned against the side panel, planning to use it to pull herself around and up the other side. For a moment she hesitated, her nerve threatening to fail her. She thought of Hans. If she didn't make it back, would he be fated to stay forever aboard the *Arabella*, working his endless passage as ship's cook, with only the mer-hund to call friend? What would become of her dear home, left to house nothing but cobwebs and dust? Would Ferdinand mourn her passing, or would he simply give one of his maddeningly handsome, rueful smiles, and go on with his life without her?

"Not if I can help it!" she roared, taking a huge breath, and plunging into the water. Beneath the surface all was silence, save for the pounding of her own heartbeat against her eardrums. When she stepped off the last stair and her feet met the sandy seabed, the water covered her entirely. It was too dark and swirly to see anything helpful, so Gretel closed her eyes and groped her way along, scratching at the wet wood of the side panels, taking enormous, slow, bouncing strides. It was more than a little terrifying having to force herself to go farther into the sea, but there was no option. She had to get free of the bathing carriage before she could head for the shore again. She could only hope that she had sufficient breath and strength and time to make the journey, for she knew she would not be able to propel herself to the surface from such a depth. She held on to her rage at Hoffman to drive her forward.

At one point something slimy and sinuous slithered around her ankle and then was gone. She told herself it was much too cold for snakes, and pressed on. She became aware of pressure building up inside her, and of a faintness that must come from using up most of the workable air in her lungs. She must not give way to panic. At last her fingers curled around the edge of the panel. She dragged herself around it, galvanized by the thought of how near freedom was. The tide must have been beginning to turn, for it was harder to make progress in the direction of land now. She clawed and scrabbled, and kicked at the melting sand beneath her feet, and at last she felt her head break through the surface. She gasped, exhaling spent breath and gulping air too soon, so that she took in an equal quantity of water. Coughing and spluttering, thrashing without thought or restraint, she flung herself through the breaking waves and onto the beach. With her last scrap of strength she crawled out of the water, coughing up brine, before collapsing exhausted onto her back. She lay where she fell, eyes shut, entirely done in, but aware of the mounting elation that follows the experience of surviving a brush with death.

"A pleasant day for a swim, fraulein."

The voice was unmistakable. Gretel ground her teeth, just the teeniest, weeniest bit. It wasn't that she was sorry he was there. She was glad. It wasn't that she did not want to see him. She did. It wasn't even that, had he arrived but a few minutes earlier he could have spared her the trouble of her waterlogged walk and helped her effect a less terrifying and considerably drier escape. She was safe, after all. No real harm done. No, none of those factors was the cause of her clenched jaw, deepening frown, and building urge to scream. What it *was* was that yet *again* the one man in the whole of Germany (including but not confined to territories off its shores) to whom she dearly wished to present herself in the best and most flattering of lights was witness to her at her absolute worst. On this occasion, she was sporting a garment so vile in its fabric, so unforgiving in its cut, and so revealing in its shape, it was as if it had been designed specifically to highlight every flaw she possessed. Highlight, expose, draw attention to, and generally flaunt. Her sodden hair clung to her head like so much seaweed. Her face had been alternately scorched, poached, and sand-scrubbed to a shining redness she suspected might be visible for several miles in any direction. She had not the aid of perfume nor powder, but instead the aroma of shellfish, and a dusting of sand.

She opened her eyes.

"Good afternoon to you, General von Ferdinand," she said. "A pleasant day to be out riding, too," she added, taking in the magnificent horse he was mounted on. She had never seen such a beautiful animal. It was ebony black, with a proud bearing and arched neck. Its mane was long and flowing, with an attractive wave to it.

"Isn't he splendid? He is a Frisian, lent to me for the day. I shan't want to return him to his owner," he said, patting the horse's velvety neck.

Gretel knew things had reached a Bad State of Affairs when she was being outshone by a horse. Even if it was a particularly fabulous one. The stallion lowered its head to sniff her curiously. With as much dignity as she could muster, Gretel scrambled to her feet.

"It appears I have been left behind," she told Ferdinand.

"An astonishing oversight on someone's part."

"I think not."

"You suspect a deliberate act?"

"I am certain of it."

Ferdinand nodded slowly, taking in the perilous position of the bathing machine and the sorry condition of its recent occupant. "It would seem that, once again, Fraulein Gretel, your talent for identifying a villain has led you into danger."

"Happily, my talent for survival is also well developed. However, I find myself ill-clad, ill-shod, and ill-disposed to effect my return to the *Arabella*. Might I prevail upon you to assist me?"

"It would be my honor," he said, slipping down from the horse. He undid his burgundy cape with the gold silk lining and wrapped it around Gretel's chilly shoulders before assisting her ascent into the saddle. He sprang up to sit behind her, taking the reins in one hand, his other arm holding her tightly to him.

It was not the most comfortable of perches, and Gretel was painfully aware of how ghastly her hair looked and how stout her legs appeared where they protruded from beneath the cape, but she would not, at that moment, as they galloped across the sands with Ferdinand clasping her close, and the fine horse carrying them away to safety, have wished herself anywhere else on earth.

⁂

Some time later, safely back aboard the ship, her hair dried and tamed, her clothes changed, herself restored to some manner of normality, Gretel shared a glass of wine on deck with Ferdinand. Her arrival had caused confusion. She had been greeted by her fellow salt-water bathers with a disconcerting lack of concern. Questioning revealed that they had understood her to have left her bathing machine moments after they had disappeared into their own, having decided against using it. Herr Hoffman had informed them that she had instead chosen to explore the island, no doubt looking for evidence of mermaids, or clues as to Frenchie's whereabouts. Indeed, they had waited some time at the tender for her to appear at the agreed hour, and some had grown quite infuriated that she had not kept the rendezvous. When Dr. Becker reached them, they felt certain that he must have seen her while searching for seabirds, but he claimed not to have. It was then that Herr Hoffman decided they could wait no longer or they might miss the tide. He had assured them a smaller rowing boat would be sent back with able men to search for her as soon as was possible.

The quartermaster had shown an impressive nimbleness of mind. Gretel surmised he must have had approximately half an hour from the time he identified her in the tender Ferdinand used to ferry her to the *Arabella* to the moment she was brought aboard and stood toe-to-toe with him. Calculating that he would have needed a full two minutes to recover from the shock of seeing her alive, followed by another eight of barely suppressed panic wherein he quite possibly believed he was on the point of being exposed as a would-be assassin, that left him no more than twenty minutes to invent a plausible excuse for his actions. He had convincingly feigned both delight and surprise at seeing her, which, given his habitually immobile features, was in itself quite an achievement. He had insisted he was on the point of sending a boat and swift oarsmen back to the island to look for her in the interior, prepared to rouse a search party from the village if necessary. When asked why he had thought she had left the bathing machine, he had maintained that one of the crew who had helped row the tender had been informed by the other crewmember also on the excursion who had been told this was so by the ostler with the draft horse. Since he spoke no German, and they spoke no Danish, confusion and misunderstanding had ensued.

Someone had suggested it was odd that the bathing carriage had been left in the sea rather than returned to dry land. To this, the quartermaster had responded that it was not his job to oversee the repositioning of an empty hut. His responsibility had been to return the passengers to the *Arabella* while the tide was favorable.

As excuses went it was pretty flimsy, but Gretel was prepared to bide her time. She knew that it would be hard to prove evil intent on Hoffman's part, but now she knew what she was up against. She knew that he had something sufficiently serious to hide to warrant attempting her murder. And what was more, he knew that she knew. She would watch him. She would wait. Such an inflammatory secret could not help but burn through whatever shrouded it sooner rather than later.

She and Ferdinand sat side by side, enjoying a passable claret and making the most of a pleasant sunset. Others were strolling about the deck or reclining in chairs here and there, no doubt happily tired if a little salty after their excursion and all with sharp appetites for the feast Hans was at that moment preparing for them. Beside Gretel the mer-hund, delighted at no longer being confined alone to the cabin, stretched out panting in the evening sun, nibbling on the remnants of yet another bone. Suddenly it left off its licking and munching to raise its head, ears pricked, and gaze up into the sails. Gretel thought it an unlikely place for a mermaid to be hiding, but followed its gaze, only to find the sea sprite sitting in a knot of rope, watching. The mer-hund wagged its tail briefly and then went back to its bone. The sea sprite pointed at Ferdinand and then got to its furry feet and performed a saucy little dance before turning to laugh at Gretel in a highly suggestive manner. It was a highly eloquent little performance that she did not care for. She mouthed "shoo" at it, and it scampered away, laughing silently still, fading into the confusion of sail and rope and masts. Gretel glanced at the general, but he seemed not to have noticed the tiny interloper. Some way off, bathed in the pink of a northern sundown, the *Fair Fortune* lay at anchor. Gretel waved her glass at it.

"No doubt you will be pleased to return to your glamorous vessel," she said to Ferdinand.

"I am in no hurry. Oh, I don't deny, she is a well-appointed ship. But there is something rather charming about the *Arabella*," he said.

Gretel harrumphed into her wine. "It is a charm that I seem alone in being unable to appreciate," she told him. "Tell me again how you came to be on Amrum. If I were a passenger on the *Fair Fortune*, I would not have given up an hour of it to visit that desolate place."

"It is the baroness's wish to avail herself of the benefits of saltwater bathing. She is under my care for the duration of the cruise . . ."

"So very good of King Julian to lend you to her. One might have thought she would have guards of her own. But then, what are families for, if not to pass generals back and forth between one another . . . ?"

". . . naturally I was required to inspect the island to ensure it was a suitable and safe place for her to visit." He turned away from the scarlet-streaked sky to look at her with such intensity she felt her composure slip a little. "I am very glad I was on hand to . . . find you, Fraulein Gretel. I do not like to think of you alone in such a state."

"You would rather keep me company in my predicament?" she asked, more sharply than she had intended.

Ferdinand turned back to the view. "I would rather see you safe," he said.

There was a moment's slightly awkward silence until Gretel found something to say in an attempt to repair the mood.

"And is the baroness enjoying her voyage?" she asked.

Ferdinand gave a small smile. "Inasmuch as she has not yet had the captain dismissed from his post, nor seen any minor crewmembers tipped overboard, we must assume so."

"She is not a woman given to revealing her feelings unless they are of the sharp and spiky variety."

"You know her well. Indeed, she has the entire ship's company on their toes at present, as she has demanded a ball be organized for tomorrow evening. A small fleet of tenders will bring an entire orchestra, no less, along with a hundred further guests, and sufficient food to feed the population of Amrum for a Scandinavian winter, I should imagine."

"I am certain it will be an affair of the grandest proportions."

The general looked at Gretel once more. "I wonder, fraulein, if you might care to attend, as my guest. Of course, if your detective work here cannot be broken from . . ."

"It can! I mean to say, it should. Oftentimes the mind functions with greater alacrity following some stimulating diversion," she told him, then added, "I should be delighted," her thoughts already racing ahead, plucking gowns from her trunk, seeking out the perfect garb for such an occasion.

Just then, the mer-hund stiffened, ears akimbo, sprang to its feet, forgetting its bone, and flung itself into the water.

From high up came the cry, "Mer-hund overboard!"

Several passengers hurried to the rail to watch the creature swim. There were exclamations and snatches of laughter. Gretel stayed put. She had no wish to be associated with the undignified animal any more than she could avoid. From the shouts and comments it became apparent that the hound had found something of interest and was returning it to the ship. A man on a rope was lowered. The mer-hund was reeled in. It bounded over to its mistress, shaking copious quantities of sea water all over her.

"Dratted dog! Must you douse me again?"

"Look"—Ferdinand pointed—"it has something in its mouth. Here, boy, what have you found for us?" he asked, gently taking the strange gray object from its mouth. He held up the saturated mass of tangles and seaweed. People stepped forward, craning their necks for a better view, all hazarding guesses as to what treasure it might be.

Gretel did not need to guess. She recognized the tight curls, the pearly glimmer beneath the sea-snail slime, the glittering thread and tiny silver bells. She recognized the unsalvageable wreck of what once had been her beloved wig.

NINE

"It was good of you to try," Gretel told Everard. They stood in her cabin, gazing mournfully at the remains of her wig. He had employed all his considerable skills and talents as a hairdresser, but it could not be saved. Gretel had suffered many mishaps and tragedies in her life, but had not, for many years, felt herself as close to weeping as she did at that moment. Here she stood, in her petticoats and corsets, about to don her very finest ball gown, on the point of leaving for what promised to be an exceptionally spectacular evening, and still she would not have the divine pleasure of wearing her wig.

"Upon my word, madam, it is vexing, but there is no more to be done."

"I understand. There it is. We must do what we can with my poor hair. I swear it is a wonder every person compelled to live near the sea does not shave their head, such is the detrimental effect of all this benighted salt," she said, raising her looking glass for another critical view of the challenge Everard faced.

"Fear not, madam, I will soon transform you," he told her, taking up his comb and lotions.

"More coconut oil?"

"I would not be without it."

As he set to, Gretel forced herself to turn her mind to business. Naturally she was gladdened to be attending the ball as Ferdinand's guest, and the prospect of at last dancing with him was most appealing, but she was a woman of action, of business, of a certain calling and reputation, and her work must take priority when the opportunity presented itself. As it did, rather unexpectedly, on this occasion. Not only would she be able to inspect Captain Ziegler's opposition—both the ship and its owner—but Herr Hoffman had again insisted he accompany the party. The captain had resisted, seeing a chance for himself to be entertained at his rival's expense, but Gretel had persuaded him to let the quartermaster go. She had found a moment to inform him of her suspicions regarding Hoffman, and she needed to see why he wanted to board the *Fair Fortune* so badly. She had held back from revealing to Captain Ziegler that she knew of his past. There seemed no necessity for it. What mattered was that she now better understood why he tolerated the quartermaster; why he needed him. Herr Hoffman would be only too well aware of it himself. She was alerted to the fact that he was capable of murder; she would not turn her back on him again. If someone was trying to drive the *Arabella* out of business, Thorsten Sommer must be a prime candidate. If Hoffman was up to some devious and dastardly deeds, might the two not be in cahoots? This was the ideal opportunity to spy on the two of them together.

An hour later, Gretel was lowered into the tender once more. The capacious skirts of her gown—the finest chartreuse silk from the Orient, cut in Paris to a design by La Coeur, and representing a sizeable proportion of payment received for her previous case—presented the crewmembers charged with her transfer from ship to launch with some difficulties, so that she was somewhat roughly manhandled in the process. She had been forced to speak plainly more than once to prevent them inadvertently sullying either her dress or her dignity. Hans appeared at the railing to wave her off, the mer-hund restrained on its leash lest it bound in after her.

"Enjoy your evening, sister mine," he called down, looking the nearest thing to cheerful he had been for several days. The cause of his good humor, and the fact that he had dared emerge from the sanctuary of his kitchen, sat next to Gretel in a cloud of powder and perfume. Gretel frowned at Birgit, who, in her opinion, was wearing far too much rouge and a gown of such unfashionable cut it was almost pitiable. Almost. When Hans had heard of the ball he had begged his sister to take That Woman with her. He rarely breathed fresh air or took a turn about the deck for fear of encountering her. If she were safely installed on a different ship for a few hours, he and the mer-hund could enjoy their freedom together. Gretel had balked, stalled, and prevaricated, not happy with the thought of suffering Birgit's irritating company herself, but he had won her around to the idea with the promise of a special after-ball breakfast in her cabin upon her return. He had also promised to securely lock up the mer-hund; she did not relish the idea of its finding its way to the *Fair Fortune* in search of her.

There followed an uncomfortable boat ride to the rival cruise ship, and more hauling and shoving as she was taken aboard.

It was sufficient to put anyone in an ill humor, but the beauty of the *Fair Fortune* quickly restored Gretel's mood. The other guests had already arrived, so that there was a pleasing air of excitement and bustle. Whereas on the *Arabella* Gretel had been among those who, it was fair to say, had little or no appreciation of fashion or elegance, here she was surrounded by exemplars of *haute couture* and lovers of fine living. Women drifted by swathed in silk and lace, their wigs (their wigs, oh! their wigs) elaborate and daringly tall, their jewels sparkling, their chatter sophisticated and urbane. Powder and perfume replaced the smell of stale ale and male sweat that Gretel had become worryingly accustomed to in the company of Captain Zeigler's men. Here, even the crew cut a dash in crisply laundered white uniforms.

Ferdinand appeared at her side, looking dangerously handsome in his own understated finery. "Good evening, Fraulein Gretel." He treated her to an elaborate bow.

She replied with a modest curtsey. It had been many years since she had risked a deep dip. This was not the time to risk being unable to rise elegantly. "Herr General," she said, deliberately turning her gaze from him. "A splendid effort. I trust the baroness is satisfied?"

"She would not venture an opinion so early in the evening."

"Ah, of course not. Better to allow time to find fault. Though I fancy she might have to look long and hard."

He offered her his hand and led her across the beribboned and bunting-strewn deck. He took her to a tight gathering of particularly well-turned-out people, at the center of which stood a large fellow, both tall and broad, his appearance suggesting good living and vibrant health, rather than overindulgence. He had a wide brow, sun-kissed skin, and a ready smile. His attire marked him as a naval man, of high rank. Ferdinand threaded through the throng. "Allow me to introduce you to the ship's owner, Thorsten Sommer. Herr Sommer, may I present . . ."

"Ah! Fraulein Gretel of Gesternstadt!" the avuncular man cried. "Your reputation precedes you. An honor and a pleasure," he insisted, kissing her hand.

"The pleasure is mine, I assure you, Herr Sommer." Gretel gestured at the loveliness around her. "You have a spectacular vessel. I am most impressed."

"She is something special indeed, fraulein, though I confess"—here he dropped his voice to a whisper and leant close to her ear—"were I forced to choose, I would say her sister ship, the *Pretty Penny*, is the more graceful of the two." He laughed loudly, the sudden change in volume startling Gretel. "But there! Parents should not have favorites, what?" His guffawing was infectious, so that others joined in, all trying to outdo one another in their enthusiasm to win the captain's favor. The more they laughed, the louder he laughed, and so it continued beyond all sense, with Herr Sommer delighting in every raucous moment. Soon Gretel felt she was surrounded by braying donkeys. She noticed Ferdinand smiling quietly. He must have known how disappointed she would be to discover the owner of such a ship, and the purveyor of such finery, was something of a vulgar character, albeit a cheerful one. The thought struck her, however, that Captain Ziegler's description of the man was at odds with the reality. Brash and loud be might be, but the man was clearly affable, well liked, and cheery. Not at all the sly character she had been given to expect.

"Come," Ferdinand said, gently taking her arm, "let us try the ballroom. The musicians make a rather better sound, I think you'll find."

And indeed they did. The ballroom was a vision of white—the linen, the drapes, the livery of the waiters and uniforms of the carefully selected crewmembers who were on hand to dance with lone ladies. Of which there were quite a few. It struck Gretel that such voyages had a disproportionate number of female to male passengers, making the women permanently on edge, and giving any single men a rather hunted look. Birgit was in her element. She wasted not one second talking to anyone who was attached to another, and blatantly turned her back on any person of her own gender who unwittingly sought to engage her in polite conversation. Gretel observed her as she worked the room, singling out the single men, offering them no choice but to dance with her, summoning waiters with more champagne for the faint-hearted, quickly ditching one after the next when the brief conversation a waltz allowed evidently yielded the wrong answers to her no doubt blush-makingly forthright questions. She could have pitied the men, had she not been happily wedded to the thought that That Woman might find An Other to pursue in place of Hans.

The following hours passed in a blur of dancing and drinking—the champagne on offer being of the most excellent quality—and exchanging decreasingly clear but increasingly amusing banter with Ferdinand and several of the other ball-goers. Such was the delightfulness of the evening that it was with some difficulty that Gretel forced herself to remember her work, and that she must make the most of the opportunity to gain further insights into the case she was charged with solving. She watched Herr Hoffman and Herr Sommer as closely as her somewhat blurred vision allowed. They exchanged pleasant-ries, and spent a little time in each other's company, but did nothing that looked remotely suspicious or conspiratorial. Nor did they leave the ballroom together at any time.

Baroness Schleswig-Holstein appeared to be enjoying the ball, though it was difficult to tell. She had grudgingly acknowledged Gretel when Ferdinand had presented her. Gretel doubted the aristocrat remembered her. In fact, she rather hoped she did not, as, on the previous occasion they had met, the baroness had accused her of theft. Better to put that encounter into the dim distant past and attempt to make a more favorable impression. Not that the baroness cared. Anyone below the rank of baron was evidently not worthy of conversation. Gretel witnessed more than two counts cruelly blanked. She pitied Ferdinand his duty of protecting the woman, but at least his work had at last given them the opportunity to dance together. And he was indeed a fair dancer.

Just as Gretel was enjoying this fuzzy reverie and considering another polka, she noticed Herr Hoffman leaving the ballroom via a side door. With a sigh she set her champagne flute down upon the nearest passing silver tray and went after him. She was not a woman built for stealth, and her ball gown did not allow for swift and effortless progress. However, such was the milling and thronging of the revelers and so great was their number that her disappearance was not noticed, and she was able to trace the quartermaster's steps and hurry along the starboard passageway and up to the main deck. One or two giggling partygoers could be heard in clandestine cuddles here and there, but they had interest in no one save each other. Gretel scanned the area for signs of Hoffman, but there was no hint of him. She made her way along the length of the ship, pausing to peer down stairwells or up rigging, but he was nowhere to be found. At last she came to the steps leading up to the poop deck. She could see the captain's cabin door from where she stood. There were lights on inside, but she could not blatantly go in uninvited. If Hoffman was inside she could not follow, and in any case, there was an efficient-looking sailor at the wheel, who would no doubt challenge her presence.

Disgruntled at having wasted her time and being thwarted in her pursuit of a man she remained convinced had something significant to hide, she turned on her heel and started to walk back to the ballroom, this time along the port side of the ship. She wondered idly if Bo'sun Brandt would be impressed with her improved grasp of nautical terminology. As she drew level with a row of lifeboats, she saw that the canvas covering on one of them was not properly secured. On closer inspection, she could see that one of its ropes had been left untied. By climbing onto a nearby deck chair, Gretel could reach the side of the small boat, lift the loose canvas, and peer inside. Had her perch not been quite so wobbly she might have contained the cry that escaped her, but the sight of Frenchie, dead and bloated, still wearing his chef's whites, coupled with her unstable footing, caused her to shout aloud and clutch at the lifeboat. The note of shock in her voice was detected by nearby courting couples, who hurried over to her.

"What it is?" asked one pink-cheeked youth. "Fraulein, whatever is the matter?"

"What have you found?" asked another.

Gretel quickly recovered her composure. Much as the discovery of the cook's body had startled her, she was not unaccustomed to such sights. Other people, in her experience, had a tendency to overreact to the presence of death, and she had no wish to spread panic through the ship. She pulled the canvas back into place and was on the point of describing a rat or some such when none other than Herr Hoffman himself appeared at her elbow.

"Well, fraulein, tell us what it is you are trying to hide," he demanded.

"I do not care for either your tone or your implication," she told him.

"It is clear something has happened," he said, in a voice even more authoritative and clear than usual, turning as if to address anyone who cared to hear, rather than speaking to Gretel herself. "Won't you tell us what it is?"

"For pity's sake, keep quiet, man," she hissed at him. "Do you want to cause hysteria among the passengers?"

A small crowd was gathering, and already excitement and suspicion were running through it like ill-trained puppies, nipping at ankles and yapping in a manner that could only serve to agitate people further.

But Hoffman was not to be stopped. With a flourish, he reached over, grabbed the lifeboat cover, and wrenched it back, exposing poor Frenchie to the nippy night air. If, as seemed his plan, he had wanted to effect a dramatic revelation, he was prevented from doing so because of the height and position of the boat, so that he was compelled to exclaim to the onlookers, "A body! A corpse!" As the crowd gasped and shrieked, he added, "A man dead, cold, murdered!" just in case anyone had missed the point. "And we find his assassin with him still!" he cried, pointing at Gretel with all the dramatic ham of a provincial amateur operatic performance.

She narrowed her eyes at him. Having Hoffman attempt to murder her was one thing; having him endeavor to besmirch her reputation was quite another. She allowed the quickly swollen crowd to have their moment of shock and frenzy, letting them exclaim and swoon and snatch up their smelling salts without interruption. When she was satisfied that as many as could fit on the deck around them had been assembled, and that all had given vent to their feelings, she cleared her throat, drew herself up as best she could on her unstable platform, and held up a hand for quiet. At last the hubbub subsided. Out of the corner of her eye she saw Ferdinand thread his way to the front toward her and several of his men taking up positions around the scene.

"There is indeed, here in this lifeboat, the body of the deceased chef known as Frenchie." There was a fresh murmur of shock, but Gretel pressed on. "He was missed four days ago from his post aboard the *Arabella*. An extensive search was mounted, but it proved fruitless."

"He must have made his way to this ship, only to be murdered here!" the quartermaster insisted. The crowd followed his thinking and glared at Gretel in the way a pantomime audience might be incited to boo a villain.

She held her nerve and said levelly, "The somewhat disturbing extent of the hapless Frenchie's cadaver, to wit the bloated features,"—there came a groaning from the crowd—"the blueness of his flesh,"—followed by gasps—"the way the eyes bulge in their sockets,"—there was the sound of one or two fainters hitting the deck—"together with the distinctive and powerful odor of decay,"—several people retched over the rails—"are irrefutable evidence of the fact that he is long dead. What is more, I would say that he did not meet his end here, but at some other place."

"So *you* say." Hoffman scowled.

"Yes, I do say, and I do so because it is obvious to a bat in a sack. A person who has had his throat slit—and this victim's head is all but severed from his body—bleeds quickly and profusely"—another brace of ladies in the crowd pitched from the vertical to the horizontal—"yet there is no blood, dried or wet, in this boat. All there is is a corpse, several days old, still clutching a bottle . . ." She paused, raising her lorgnettes to her eyes for a closer look. ". . . of brandy. Whoever murdered him did it somewhere else. Whoever murdered him then moved him into his current position for reasons as yet unknown. Whoever murdered him was not me," she added, pointedly looking at Herr Hoffman.

General von Ferdinand stepped forward, issuing orders for his men to move the passengers away and rope off the area. He sent word to the captain to tell him of the discovery, and a messenger gull was organized to inform Captain Ziegler that his errant chef had been located. With a great deal of muttering, Herr Hoffman relinquished his position as Gretel's prosecutor and took himself off to organize the tender for the return trip to the *Arabella*. The ball, it seemed, had come to an unexpectedly early finish, much to the displeasure of the baroness. She steamed onto the deck looking for someone upon whom to vent her ire. She found Gretel.

"What is the meaning of this?" she spat. "Why am I compelled to cut short my entertainments?"

"We have discovered the body of a missing person, baroness," Gretel told her.

"Who was this . . . *person*?"

"He was the chef from the cruise ship *Arabella*."

The baroness tutted loudly. "I fail to see why a person of no consequence should alter my plans, be he alive or dead," she said.

Gretel quelled the urge to punch the baroness on her pointy Findleberg nose.

"Whether or not Frenchie's demise warrants your sympathy, baroness, the matter of murder is always of consequence."

"Murder, you say?" This information at least seemed to penetrate the woman's ironclad soul. "Are you sure? Herr General, are you of the same opinion? Could the man not have died at his own hand? Or in a drunken mishap, perchance?"

Ferdinand shook his head. "Such an injury could not have been self-inflicted, baroness. This is indeed a serious matter and will need investigating. We are fortunate to have Fraulein Gretel to assist us," he explained, turning to offer the detective one of his most handsome smiles.

Gretel felt a pleasing warmth travel from her throat to the very tips of her ears. It was a warmth of such quality that it could not be cooled even by the icy, disapproving stare of Baroness Schleswig-Holstein.

What did bring her up short, however, what sent a chill sprinting up her spine, was the eerie, distant singing that suddenly filled the sky. All present gasped and turned in the direction from which the sound came, straining to spy its point of origin in the gloom; but the dark was too deep, the sea too wide, the horizon too far. There was nothing that could be seen, but still the ephemeral song continued, growing louder and clearer. Two nearby sailors cursed. Another began to pray. Passengers who had been persuaded away from the drama of a dead body reappeared, as if drawn by the siren's call. Soon the deck was crowded once more, and all the company was silent and enthralled. They could do naught but listen as the bewitching notes cut through the night air. The moment was rare and particular and none who had been there would ever be able to forget it.

What they would also remember, whether they wished to or not, was the more raucous, discordant sound coming from the direction of the *Arabella*: the mournful howling emitted by the lonesome mer-hund locked in Gretel's cabin.

TEN

Captain Ziegler's fury was quite something to behold. Gretel sat in his sumptuous cabin, still in her ball gown, allowing him to rant and rave, reasoning that his outburst was a storm so violent it must soon blow itself out.

"Disaster is heaped upon catastrophe, I tell you! The days pass and your presence does nothing to bring about a resolution of these vexing matters. God's teeth, and hang me for a liar if the situation has not worsened!" he raged, banging his fist down on the very fine mahogany of the desk before him. "'Tis not enough that my cook goes missing, he must be found mutilated and murdered and apparently placed upon my rival's ship."

"A fact some might say indicates the involvement of Herr Sommer."

"The man is many things, fraulein, but a fool is not one of them. Why would he implicate himself in such a manner? No, it is more likely seen as a clumsy attempt to blacken his name. Well, the effect is the opposite. 'Tis my name, that of my ship, that is sullied. Do you not see that?" Without waiting for an answer, he thundered on. "I brought you here, at no small expense . . ."

"Ah, a matter we have not yet fully discussed, if I might remind you . . ."

". . . you gave me assurances, woman. The case will be solved . . ."

"And so it shall."

"Before my ship is devoid of crew? Two more men jumped ship on hearing the news of Frenchie and the mermaid's singing. Two more! Much more of this and I shan't be able to sail."

"Could not others be pressed into service for the time being?"

"The *Arabella* is no rowing boat or canal barge. Such sails as she boasts require a number of men to work them. When I fall below that figure, will you be ascending the rigging, fraulein?"

Gretel took a deep, slow breath and rose from her seat. It had been a long night. The happy revelries of the ball had required a certain exertion. The heightened tension of the discovery of a dead body, and the ludicrous accusations that followed, had drained her. She was weary and had had quite enough of being bellowed at.

"Captain Ziegler," she said, levelly holding his wild-eyed glare, "I will allow that circumstances are testing." She held up a hand to ward off his interruption. "Be that as it may, the measure of a man is surely not what manner of trouble he finds himself in, but in what manner he finds his way out of it. And I contest the notion that matters have worsened of late. True, we have lost a good man, who also happened to be an excellent cook, but even in death Frenchie can tell us much."

"How so?"

"To begin with, there is the way in which he met his end. His throat was slit with a large blade, and that weapon must be found."

"Huh! Every man worth his salt keeps a knife. How will we know which it was?"

"It will be the one missing. By which I mean, no murderer will keep the murder weapon close to him. Look for a man who no longer has a knife, or has recently acquired a new one. Secondly, the fact that Frenchie was placed where he was suggests a complicated mind at work. This was no random act, nor a killing done in a moment of passion or rage. The perpetrator wanted Frenchie out of the way—and we must ask ourselves why that might be the case—and once he was dispatched, they sought to use his corpse to obscure both their identity and their purpose. Their attempt to implicate me in his demise was nonsense, of course, but it served to swell the confusion surrounding his discovery. And then there is the bottle the late cook clutches still."

"Ah! I have that!" cried the captain, pleased with himself. "The murderer wanted to make it look as if Frenchie was drunk at the time he met his end. Perhaps violent in his cups, so that the villain could claim he acted to save his own neck."

Gretel smiled indulgently as she gently strangled this weakling of a notion with her own robust logic. "The bottle was empty. The stopper in place. What drunkard would carry with him a bottle full of nothing? No, I inspected his grip. Frenchie held that bottle with his dying grasp, knowing even as the life bled from him that his clutch *post mortem* would be too stiff for another to undo. Particularly if that other was in a hurry. The act was deliberate. It was meant to signify something to whoever found him. I intend discerning that something."

The captain looked sorrowful and shook his head. "It should not have come to that. An honest man's heart stopped, his life at an end, to further the cause of some unscrupulous person, damn their eyes."

Gretel toyed with the idea that this might be the moment to reveal her knowledge of the captain's previous identity. It seemed a little rich for a man who had, in years gone by, made his living doing precisely the deed he now described with such loathing not to acknowledge this double standard. But then, he was her client, his past was not her business. It was his future she must concern herself with.

She looked down at the chart upon the desk between them. A small model marked the position of both the *Arabella* and its grander competition. All around was mostly empty sea, but there were two tiny islands a way off to the west, and Gretel wondered if it was on the closest of these that the mermaid had sat and sung. It kept coming to her that the elusive creature was connected to Hoffman's skulduggery somehow, and therefore to Sommer, too, if her instinct was correct. "It seems to me that the placing of Frenchie's body aboard the *Fair Fortune* was a double bluff, designed to look like a ham-fisted attempt to implicate the ship or its connections, so that it would do just the opposite, as you have so astutely noticed. Therefore, I believe that someone on that ship is working with someone on this ship to blacken your reputation, scare off your crew and passengers, and put you out of business. As you know, I suspect Herr Hoffman of being involved. He is the common factor. It may well be that he is working with your rival, Thorsten Sommer, though I have no proof of this as yet. However, this is the line of inquiry I shall follow."

"You suspect Sommer?"

"I do, though, as I say, without foundation, thus far."

"Aye, the fellow is sly, I've always held so. And no doubt he would be pleased to see me and my ship gone from these waters."

At that moment there was an urgent knocking on the door, and Will appeared, a messenger gull perched on his arm.

"Sorry to intrude, captain, but I thought I should bring him to you direct," the boy said, holding the enormous bird as far from himself as his physique allowed.

"You did right, Will. Let me have him." The captain stood and detached the message from the gull's leg. It squawked loudly before flapping over to a gull perch on the far side of the room and settling to preen its feathers. Will looked mightily relieved to be rid of the thing.

"Hell's eyes and damnation!" Captain Ziegler thrust the note into Gretel's hand. "It is from Sommer himself. See if that don't blow your theory out the water, fraulein," he told her.

Gretel read the message aloud.

"'First mate and Sailor Shultz missing. Crew and passengers in state of panic. Putting in at port of Nordstrand.'"

❄

As Gretel left the captain's cabin to return to her own, the stars in the night sky twinkled merrily as if everything were peaceful and lovely and all was right was the world. Except that it was not. At least, not the part of the world Gretel inhabited. Two crewmembers were missing from the *Fair Fortune*. The suggestion was not that they had availed themselves of a tender and sailed away, but that they had vanished, as mysteriously and suddenly as poor Frenchie. Had they, too, met an untimely end at the hands of murderers? Or had they been lured to a watery death by the mermaid? Either way, Gretel could no longer reasonably hold the view that Thorsten Sommer was behind the disappearance of Captain Ziegler's crew. The loss of his first mate was no minor inconvenience. The setup aboard the *Fair Fortune* differed from that of the *Arabella*; there was no captain as such, but a combination of owner, or master, and first mate. Herr Sommer did not, in fact, hold the title of captain himself, and the first mate therefore had charge of the ship. Without him, they could not continue to sail, and therefore had been forced to go directly to the nearest harbor big enough to take them. This did not smack of a cunning double bluff. This smacked of something of a disaster, for the crewmembers most of all, for Sommer's future business decidedly, and in a horribly damning way for Gretel's theories regarding the case.

So late was the hour that the deck was deserted, save for the lone crewmember who had the watch, and another at the wheel. Gretel was on the point of descending the ankle-twist-ingly steep stairs when the sea sprite landed on the handrail in front of her.

"Well?" it asked. "Did you solve my little puzzle, or are you as silly as you look?"

Gretel felt this was not a position someone covered in purple fur could safely take, but decided against commenting as such. "It wasn't really very difficult," she replied. "Though I confess the information was interesting."

The sprite shook its head, grinning. "Without my help, it would have taken you ages to work out who our glorious cap-tain used to be, wouldn't it?"

"Undoubtedly," she said, watching the unsettling way the little creature was eyeing her lorgnettes. "I rather think you must have enjoyed life aboard a pirate ship," she went on. "Lots of sparkly plunder for you to filch, one would imagine."

"I don't take things to keep, you know," it insisted. "I don't want them for myself."

"No? What, then? Do you sell them?"

"Of course not; who would I sell them to? Nobody's going to buy something from someone who doesn't exist, are they?"

"You may have a point. So why take things in the first place?"

"I like to . . . move them around." The sprite hopped off the rail and circled Gretel, running a silver-nailed finger along the silk of her skirts as it did so. "I like putting them in places they shouldn't be and then seeing what happens. You wouldn't believe the fuss sometimes." It chuckled; a sharp, impish sound that caused the hairs on Gretel's arms to stand up.

It struck her that the sprite was nothing more than a naughty child, desperate for attention. Although in its case, unlike a child, it could not gain that attention, which must make its existence—or nonexistence—a lonely one. Gretel wondered why it had singled her out for communication. It must, after all, be able to watch everyone on board as much as it liked.

"Tell me," she asked, "on the night of the great storm, a little while back . . ."

"Huh! Call that a storm? That was nothing."

"Nonetheless, you know to which night I am referring?"

"Of course."

"I know you would have been on deck. A . . . person such as yourself could not possibly be frightened of a bit of weather."

"I'm not frightened of anything," it told her, jutting out its velvety chin.

"Indeed. And during that night, did you happen to witness anything . . . unusual?"

The sprite did not reply at once, but seemed to be considering how much, if anything, to reveal about what it had seen. When it finally did speak, it was, much to Gretel's annoyance, to deliver another puzzle.

"To understand, look close at the hand, and remember that special drink: the answer is clear, though it's not kept near, and it's never the person you think," it sang, before flitting away into the darkness.

"Quite. Thank you so much. Exceptionally illuminating. Inordinately helpful of you," Gretel muttered as she made her weary way belowdecks. By the time she reached her trunks in what she now accepted was their permanent lodging in the passageway, her temper was frayed at the edges, her patience threadbare thin, and her good humor worn right through. As there was unlikely to be anyone else stirring at such an hour, she removed her ball gown and birdcage where she stood, taking advantage of the fractionally larger space, before entering her cabin wearing only her petticoats, shift, and corset. Hans lay on the floor in his chef's garb, still clutching a wooden spoon, the fumes of his snore-borne breath suggesting that the news of Frenchie's body being found as it had been had driven him to even more drink than usual. Gretel was horrified to see the mer-hund stretched out upon her own bunk.

"Well, really!" she huffed. The hound stirred at the sound of her voice, grinned sheepishly, wagged its tail, rolled over, and went back to sleep. Gretel knew there was no way she could make the climb to the top bunk. She sat heavily on the wooden stool and plucked off her shoes. As she sat rubbing her aching feet, she repeated the sprite's rhyme to herself just to make sure she would remember it. There seemed little sense to it, and it was galling to think the creature might be holding back some useful information. The plain truth of the matter was, Gretel had made no discernible progress with her investigation. The *Arabella* was losing crew; the captain was losing his reputation and in danger of losing his business, and would soon lose tolerance for paying a detective who failed to detect anything worthwhile. Hoffman was still at the center of things; Gretel's mind had not changed about that. That Sommer was also involved now seemed less likely. That the mermaid was in some way linked to what was going on seemed one of the few sure things remaining.

"In which case," Gretel said to herself, *"cherchez la femme."* She got to her feet again and clambered over her brother. She fetched a simple day dress from her trunk outside the door and wriggled into it, wrapping a shawl around her shoulders.

"Hans," she called to him, then again, louder, adding a gentle nudge with her foot. "Hans! Wake up!"

"What? What's that? Who's there? Dash it all, Gretel, I don't need kicking like a lowly mutt."

"I can't kick him, he's up on my bunk. Anyway, it wasn't a kick, just a bit of gentle encouragement."

"Says you. Felt like a kick from down here," he told her, puffing as he twisted and heaved himself into a sitting position. "It's still dark. The middle of the night. What on earth is it that can't wait until a sensible hour?"

"Aside from the fact that your stinking mer-hund is in my bed, d'you mean? Never mind that now. Get up and come with me."

"Where are we going?"

"To the kitchen. We need provisions."

"We do? Why?" he asked, his knee joints cracking in protest as he stood up.

"Drink—ale would be best, I think. And bread, cheese, some cold meat. Bring a knife. And matches of some sort. A lantern, too, of course."

"Of course. What for?"

"Stop asking questions and come along. Not you!" she barked at the mer-hund as it tried to follow.

"No need to snap at the poor thing," said Hans. "He doesn't want to be left behind."

"He can't come."

Hans frowned petulantly. "Right, that's it. I am not moving from this spot until you tell me where we are going, why we are going there, and what's wrong with his coming with us."

Gretel sighed. "Very well. I have work to do and I require your help to do it."

"You do?"

"I do. You are going to have the thrilling opportunity to play captain in charge of your very own vessel."

"I am?"

"You are. We are going to find that dratted mermaid ourselves, right now."

"We are? Well, in that case, we'll need a mer-hund, won't we?" He waited for her reply, eyebrows raised, hand gesturing unnecessarily at the damp dog on Gretel's bed. By way of strengthening its own case, the mer-hund yawned elaborately, stretched its front legs, and wagged some more.

Gretel considered the situation. It was doubtful that anyone ever actually *needed* a mer-hund. What was certain, however, was that if they left the thing behind, it would start barking and howling and kick up sufficient rumpus to wake the whole ship.

"All right, bring him. But he's your responsibility. It's up to you to keep him in check. And keep him quiet. And for pity's sake, keep him from licking me when I least expect it; it is singularly disturbing." She turned and hurried along the passageway, Hans and his loyal companion following.

"Tell me, sister mine," Hans asked in a stage whisper, "exactly what sort of vessel shall I be in command of?"

"You'll see, Hans," she told him. "You'll soon see."

ELEVEN

The lifeboat Gretel had selected for their enterprise was the only one that was not visible to the person at the wheel of the ship. This meant that, if they trod lightly and moved carefully, they should be able to lower it without being seen, so long as she first took care of the sailor on watch. This did not prove difficult. By now it was nearly four o'clock in the morning, so the man was already fighting sleep. Ten minutes of sharing brandy with Hans while listening to him chunder on about the finer points of seven-card whist rendered him helpfully unconscious.

"Right," Hans whispered as he caught up to her beside the lifeboat, "he's down for the count. What now?"

"Put the food and drink in the boat. Good grief, we're only going to be a few hours—you've brought half the contents of the kitchen."

"I was instructed to provide us with provisions, and that's what I've done. See here—a little ham, French loaf . . . Frenchie used to make them better, but I'm improving. Poor Frenchie." For a moment Hans's face contorted and tears threatened, but he brought himself back from the brink by focusing on the food. "Not a bad batch, if I say so myself. And ale, and some cheese. Couldn't decide . . . Emmental or Brie? I'm not a great fan of either, truth be told, but, ha, any port in a storm, eh? Not that I brought any port. Though I could nip back and get some . . ."

"Hans, please, stop talking." She took the bundles and baskets from him and loaded them into the boat. "Now, you take this rope, I'll take the other one. We have to let it down so it swings over the side, then we can get in. After that, we lower while we are seated. Come on."

The maneuver went surprisingly smoothly. The winches on the boat allowed them to position it without mishap. Getting from the ship to the boat while it dangled was a more challenging task, however, particularly when attempting to perform it *sotto voce*. There was a fair number of muttered curses as first Hans, then Gretel, then the mer-hund made the nerve-testing step over the side with the lifeboat swinging unhelpfully. Once in, they continued to lower away, slowly letting out the rope. At one point, Hans became distracted by the mer-hund's excited wagging and got behind the movement so that soon they were at an alarming angle. A great deal of hissing and urgent gestures on Gretel's part rescued the situation, and within minutes they were safely upon the water. The moon was full and the stars still bright, with the promise of daybreak imminent upon the horizon, so that there was sufficient light for them to be able to see what they were about. Releasing the ropes, they picked up the oars, rowing inexpertly but surprisingly effectively in puffing silence until they were at a distance from the ship, and to its stern, which Gretel deemed out of sight and hearing.

Hans beamed. "That went rather well, I think. We are launched! Though I have to say, I had hoped for something a little more 'ship' than 'boat.'"

"This is perfectly adequate for our needs," Gretel told him.

"And what are they exactly? How does one set about a mermaid hunt?"

"While in the captain's cabin I examined the charts," she said, slightly overstating the case, but keen to imbue him with confidence in their expedition. "I identified two small isles, both within striking distance of the *Arabella*, and both possible locations for the singing mermaid that was heard last evening. According to the charts, the islands lie due west," she explained, pointing in that general direction. "All we must do is pull directly away from the rising sun, holding our course straight and true."

"Sounds simple enough. How far are these islands?"

"Oh, no distance at all," Gretel replied, thinking of the thumbnail space on the map between the ship and their intended destination. "With steady effort I calculate we should make landfall by late afternoon."

"Gives us time for a few snacks, then," said Hans, eyeing the provisions.

"We must put a number of miles betwixt ourselves and the *Arabella* first. I don't want anyone on board knowing what it is we are about. I wish to locate the mermaid unannounced."

"So you really believe there is one? Only you seemed somewhat skeptical when we began our cruise."

"It is my job to be skeptical. She may be real, she may be fake; either way, she is implicated in the various disappearances and

I intend to question her and obtain answers. The time for bold action has come. Now I suggest you save your breath for rowing."

Together they turned the boat about so that they were pointing as west as they could be, the sun their only compass. The vessel was small compared to its mother ship, but felt dauntingly hefty when being powered only by two Bavarians, neither of whom had any boating experience to speak of. The mer-hund stood in the prow, like some ill-fashioned figure-head, gazing intently out at the open sea ahead. After a short while, the rowers found a modicum of rhythm and the lifeboat cut through the calm sea in a pleasing way. Within an hour, the *Arabella* was a toy ship in the distance, which was a good thing. What was less good, Gretel decided, were the blisters that were already blooming on her hands, the aching of her lower back, and the clamminess of the shift beneath her dress. When Hans suggested a pause for refueling, she did not argue. She quickly scanned the far horizons with her lorgnettes to satisfy herself they could still not be seen by any passing ships and then instructed Hans to break out the supplies. They let the boat drift and bob gently as they tucked into bread, ham, and ale. The sun was lifting above the sea now, casting a dove-gray light upon the water and a helpful illumination all around them.

Hans waved his baguette in the direction of the ship. "Soon be serving breakfast on board." He shook his head slowly. "I can only imagine the muddle. Kitchen left in charge of the sous chef and two lads who don't appear to know a ladle from a lentil."

"I'm sure they will provide an adequate service in your absence, and the passengers will be all the more appreciative of your efforts upon our return."

"Poor old Frenchie." Hans paused in his chewing for a few seconds. "Still can't get over him being found like that. Such a horrible death. So brutal. Who could have done such a thing?"

"We are indeed dealing with heartless people."

"A bit worrying to know we are sharing a ship with them."

"Which is why I have turned to the mermaid for answers. If she . . . it . . . is in cahoots with Hoffman, as I suspect she may be, I must extract a confession from her."

"Well, she's hardly likely to just tell you everything you want to know, is she?"

"Most people can be persuaded."

"Torture, you mean?" Hans's eyes bulged and he took a swig more ale. "Have to say, sister mine, I don't like the sound of that. Dash it all, defenseless creature, mythical being, rare as hen's teeth, an' all that. Not sure I'm comfortable with you . . . how do you torture a mermaid, exactly?"

"Do be sensible, Hans. I have no intention of torturing anyone. I simply meant that every man has his price and I don't see why a mermaid should be any different."

"Why don't you just try to buy off Hoffman, then, if you think he's at the bottom of things?"

"Firstly because I don't yet know what 'things' are. By which I mean, I know he is involved, but if he is not working with Thorsten Sommer to put Captain Ziegler out of business, I have no motive for his actions, as yet. Secondly, because he has already attempted to kill me once, which suggests he would prefer doing away with people who threaten his plans, rather than negotiating with them."

"But you have no proof?"

"Not of his attempt at murdering me, nor the killing of Frenchie. What would help is some tangible evidence, such as the murder weapon."

"That would be handy, I can see that. A slice more cheese? Here, let me cut it for you," he offered, hacking at the lump, tutting as he did so. "Poor quality knife, this. Frenchie would wince to see me use it, but the only decent blade in the galley was his own, and I've not seen that since the day he disappeared. There you are, nice bit of Emmental—good choice after all, it seems. Lacks a spoonful of pickled cabbage if you ask me, but, ha, worse things happen at sea, eh?"

Gretel felt a small muscle in her jaw begin to twitch.

"Hans, are you telling me Frenchie's own knife went missing the night he was murdered?"

"Isn't that what I just said?"

"You might have mentioned it sooner!"

"Why? He's hardly likely to have cut his own throat with his own knife, is he?"

"No, but someone else might well have. In which case we know which knife we are looking for."

"Most likely at the bottom of the ocean by now, one would have thought. Shame, though, splendid cooking implement, curved blade, as I recall, and a rather attractive bone handle with a silver end. Pass the ham, would you?"

Gretel had to admit that for once her brother was probably right. This news was dispiriting. It meant one of the few possible pointers to the identity of the murderer—i.e., their own missing knife, or recently acquired new one—no longer held water. If Frenchie had indeed unwittingly provided the means of his own death, the killer would almost certainly have lobbed it over the side, and there was an end to it. Suddenly their mission to find the mermaid had become even more important, for it seemed no other avenue of investigation was left them. Gretel dusted crumbs off her hands and skirts and packed away what little remained of the food.

"Right, let's get back to rowing. The sooner we find that island, the happier I shall be. Look, the sun is properly risen now, so it's as plain as day in which direction we need to steer. Come along, brother dear, let's see what you're made of," she added by way of pep talk. She knew Hans's habit was to take a postprandial snooze, but now was most definitely not the time.

After a further hour of effort they had lost sight of the *Arabella* completely, but there was still no sign of any islands. The morning had cooled somewhat and a breeze had got up. Gretel was doing her best to ignore her own discomfort when Hans began to whine that it must surely be lunchtime by now, and that a person could not be expected to work at full strength when in need of sustenance. It was clear their progress was slow and getting slower as they tired. Gretel shipped oars and examined the equipment stored in the boat.

"If I'm not very much mistaken," she informed Hans, "this is some manner of mast, and these sheets must be sails. Now that there is a light wind, let us see if we cannot harness its power."

Hans needed no further persuading to stop rowing. In the absence of any helpful instructions, the reconfiguration required more than one false start, but eventually the mast was slotted into the brass ring in the center of the boat and secured by bracket and screws. The cat's cradle of rope proved a trickier puzzle to solve, but solve it they did, fighting with the flapping sails until they were at last tied in place. A celebratory snack would have been most welcome, but there was no chance of such relaxation. The breeze had upgraded itself to a gusty wind, which filled the sail, sending the boat racing across the water.

"For pity's sake, Hans, steer the thing! We are going the wrong way," Gretel yelled.

"Steer it with what?" he wanted to know, as the answer, in the form of the swinging boom, hit him squarely in the belly. "Ooof! Dash it all, Gretel, do something."

"That bit of rope, by your feet, grab hold and pull."

Hans did his best to comply with his sister's wishes, but the lurching of the lifeboat, the swinging of the boom, added to the scrabbling mer-hund's getting in the way, prevented him.

At last Gretel got hold of the vital controls herself, hauling on the rope so that the sails filled again and the boat turned sharply around. Twice.

"Other way!" Hans shouted above the noise of the ever-strengthening wind.

"This is impossible!" Gretel declared. "The wind is too forceful. We are being sent horribly off course. I can't keep the thing facing the right way."

As she spoke, the boat tilted and tipped alarmingly, flinging its occupants to one side. For a moment, as they lay like beetles on their backs in the well of the thing, she feared it would capsize and it would be all up for Gretel (yes, *that* Gretel) of Gesternstadt. She refused to meet such a ridiculous end. Summoning all her strength, she clambered to her knees and then propelled herself at the sail, grabbing and pulling at the thing in a desperate effort to bring it down.

"Undo something, Hans, quickly!"

"Undo what?"

"Anything! Everything! We have to get this sail down before the wretched boat tips over."

There followed an undignified and uncoordinated struggle, which mercifully resulted in the sail being detached from the mast. So detached that a particularly fierce gust of wind whipped it from Gretel's grasp and carried it away out to sea. They watched it go, aware that losing their one and only sail was something they would probably come to regret, yet knowing there was nothing to be done about it. The mer-hund, as if sensing their dismay, barked energetically at the dwindling thing until it had vanished altogether.

At least now the lifeboat ceased behaving like a bucking bull and settled down to being merely jostled uncomfortably by the wind. Gretel and Hans took up their oars once more and rowed. Their rhythm was noticeably slower, their puffing louder, and a tense quiet replaced their earlier optimistic chat. Gretel had a horrible feeling that they had been sent badly off course. While they could now continue in a fairly steady westerly direction, there was no telling how far north, or quite possibly south, they had traveled during the disastrous experiment with the sail. Without compass, chart, or proper sailor, they would remain ignorant of their position. The only course left them was to hold their nerve and row on.

⁂

By the next afternoon, Gretel had to admit to herself that they were in something of a tight spot. Despite valiant rowing on Hans's part, and carefully chosen words of encourage-ment from Gretel—after severe blisters had forced her to down oars—they had found not so much as a rock. They had passed a cramped but tolerable night in the boat, time spent in their cabin having at least prepared them for sleeping in limited space. The weather had been mild, and the sky clear and star-studded, so that there was no fear of a storm to blow them farther off course, nor giant waves to swamp them. The next morning, however, these clement conditions had passed beyond pleasantly warm into horridly hot. The rations had provided a meager breakfast and a pitiful luncheon, and now only a flagon of ale remained. Hans had rebelled against rowing a stroke more without a nap. Gretel had attempted to persuade him into action, but he had become agitated and worryingly pink beneath the harsh sun, bandying about such words as "slave" and "galleon" so that she was forced to let him sleep. There was now not a whisper of wind, and the lifeboat merely sat upon the water, not even bothering to bob or pivot. The mer-hund kept itself cool by plunging into the sea at irregular intervals, returning to shake salt water over its companions, who soon came to welcome the refreshment this provided.

As her brother's snores rumbled out over the open ocean, Gretel took stock of their situation. They were adrift on the wide, wide sea, with scant supplies, having informed no one of where they were going. Or rather, where they had intended going. They may well have missed the islands and now be rowing into a hundred leagues of empty water. Or they might be traveling in circles, given the disorienting effects of the wind of the previous day. It was sobering to realize this was their best hope. The heat was becoming an issue. So much so that Gretel had already removed her dress and corsets and sat in her petticoat and chemise. Her shawl she had fashioned into a surprisingly stylish headdress in order to keep her brains from boiling. The glare as the relentless sun bounced off the surface of the sea was making her squint. Sitting there, she wondered if there were not a less taxing manner in which she could earn her living; something that did not involve quite so much peril.

She thought briefly about Ferdinand. What would it be like to be the wife of an Uber General? She would no doubt be required to accompany him on formal occasions, to step out decoratively on his arm, to entertain minor dignitaries and army officers in their—one would hope—comfortably appointed quarters. He might expect children. That was a worrying thought. She could not call it an unreasonable expectation, but the resultant ballooning of her already capacious waistline, followed by, as she understood it, the withering of all parts previously full or taut, repulsed her. Altogether, this ruination of her embonpoint, and quite likely her nerves, and the years of caring for the baffling creatures that were children, did not hold a great deal of appeal.

She closed her eyes and let the brilliance of the oceanic light dance on her lids, forming restless blotches she recalled seeing once before after overindulging in Hans's vintage plum brandy. Would she end her days thus? Would they be found months from now, dried to husks by the sun and salted like so much Nordic cod? Would they be found at all? The notion that their disappearance might remain forever a mystery filled her with despair. They would be written off as two more persons missing from the *Arabella*, nothing more. She refused to be lumped together with sailors and chefs and galley boys and spineless crewmembers afraid of mermaids. She simply could not let it happen.

She shook Hans roughly. "Wake up," she told him. "We must row again."

"We?" Hans asked pointedly as he dragged himself to sit between the oarlocks. "I don't recall the last several hours rowing having much 'we' about them."

Gretel tore off two strips of fine Moroccan cotton from the hem of her petticoats, wound them around her blistered palms, and picked up her oars. "*We* are going to row, and *we* are going to keep rowing until we find land, be it a mermaid-infested island or the very West Indies themselves. Now, pull!"

The hours crawled by. The boat crawled forward. Gretel began to have the sense that any progress was in fact an illusion, and that they were merely dipping their oars into the same patch of sea over and over again. At one point Hans became convinced that he could see a huge creature moving beneath the water, circling their boat in a menacing and purposeful fashion. Only after the mer-hund had dived in and swum about cheerfully would he accept that his eyes were playing tricks on him. The sun dipped toward the distant horizon, causing them to row all the more determinedly at it, their only marker in the vastness of the ocean. But even as it set, its colors bleeding into the darkening sky, still there was no sight of land.

That night they finished the last of the ale. With no food left, things took a turn for the morbid, with Hans so hungry he began reciting tales of cannibalism among castaways. Gretel assured him that they were a long way from having to eat each other yet, but she did not care for the way he was sizing up her calves. Meanwhile the mer-hund seemed to exist quite well on sea water. Gretel wished the human constitution were so well adapted, and then sulked at the realization that she was now envying the wretched hound. The darkness provided at least a soothing respite from the beating sun, and exhaustion aided their sleep. When they awoke again at dawn, it was Hans who voiced the dark thought they were both thinking.

"No breakfast."

It wasn't as if Gretel had not missed a breakfast or two in her life, nor that they weren't both sufficiently well fed and well covered to survive without a meal or several. What struck home was the doom behind these two simple words. He might as well have said, *No breakfast, nothing to drink, no chance of any lunch or supper or even so much as a light snack between us and the end of forever.*

As if detecting the dolorous mood of its owner, the mer-hund leapt once more into the sea, disappeared into the depths for a gaspingly long moment, and then returned with a fish in its jaws. It clambered back aboard and released the thing, which flapped and floundered upon the deck of the boat. Hans, demonstrating a startling turn of speed, swung his oar inward and whacked the hound's catch on the head. It lay still. He picked it up and grinned at his sister.

"Breakfast!" he declared.

Gretel frowned. "You're welcome to it," she told him grumpily. "I refuse to have anything to do with it unless I am provided with lemon and a napkin."

"These are desperate times, Gretel. We have to make do."

"I still have standards to maintain. We cannot allow ourselves to sink to the level of barbarians."

She looked at Hans looking at her. His eyebrows shifted upward eloquently. Her state of undress, her outlandish head-gear, her browned and flaking skin, her salt-encrusted hair . . . one might reasonably have concluded that any standards she once had laid claim to had hurled themselves overboard many hours earlier.

"I have no appetite," she insisted, scowling at the fish.

"Come, come. You can't argue with its freshness. Think of it as smoked salmon. I'll slice it thinly. I could even light a cigar under it—that should give it a bit of smokiness, one might think."

Whether or not this would have rendered the fish edible they were not to discover, as at that moment the sky darkened, with clouds scudding overhead appearing apparently from nowhere, bringing with them a wind that quickly stirred up waves. As if that were not excitement enough to manage, it began raining heavily.

"Quick!" Gretel shouted. "Catch the water. Use anything you can find!"

They both grabbed empty ale jars and the single tin cup that had been in the food basket, holding them up to the heavens to receive the blessed rain. The temperature dropped swiftly. It was a welcome relief to feel the cool rainwater washing over face and body, removing salt, sweat, and grime. Soon there was an inch of water in the bottom of the boat. Then two inches. Then several. It quickly became apparent that what at first had seemed to be lifesaving rain could well be the finish of them.

"Bail, Hans. Bail!" Gretel urged.

They set to their task, bent double, scooping the water out with cup or jar. The waves were of noticeable size now, so that every now and again one flopped over the side of the boat, adding to their problems, and infecting with salt what drinking water they tried to secure. Gretel straightened up, stretching her aching back, cursing herself for a simpleton to ever have undertaken such an enterprise. As she did so, she saw something in the distance that caused her to yelp.

"Land! Look, over there. It is, it's land!"

Hans agreed. "Certainly looks solid enough. Trouble is, how do we get to it?"

He had a point. The conditions were such that their enfeebled efforts at rowing stood little chance of taking them anywhere at all, let alone to some specific and dauntingly remote point. Gretel set her jaw. She knew a Last Chance when she saw one, and she wasn't about to let it get away.

TWELVE

We need another sail," she said.

"What?" Hans shook his head. "After what happened last time? And anyway, we don't have a spare."

"Necessity, brother mine, is the mother of invention, the sister of resourcefulness, and the second cousin twice removed of ingenuity. Here, take hold of this," she said, handing him the corset she had removed many long hours ago. Using the stays, they fastened the helpfully capacious garment to mast and boom. At once the wind caught it, sending the boat sculling across the sea. This time Gretel was ready for it. Feet braced against Hans, who was in turn wedged into the narrow pointy end of the boat, still bailing, she leaned back and hauled on the silken stays, bringing them about.

"Here we go!" she cried as they traveled with exhilarating speed in the direction of the land they could now quite plainly make out, even through the continuing rain. The choppy sea made their ride a bumpy one, causing the lifeboat to bounce and leap, and the mer-hund to fall more than once into Gretel's lap. The rain poured down her face, the noise of the wind filled her ears, but she let nothing distract her from her task. She kept her target in sight, shifting her weight in the little boat, heaving on the makeshift ropes to control the magnificently expanded sail, so that soon they were within clear sight of a beach.

"Hold tight!" she warned. "There may be reef or rocks in the shallows. We are about to make landfall, and at a fair rate of knots!"

There followed several moments of tumultuous progress, during which Gretel entirely lost her dominion over the vessel, the stays pulling free of her hands, so that the occupants of the boat were thrown this way and that as it turned and tipped and dropped into the gully of a wave, or leapt from the top of another. At last, with an almighty lurch, the lifeboat was cast up upon the shore. Battered and bruised, Gretel pushed at Hans, urging him to get out quickly and grab hold of the boat, which they then hauled as far up the blond sand as they could. Exhausted, the two lay on their backs, panting like sprinters, their heads swimming and stomachs knotting from the confusion of moving from fairground ride to static land so suddenly. Even the mer-hund subsided next to them.

It was a while before Gretel could summon the strength to sit up. Looking about her, she saw that they had come to a place depressingly similar to Amrum. Empty beach stretched away on both sides. Behind them lay dunes and then tufty tundra, fading to nothing in the distance. The rain had dwindled, the bulk of the storm clouds having either deposited their load or moved out to sea.

"Any notion where we might have been washed up?" Hans asked, still spreadeagled, his eyes closed.

"An island, I think. A fairly small one, by the look of it."

"One of the ones we were aiming at, perhaps?"

"Perhaps. Or perhaps not. Too soon to tell," she said, getting wearily to her feet. The sky was clearing, so that she was able to see the sun once more, and struggled to work out from its position what the time of day might be. A loud rumbling from Hans's belly offered a far more accurate measure. It was past the breakfast they hadn't had and heading toward the lunch they weren't likely to get. It would be all too easy to sink back onto the damp sand and give in to despair.

Hans shifted at last, rubbing his eyes with salty fists, which did nothing to improve his humor.

"Dash it all, Gretel, *a few hours*, you said. *No distance at all*, you said. We've been adrift, becalmed, storm-washed, sunburnt, and now marooned. I'm not sure I signed up for this."

"Don't be such a defeatist, Hans. One cannot simply throw up one's arms after a few minor setbacks."

"Minor? What would you consider major, I wonder? Must we be savaged by sharks? Stung by poisonous jellyfish? Devoured by a kraken?"

She narrowed her eyes at him. "You are drifting into a drama of your own imagining. We are safely delivered on dry land, and if I'm not very much mistaken . . ."

"Oh! That'd make a pleasant change!"

". . . this looks precisely like the sort of place a mermaid might be found."

"I'd rather find a good butcher's shop."

"It's no good wallowing in self-pity. Get up, come along." She grabbed his hands and pulled him to his feet. "This is your chance to prove yourself a man."

"I was unaware there was any doubt in the matter."

"I need you, Hans. Your hour has come."

"What is it you want *this* time? I mean to say, first I must cook for the entire ship's complement, then I have to propel that blasted boat, now . . . what?"

"We need wood for a fire."

"To what end? We've no food to cook on it, and I refuse to sing campfire songs to entertain you. There are limits, you know."

"We need to build a beacon. When night falls we will light it. The weather looks set fair again: our signal will be seen by any vessels in the area, and they will come to our aid."

Hans brightened fractionally.

"Well, I suppose that might work . . ."

"It is our best hope. Now, there don't appear to be too many trees, so I suggest you work your way down the beach, see what driftwood is to be had."

"And what will you be doing?"

"We set off in search of a mermaid, and if there is one on this island I intend to find it. Come along," she called to the mer-hund, "time to set to work." But the animal merely gave her a baleful look and slunk into the dunes, from where he could be heard vomiting copiously.

Hans shook his head sadly. "Well, who'd have thought it, sick as a dog. Ha! I say, that's quite funny, don't you think? Sick as a—"

"Would you like me to remind me how much you paid for that creature?" Gretel asked sternly. "No. Thought not."

"I'll fetch wood," Hans said meekly, turning to plod over the sand. "Just don't get lost," he called over his shoulder as he went. "Don't want to have to come searching for you."

"Don't worry about me," she replied with more confidence than she felt, taking off her shoes and leaving them in the boat, as they served no purpose now other than to collect sand as she walked. Secretly, she feared there would be no mermaid, and that no one would see their fire. She shook such dismal thoughts from her head and replaced them firmly with brighter ones. They would be missed. They would be searched for. They would be found and rescued. She was certain of it.

The going was easy while she followed the broad beach. Her dress having been soaked through by the squall, and the weather being warm again, she still wore only her petticoats and chemise. She removed her headdress, tying the shawl around her waist, and unpinned her tangled, salty hair. It refused to hang free and wild about her shoulders in an attractive manner. Instead it merely descended about her ears in matted clumps. She thought fleetingly of Everard and promised herself she would pay him whatever he asked upon her return to the ship to render her fit for society once more.

After an hour or so, she met a narrow stream that ran from the interior down to the sea, and was able to refresh herself with a good drink. At this point, the shoreline changed dramatically, becoming a thing of rocks and cliffs, so that she was forced to climb up to a high path above. The altered terrain was hard on her bare feet but would have been impossibly slippery in her shoes. The elevated viewpoint at least enabled her to scan the sea for ships. She did not allow herself to dwell unduly on the vastness and emptiness of the ocean, but instead reasoned such uninterrupted seascape must surely mean their beacon would be visible at a very great distance. Surely farther than they could have traveled in their little boat. Particularly if anyone with a half-decent telescope was looking for them. She liked to think several such people existed, and succeeded in listing Captain Ziegler (if only to retrieve his lifeboat), Dr. Becker (with his ever-present binoculars), and of course Ferdinand (just because the thought of his searching made her feel a smidge less flimsy).

Her route took her to a rocky promontory that looked encouragingly like mermaid territory and indeed resembled the shadowy shape of the rocks on which the first singing mermaid of the cruise had been sighted. She offered up a silent prayer and an on-account thank you to anyone who might have influence over such things that just this once luck might go in her favor. It was entirely possible that the lifeboat had borne its landlubbing occupants in a southerly direction, so that their journey had converged with the course of the *Arabella* some days earlier. Gretel looked about her. There were rocks, with tenacious grasses and flowers clinging to crevices, and then there were more rocks, nearer the cliff edge, before a now dizzying drop to the sea below. The path ahead twisted around a high upward reach of gray stone, so that to proceed she had to walk horribly close to the edge, but she had no choice other than to continue. Flattening herself against the rock face as best her shapely physique would permit, she crept on. Looking down was definitely a bad idea, but there was nothing out at sea on which to fix her gaze. In the end she found turning her head in the direction she was going and squinting into the sunshine the pick of her options. In this way she was able to round the point and step onto the mercifully wider stretch of path on the other side. To her delight, the first thing she saw was the entrance to a cave, the arch of which was prettily decorated with seashells and white pebbles. Seaweed in a variety of subtle shades and hues was draped around the opening, and sprightly shrubs and flowers had been trained along the path that led to it. Gretel had never seen a mermaid's home before, but this could surely be nothing else. Cautiously, she ventured in. The interior was dark as night after the brightness of the day outside, and her eyes struggled to function.

"Hello?" she called, her voice echoing eerily in the cavernous space. "Hello, anyone home?"

There was no reply. She took a few more tentative steps. As her eyesight adjusted, the half-light within revealed the full beauty of the magical dwelling. While the outer rock was dark, sea-weathered, and rugged, the interior was altogether different. The cave appeared to have been formed inside a layer of pale blue crystal, so that even in the low light provided by the entrance and several high holes, all the walls glittered and twinkled. The effect was bewitching. Ledges had been fashioned here and there at various heights, some thatched with seaweed and reeds, others lined with moss, providing comfortable places to sit or lie. Shells of oysters, razor clams, mussels, and other exotic sea life were arranged in careful displays. This was clearly the home of someone who appreciated beautiful things.

Gretel saw that the far side of the cave contained a pool, and the manner in which the level of it undulated suggested it was affected by the tide. She decided this must be a point of ingress and egress, leading to the sea itself.

"Hello?" she called once more. "Is there anyone here?" All the answer she received was the echo of her own voice. Her initial euphoria at finding what could only be a mermaid's home quickly evaporated when she accepted that the place was empty. How long did such creatures spend out at sea? When might she return? It could be many hours. Days, even. Gretel knew she could not expect Hans to endure famine upon the island for a second longer than was absolutely necessary. They must light their bonfire, and would likely be rescued the same night. Her only hope was, on being collected, to ascertain exactly where they were, and arrange to be brought back to the island by an experienced sailor. Surely there would be plenty in the region willing to undertake the task so long as they were paid sufficiently. And so long as they were not superstitious about mermaids.

With a sinking heart, Gretel picked her way back across the shiny floor of the cave, and was just about to leave when she heard the sound of splashing behind her. Turning, she saw that the water in the pool was disturbed. She hurried back, clambering as close to the edge of it as she dared. There were bubbles, almost as if the water was boiling. This activity was accompanied by a curious smell that put Gretel in mind of lilies. With a sudden whooshing, the surface erupted into a great fountain, causing her to stagger backward and ultimately fall heavily onto her rear. Out of the water emerged the most exquisite being she had ever set eyes on. The mermaid—for mermaid it most certainly was—had fine features, a broad brow, and green eyes that were wide-set. Her hair was long, rippling waves of dark gold, gleaming even though heavy with water. Her sodden locks clung to her slender body, affording her a little modesty. Her upper half was indisputably human and female and gorgeous. From the waist down she was pure fish, albeit one whose scales glistened prettily, iridescent green and blue, and her tail was sinuous and graceful as she moved out of the water. She did so in one surprisingly fluid movement, an upward lift propelled by her powerful tail, so that she came effortlessly to sit decoratively on one of the moss-filled ledges.

"A visitor! How simply lovely," the mermaid exclaimed, her voice mellifluous, each word carrying with it a sweet smile.

"Forgive me for entering your home uninvited," said Gretel.

"You are so very welcome. I seldom receive callers."

"I find that hard to believe," Gretel told her, and meant it. The creature before her had a mesmerizing quality, so that any who looked upon her could only desire to go on doing so. It seemed to Gretel that if anyone knew of the mermaid's existence and the location of her grotto, they would become frequent visitors.

"Sadly, many people are afraid of me," the mermaid said. "Imagine that. Afraid of little old me." She tilted her head, peering up through long lashes, her expression one of innocent bewilderment.

"There are superstitions regarding . . . your kind."

"Such a shame. It would be so much better if people made up their own minds about things, instead of doing what is expected of them. Don't you think so, Frau . . . ?

"Fraulein Gretel, of Gesternstadt. Do you have a name?"

The mermaid smiled broadly at this. "We have many names, my sisters and me, but all of them make us out to be dangerous in some way. Really"—she shook her head, causing her flowing hair to move in a very attractive way, and tiny specks of crystal to fall from it, catching the beams of sunlight that fell from the glassless windows high above—"such silly nonsense. How could *I* be dangerous?" she asked, giving a tiny, tinkling laugh.

Gretel knew a thing or two about what was dangerous and what was not, and quickly decided that, however appealing she might appear—or indeed precisely because she was so bewitchingly glorious—the mermaid had the potential to be extremely dangerous. She had seen for herself what such allure could do to a man. Seen what strong, apparently moral men of integrity could be reduced to doing for the sake of such loveliness. And if that loveliness was possessed by one with, perhaps, a grievance, or too few scruples, or too much time on their hands . . . the outcome was often disastrous.

"But of course, I do have a name," the mermaid went on. "The thing is, I'm not allowed to tell it to you."

"Oh?"

"No, I can only give my name to someone who pledges me their heart. So you see, it wouldn't really be appropriate."

"Quite, quite, no, I understand. Good thing my brother is not with me. He would undoubtedly have pledged you his heart, lungs, liver, even his stomach, in a trice."

The mermaid laughed again. "You are funny! I like people who can make me laugh."

"You say you receive few visitors . . . fraulein . . . but I would hazard a guess that there is one regular caller of late. One who is not in the least bit afraid of you. One who sought you out, in fact."

"Well! Fancy you knowing that. Have you been spying on me?"

"I have not. But I confess I have been looking for you."

"Oh, really? It is quite unusual, a *woman* wanting to find me."

"I have my reasons, and they are specific, material, and important."

The mermaid picked up a carved clamshell and began languorously combing her hair with it. "How very mysterious," she purred. "I think I quite like the sound of being important."

"Tell me, your recent guest, did he approach you with a special request regarding your rather marvelous singing?" Gretel asked, attempting a little flattery, but aware it was not her forte.

The mermaid continued to appear relaxed and unconcerned by Gretel's line of questioning, and yet there was a minute alteration in her expression. Her eyes seemed to harden just the tiniest bit.

"It is a harmless enough request," she said. "We are quite famous for the beauty of our song; that is no secret."

"Indeed. Nor is it a secret that many find that same singing unbearably sad. Some are driven to run from it, others to throw themselves into the sea as if irresistibly drawn to it."

"Poor things!" The mermaid's eyes now filled with salty tears. "I have no wish to cause anyone pain, Fraulein Gretel. Surely you believe me?"

"I have no reason to suppose that you deliberately set out to frighten men out of their wits. I do, however, suspect that you would not be persuaded to sing against your own will or inclination. Forgive me, fraulein, but you do not strike me as a person given to doing anything not of your own desire."

The mermaid smiled sweetly again, the tears vanished. "But I love to sing! Why ever would I not want to? It brings me joy to sit on the rocks overlooking the sea and send my music out across the dark, dark water."

"Let me put it this way: even if we accept that it is not your intention to cause trouble or dismay, the person who came here to ask you to sing knew exactly what he was doing. He knew that many sailors cannot abide the sound of a mermaid's voice; that they fear it portends death or shipwreck or madness. Some will refuse to sail on a ship once they have heard your music while aboard it. I come from the *Arabella*, which is suffering from a depleted crew, several members of which have either left or disappeared as, we believe, a result of what they have heard." Gretel knew herself to be stating facts rather baldly, and that some of these facts were speculation at best. This mattered less, she decided, than prodding the mermaid's conscience, if she had one, into revealing what needed to be revealed. "What was it that your visitor promised you in return for this service?"

"*Service!*" The mermaid bridled. "I am not some washer-woman or laborer!" Her eyes flashed dark and deadly. "I am not some lowly peasant to be hired by the day!" As her temper slipped, so did her mask of sweetness, revealing a frightening glimpse of the true nature of the creature beneath.

"Be that as it may, you reached some bargain, did you not?"

"Why should I tell you my business? What right have you to come poking your red shiny nose into my affairs?"

Gretel took a breath. It was not, at that moment, anything like an even match. Had she been at her best, elegantly turned out, properly coiffed and fashionably dressed, things might have been different. As it was, she had no hope. In front of her, glowing with anger but still radiantly beautiful, sat the mermaid, slender, sparkling, and lovely. She herself was salt-scrubbed, sunburnt, mad-haired, and even more madly clothed. If the mermaid was going to start bandying about insults, Gretel was bound to lose that contest. She rose above the slur.

"I was called to the *Arabella* by her captain, who fears for his men and his livelihood. I am a detective, and the task I have undertaken is to help him. You, fraulein, wittingly or not, are the cause of much of his woe. That said, there is another who wishes disaster and ruin upon him, and that man is the very same who pays you to sing. What has he given you, and what is his name? Or would you like me to tell you precisely what a man looks like when he has been dead three days with his throat slit? I warn you, I shall spare no detail," she insisted. She well knew that she had implied that the mermaid's singing had been somehow responsible for a person meeting such an unpleasant end. She also knew that this was unlikely to be the case. She further knew that the notion of such culpability, coupled with the threat of a graphic description of the gruesomeness of such a death, might be sufficient to shock the mermaid into cooperation. In this, as in so many things, Gretel's instinct proved to be correct.

"I don't know his name!" she insisted, her expression now a mixture of sulkiness and alarm. "He never gave it to me."

"What did he look like?"

"He came only at night and wore his hat low. He never plainly revealed his face to me."

"And what bargain did you strike with this shadowy figure?"

"He asked me to sing, out on the promontory, on certain nights."

"He gave you dates and times?"

"He did."

"And were you always to sing here, on this island?"

"Not always. Sometimes I was to sit on another. I can swim quite a way with no difficulty at all, you know," she said, running a hand down her powerful tail.

"And did he tell you why he wanted you to sing?"

"He was reluctant, at first. But I persuaded him, eventually. I have my little ways," she explained with a coy smile.

"I can well believe that. So, what was his purpose?"

"He wanted rid of the cruise ships."

"You mean Captain Ziegler's cruise ship?"

The mermaid shrugged.

"He did not specify the *Arabella*, you are certain of that?"

"He just said cruise ships. He gave me no names. He said he wanted me to sing to frighten the sailors and scare them away. I asked him why, but he was very stubborn on that point. He simply would not tell me more."

"And what did you gain from this arrangement?"

"Oh, he paid me handsomely."

"Did he indeed?"

"I am not a silly creature. People often think that of us, too. Dangerous and silly. It is horrid to be considered so, and really not true at all. I wouldn't do what he wanted for pennies. I'll show you," she said, and in one startlingly swift movement she flung herself back into the pool and disappeared into its depths.

Gretel could do nothing but wait. She stared at the point where the creature had vanished for what felt like an unreasonably long time.

At last the mermaid broke through the surface, sending a shower of water over Gretel as she leapt out to sit once more on the crystal rocks, this time closer to her interlocutor.

"Here, see?" She held up a leather pouch, which she untied, tipping the contents out onto the cave floor beside her. Gold coins gleamed in the eerie light. Many of them.

"That's a fair amount of money, fraulein. You certainly know how to obtain your due. But tell me, what will you do with it?" She gestured at their surroundings. "You surely have everything here you could want or need."

"Oh, this place." The mermaid shook her head. "It is all very well now, in the summer months. It is pleasant enough *now*. But come winter . . . I cannot properly tell you how cold this cave becomes. Nor how bitter the winds that chase across this island. Nor how frigid and dark the sea." This time the tears that filled the mermaid's eyes betrayed a genuine suffering.

"I think I can imagine," Gretel told her, thinking of the bleakness of Amrum, the ferocity of the changeable weather in the vicinity, and the vast emptiness of the sea.

"Well, I've had enough of it," the mermaid told her. "I want to go somewhere *warm*. Somewhere where the sky is blue more often than it is gray. Where the winter nights are not so very long. I want to live in a place where I can dry my hair in the sunshine and feel the sun warm my body. And when I get a little too hot I can slip into the warm sea. A sea that is filled with light and color. Even I cannot swim such a distance but would require a vessel to take me where I wish to go. That is what I want, Fraulein Gretel. That is why I agreed to sing."

"You are saving for your passage, I see. It would take a fair amount to travel to such a place, but I deduce, judging by your current wealth, and given that you surely intend singing some more, you will soon have sufficient for your ticket. What may be harder to find is a captain willing to let you aboard his ship."

The mermaid looked perplexed. "But my money is as good as anyone else's."

"That is as may be, but you must understand that the talent that has earned you your riches may also be the thing that prevents you from getting what you desire."

"I don't see how. I can promise not to sing."

"But how are you to be trusted? Word is spreading fast in these parts that there is a mermaid, a singing one at that. The more people hear of disappearing sailors and mysterious deaths, the less likely any one of them is to let you on their vessel. How could they take the risk? In truth, you need not sing so much as a single note; your presence alone could be enough to send half the crew overboard."

"But that is ridiculous," the mermaid replied, her face showing the extent of her growing consternation. "I am a harmless creature. They surely would not give way to such superstitious fears."

Gretel sighed, the sound floating mournfully around and around the interior of the cave. However much the mermaid denied accusations of being dangerous and silly, it was hard to defend her against either charge. Her plan had been quickly formed and poorly thought through. When the mysterious visitor had offered her money to sing, she had seen a way of obtaining her greatest wish, but she had not applied logic and sound thinking to her plan. She would most likely end up with a pile of gold that was useless to her and be forced to remain forever precisely where she was. The mermaid's plight struck Gretel as quite pitiful. It was also quite open to manipulation.

"How would it be, fraulein," Gretel asked her gently, "if I were to find you a captain who would be willing to take your gold and convey you swiftly and safely to the more tropical climes you seek?"

"How do I know you won't trick me? How do I know you know such a person?" The mermaid stuck out her bottom lip. She was struggling to be brave, for it trembled noticeably.

"I will bring him here to meet you. You may talk with him your-self. I will bear witness to any agreement forged between you."

There was a pause while the mermaid considered this sug-gestion, evidently searching it for hidden traps.

"Why would you do this for me?" she asked Gretel.

"As I believe I mentioned earlier, I am here as part of my duty as a detective. I have a case to solve, and solve it I shall, and removing you from these waters would go a very long way to achieving that end."

"Very well. Bring this captain of yours. But be quick. I am due to be called upon by my benefactor very soon. If he arrives before you do, I will consider you having failed me. I will take his money and take my chances with it. If this cooperative captain of yours does not come to me, in person, in good faith, I must make as much money as I can. The only course left to me will be to raise sufficient gold to soothe the fears you speak of. Even though that might take me a great deal of time. And who knows how many silly sailors will disappear because of it. I will never give up, do you hear me? One way or the other, I will have what it is I want."

"In that case, fraulein, I will take my leave. I must return to the *Arabella* as quickly as possible. All I ask at this point is that you refrain from singing tonight. I wish to attract a vessel of some sort to the island so that I might be taken off it. If you are endeavoring to frighten them from it at the very same moment, I may not succeed."

The mermaid flicked her hair over her shoulder and slid onto her mossy bed, where she reclined decoratively. "I don't much feel like singing this evening, anyhow," she said.

"I will bid you good night, then," said Gretel. As she reached the entrance to the cave, she heard the mermaid call after her.

"Two nights and two days, fraulein. Return swiftly, for I will wait no longer."

THIRTEEN

By the time Gretel reached the beach and the lifeboat, dusk was descending. Hans was nowhere to be seen, but his footprints were clearly visible in the sand. Muttering curses, Gretel trudged in his wake. On her journey back from the mermaid's home, she had paused at the freshwater stream to drink, but had had nothing to eat since the previous day and her energy levels were lower than low. The last thing she needed was to have to hunt for her brother. She made her way along the shoreline. As she rounded a curve, the sand banked steeply inland, and the dunes were replaced by more rock, rising to cliffs. These were similar to those she had encountered in the other direction, but lower. She kept doggedly to Hans's footsteps and soon saw his familiar form, recumbent upon the sand, the mer-hund dozing beside him. She reached them somewhat out of both breath and patience.

"Hans! This is no time for sleeping," she snapped.

"Not asleep," he insisted without moving. "Merely resting my eyes." He had fashioned a hat out of his kerchief, which sat knotted upon his head in a ludicrous style.

"You were supposed to be collecting wood for a fire," she reminded him.

He waved a pudgy paw to his right. "Done," he told her.

Gretel ground her teeth. "Three planks, a rotten bough, and a clump of seaweed do not a woodpile make."

"That's all there is. Unfavorable tides, one must suppose. Or winds. Or currents. Or some such. I gleaned every splinter available, I promise you. There is no more to be had."

Gretel detected a slur in his words. She leaned over her brother and sniffed. "You've been drinking! Do not tell me that all these tortuous hours, you have been in possession of a hip flask."

"I have not." With some effort, he sat up, and as he did so he lifted a bottle to show her. "I found this. While I was looking for the wood. Over there, in a tiny little cave."

She snatched it from him and took a swig. "Brandy!"

"Rather a good one, too. There's loads of it, all carefully packed in wooden crates. Doesn't look like flotsam or jetsam to me, have to say."

Gretel drank a little more. Her stomach knotted at the unexpected arrival of alcohol when it had been anticipating food. Nausea swept through her briefly before being replaced by a pleasant fuzzy warmth. She savored the dark flavors. The familiar dark flavors, for this was not, she realized, the first time this particular brandy had passed her lips.

"Hard to come by," Hans noted, "that sort of quality. French, I'd say. Variety of booze that import tax usually makes maddeningly expensive. Somebody must have come all the way out here and put the stuff in that cave," he went on, shaking his head. "I can't imagine why anyone would want to do that."

"Oh, but I can, Hans," she said. "I can."

※

An hour later, with darkness proper having fallen upon the little island, Hans took his cigar lighter from his pocket and put a flame to the pyre they had built. It was not high, it was not broad, nor did it consist of anything much in the way of good wood. It did, however, contain quantities of liquor, so that it caught with an eyebrow-singeing *woomph*. Gretel pulled her brother back to a safe distance, where he stood and watched the impressively tall flames while she watched the horizon. For what seemed like an age, there was nothing, save for the expanse of dark water and the sound of the ebbing tide lapping at the shore. Which was all but drowned out by the roar of the fire. Every time the blaze dwindled, Hans emptied another bottle of brandy onto it. On each occasion there was an exciting flaring, greeted by a childish cheer from Hans and a whimper from the mer-hund, followed by a rekindled inferno, which gave off rather enjoyable fumes.

Hans beamed. "Puts me in mind of a little French restaurant Wolfie and I frequented in our youth in Nuremberg. Can't recall the name of the place, but they did a splendid *crêpe suzette flambé*. Smelled exactly as this does. Though with more sugar, perhaps. Quite fancy a crêpe now, I don't mind telling you. Quite fancy anything, in fact. If our fire is not observed by any passing ships we will have to set our minds to the matter of finding food, sister mine. There is no avoiding the matter," he said solemnly, his stomach growling to underline the point.

At that moment, Gretel glimpsed a tiny shape out on the horizon, picked out by the beams of a helpfully bright moon.

She lifted her lorgnettes to her eyes. Still it was hard to make anything out in the darkness, but slowly the shape moved closer.

"There is something there!" she told Hans.

"A ship? Is it your fellow Ferdinand on the *Fair Fortune*, d'you think?"

"Alas no, it is far too insignificant a vessel."

"The *Arabella*, perhaps?"

"Too small even for that, I fear."

"Oh, might it be a fishing boat? Yes, I'll bet it is a fishing boat. My money's on a fishing boat!" he cried, hopping about excitedly.

Gretel lowered her glasses to scowl at him. "Hans, this is not a gambling opportunity. Neither of us has any money. What is at stake here is our very lives, so for pity's sake stop jumping up and down like a rabbit with a flea and make yourself useful. Feed that fire some more, quickly. They must not miss our distress signal."

"Right you are!" He dashed off to the store of bottles as instructed.

Whether or not the occupants of the passing vessel would have spotted the resultant blaze became a redundant question, as they most certainly heard the blast that followed Hans's decision to tip an entire crate of bottles onto the pyre. The force of it blew him and Gretel off their feet, which was no small achievement in itself. The mer-hund ran for cover, showing a fair turn of speed, but still losing some of its fur before it outran the showering sparks and embers. That nobody lost an eye to a flying sliver of glass was little short of miraculous. Gretel landed on her front, the force of the explosion pressing her hard into the wet sand, so that when she stood up she found she was coated in the stuff. Her clothes bore scorch marks. Aside from this, she had escaped injury. Looking around, she saw Hans on his backside. He had been thrown onto his rear and therefore bounced like a beach ball to a safer remove. He appeared a little stunned, but otherwise he too remained unscathed. Wiping sand from her lorgnettes, Gretel searched for the boat once more.

"It's coming this way! They must have noticed our signal!" she cried.

"What's that?" asked Hans, the explosion evidently still ringing in his ears.

"We are saved!" she bellowed at him.

"Good-oh! And are they fishermen?" he wanted to know.

"I . . . don't think . . . so," she replied as she gained further clues to their identity, the closer into focus they sailed.

It was a plain boat, with no flag hoisted, and was powered by a modest sail, backed up by oars. There were three fellows in it. The nearer they drew, the more disappointing they appeared. These were not the gallant and handsome rescuers a person might reasonably have hoped for. Not a burgundy cape nor manly stance among them. Their age averaged no less than fifty. All three were poorly dressed, their garments apparently having been selected for their drabness. Indeed, they seemed to have been attempting to out-drab one another. It was a close thing, but the skinniest one at the front would most likely have taken the prize. There came a point when Gretel realized that this was not a medium-sized boat far away, but an insignificant one close up. They had no need of an anchor, but simply ran the thing through the shallows until it was grounded. They proceeded to clamber out, hauling it a few strides farther up the beach so that it would not float again without their assistance. It was, in point of fact, only fractionally larger than the lifeboat it now shared a shore with.

In her many years as a private detective, and indeed in her many years as a woman of good sense and sound reason,

Gretel had learned a thing or two about mankind. One might chatter on at length and as much as one liked regarding the dangers of judging a book by its cover, but the fact remained that first impressions usually gave a pretty good indication of the manner of person with which one was dealing. On this occasion, with these particular persons, first impressions were of the off-putting variety. Aside from their ragged and unbecoming attire, the men were all hirsute of arm or regrettably exposed chest, stubbly of chin, and gimlet-eyed. Another common factor was a salty odor that traveled from them on the inshore breeze in Gretel's direction. The trio represented a range of physiques, but not one could have been described as attractive. The first man to step forward was tall, but not in an appealing way, as he was so thin and frail as to give the impression that were he to fall, his bones would snap and shatter like *langue du chat* biscuits dropped upon a stone-flagged kitchen floor. The next was of average shape and size, but his color was so pale, and his face so afflicted with pustular spots and pimples, that it was hard to regard him for more than a few seconds without feeling queasy. The last was short and wide, and seemed to wobble as he walked, as if it was only his filthy clothing that held him together, while he himself was made of a material altogether unwholesome and decidedly unattractive. Aged milk curds, perhaps. Or semolina. With a thick crust of furry, green-blue mold.

Hans strode toward them, hand outstretched in welcome. "Well, you fellows are a sight for sore eyes!" he enthused, snatching up their own hands and shaking them enthusiastically. "We were in a pretty pickle until you came along, don't mind telling you."

The men remained silent, apparently rendered speechless by the surprise of finding two disheveled, lightly charred strangers on the shore. It was only now that Gretel became aware of the fact that she stood before them in her petticoats and chemise, minus corset, barefoot, her hair a tangled mass of salt and frizzing knots, and sand stuck to her face. Her brother also presented a picture of madness, with his sooty eyebrows, handkerchief headdress, damp and pungent clothes, breathing brandy fumes all over them in his effusive greeting.

While their shock was understandable, however, their lack of inquiry as to the hows and whys and wherefores that had precipitated Gretel and Hans being on the island struck her as odd. As did the fact that they had been traveling in such a small boat upon such a large ocean. One thing was certain: these were no fishermen. She noticed Mold casting sideways looks at the bonfire and frowning at the shattered glass and bottle shards strewn about the place. The aroma of flambéed brandy hung over them all like a shameful secret.

Gretel cleared her throat. "We are, as my brother says, tre-mendously pleased, not to say relieved, to see you. We were shipwrecked here after a storm blew our own small boat off course, and were forced to signal for assistance," she told them, despite having the distinct feeling that they cared not one jot how she had come to be there.

"Thought we might be marooned," Hans put in. "Left here to fend for ourselves for years and years, existing on winkles and barnacles and gnawing on the odd seagull, that sort of thing. Would have been a sorry state of affairs—not enough wood to build a shelter, I can tell you that. We were fortunate to find the brandy that fueled our fire, else we might never have been seen."

The word "brandy" caused small but telling reactions among the men. Mold looked again toward the fire. Pustule started scratching at his chin, his dirty nails raking at the bristly skin and threatening to scrape the tops from a handful of his worst boils, so that Gretel had to swallow hard to maintain her composure. Cat's Tongue drew himself up, making his body even more weedy and unstable. Such minute responses might have gone unnoticed by most people. But Gretel was not most people. She was a detective, and at this precise moment she detected smuggling. These men were here for the stow of tax-free alcohol, she was convinced of it. Why else would they be in such a place at such a time of night and exhibit such shifty mannerisms? If her instinct was right—and it rarely failed her—she and Hans were in great danger. There was a great deal of value in the stash of liquor. Or at least, there had been, before the major part of it had been burned up or exploded. A fact not likely to endear them to their potential rescuers. She knew the situation required handling both delicate and dextrous. If they gave these men the slightest hint that they knew what skulduggerous enterprise they were embarked upon, their lives would once again be imperiled.

"Exceptional quality, that brandy we found," Hans informed them cheerfully. "Tried a sip when we happened upon it. Not your usual cheap stuff, oh, dear me, no. Expensive, I should say. Worth a bob or two. Wouldn't you agree, Gretel? Particularly fine brandy, eh? And a goodly amount of it, hidden away."

Before Gretel could form a response, Cat's Tongue thrust his scrawny face close to her own, though he had to stoop to do so.

"What business have ye here?" he demanded. Gretel rolled his accent around in her mind and detected several Hamburg generations, diluted by a more northern influence, most likely Danish.

She kept her voice level and even mustered a small, placatory smile.

"As I said, we were blown off course, and—"

"Ye ain't sailors," he said.

"I congratulate you on the keenness of your deduction, Herr . . ." When no name was forthcoming, she pressed on.

"My brother and I were . . ." Here she was forced to pause once more. The phrase "mermaid hunt" seemed suddenly completely unbelievable, and yet it was the truth, and the only one she had. "We were searching for the source of some particularly unusual singing."

"Singing?" Cat's Tongue and Pustule exchanged incredulous glances. Mold was not, apparently, worthy of inclusion in this silent dialogue.

"Precisely that," said Gretel, still smiling. "We have come from a cruise ship, sailing out of Bremerhaven . . ."

"What cruise ship might that be?" Pustule took it upon himself to ask. Despite their differing physiques, his voice and his singular accent strongly suggested he must be brother to Cat's Tongue.

Hans, seizing a question that for once he was able to answer, blurted out, "The *Arabella*. Fine little ship. Do you know of her?"

"Did Hoffman send you?" Pustule demanded, pushing his sibling out of the way so that he might thrust his own unlovely visage at Gretel. This was, she decided, an unfortunate technique for conducting a conversation, for close up his appearance was so distracting, it was difficult to remain engrossed in the subject being discussed. However, she did her best, keen to reply before Hans said anything that could dig them deeper into the pit of trouble in which they found themselves.

"The ship's quartermaster?" she asked, convincingly baffled. "Why, no. We acted upon our own accord."

"Oh?" Pustule seemed unconvinced. "And the wind just happened to blow you onto this island . . . ?"

". . . this very island?" Cat's Tongue repeated the accusation and both brothers nodded vigorously.

"Well, yes, it did. As you so astutely noticed, we are not sailors, and had difficulty directing our boat, particularly during the squall."

"And what found ye here?" Cat's Tongue wanted to know.

"Aye." Pustule was not to be outdone in the business of clever questioning. "What found ye here?"

There followed a hesitation, which, as is so often the case, was in and of itself an eloquent thing. That they had found brandy was a fact Hans had already divulged. Quite what she and he thought that brandy to be, how it had come there, and what their recently arrived visitors had to do with it were the facts now in question. Gretel could see Hans opening his mouth, on the point of blathering on about mermaids and high import taxes again. She observed Mold picking up a bottle bottom and turning it over and over in his flaccid hands. She noticed the Brothers Grime hold their bodies tense and still while their minds whirred and spun, filling the little silence with dangerous conjecture and conclusions. Much of which might— more by chance than skill—have been accurate. It was not the first time circumstances had demanded that Gretel produce a convincing story to explain her actions, buy herself some time, and effect her escape from a threatening situation. Her mind was, by its nature, adept at invention and postulation that was both plausible and intelligent. However, that same mind was slave to her body, and could only function at its highest level when its corporeal home was in tip-top condition. Gretel was tired, thirsty, hungry, aching, sore, bedraggled, and in all manner of ways very far from either tip or top. As such, in this instance, her mind offered up nothing. Nought. Nix. Nil.

Pustule's face darkened.

Cat's Tongue's hand dropped slowly to the dagger hilt in his belt.

Mold took a short, stout step forward.

Just when things were moving from tricksome to downright ticklish, help arrived from the most unexpected of quarters. The mer-hund, singed fur and all, came charging forth from its hiding place among the rocks. It barreled into the group with a fearsome growling and barking, baring its teeth, belching fishily as it leapt into the fray. The men shouted in alarm. Cat's Tongue drew his blade, causing Hans to react with the instinct of a parent, which overruled his natural talent for self-preservation. He flung himself atop his precious pet's would-be assailant, knocking him to the ground and causing him to drop the dagger and squeal in anguish beneath Hans's great weight. The two struggled, the thinner wriggling from under the fatter and then turning to beat him with furious fists. The mer-hund had by this time clamped its powerful jaws around Pustule's left leg, making him scream and yelp in two languages. The night was filled with men's shouts and curses, the growling of the hound, and the gibberish of Hans.

To Gretel's horror, Mold drew a pistol from his rancid trousers. His aim looked dangerously poor, as he waved his weapon wildly. She knew she must act. She filled her lungs with sea air and bellowed in her most authoritative voice, "Will you be quiet!!? Put that down now! Stop making such a terrible racket! What do you think you are doing?! What would your mothers say if they could see you now?" Her tone cut through the fug of male bravado and found its target in the small boy that dwells in the heart of every man, however grown, however fierce. All four men stopped what they were doing and stood—or lay—shamefaced, heads drooping under the force of Gretel's disapproval. "I have never in my life," she went on, "seen such behavior! Hans, take control of your creature. You, uncock that pistol. And you with the dagger, unless you plan to fillet a fish with it, I insist you put it away. Such manners! Such rudeness! Here is a woman in distress, at the mercy of your gallantry, and yet you brawl and scream oaths like common ruffians." The confusion of being accused of being precisely what they were brought the smugglers up short. They did as they were told. Gretel pressed home her advantage.

"Now, I intend fetching my day dress and shoes from the lifeboat, and then, if it wouldn't be too much trouble, my brother and I would be exceedingly grateful if you could take us to something that passes for civilization in this region. We are in need of sustenance and refreshment, and a bed for the night. In the morning we will send word to the *Arabella* of our whereabouts. I promise you, your assistance will not go unrewarded," she added, appealing to their greed as well as their altruism, certain in the knowledge that the former was bound to be larger than the latter.

FOURTEEN

Keen as she was to leave the island, Gretel found herself a reluctant passenger on the smugglers' boat. It was not large enough to accommodate them all, so that Hans and the mer-hund were made to travel in the *Arabella*'s lifeboat, which was towed behind. There had been some argument about abandoning the hound, but Hans refused to budge without it, Gretel refused to leave without him, and their rescuers—for such they had now become, willingly or not—after much muttering between them, evidently deemed it better for their own plans if the pair were removed from the island. Their acquiescence in the matter was unnerving. Their interest, Gretel decided, must surely lie in making certain their plans were not thwarted, and to this end who knew what they might be prepared to do. She had to remain on her guard for the slightest indication that she was about to be tipped into the sea. The crates of brandy that had not been used to feed the signal fire were swiftly stashed in the bottom of their boat. The men had offered no rationale or explanation. They had no need to, for Hans had loudly declared it would indeed be a shame and a waste to leave such expensive liquor behind, especially when whoever put it there had clearly forgotten about it.

The night was black as licorice now, with few stars and a dull, cloud-strewn moon. Gretel knew they were at the mercy of these dangerous men, as only they could safely navigate in such conditions. However much she wanted to be free of them, she did not relish the prospect of being adrift at sea again. She was seated in the rear of the boat, which at least meant she was situated between the rope that connected Hans to them and Cat's Tongue's sharp knife. She was weary to her bones, but sleep was out of the question. She must remain awake. She must remain vigilant. One feeble ship's lantern was all that illuminated their vessel. It threw a patchy light across the faces of the crew, swinging slowly with the rocking of the boat, so that they were revealed in turn, each one more grim-faced and fierce than the last. All of them staring hard at Gretel.

The plain truth was that they were all—with the exception of Hans—engaged in a dangerous charade. Were any of them to voice aloud the word "smuggling," it would be all up for Gretel, her brother, and even the wretched mer-hund. Gretel knew well enough what it was the men were about. They knew that she knew. She knew that they knew that she knew. They knew she knew this. Hans knew nothing. They all must maintain the pretense that nobody knew anything.

Two hours of this tense journey brought them to another island. This one was larger than the last and boasted a small harbor, into which they put. The quayside was all but deserted, the hour being late. The men bundled their passengers along in front of them and took them to an inn. It looked presentable enough, and from it came the low hubbub produced by gentle drinking, eating, and conversation. Hans spotted the sign declaring it to be the Star and promising good ale, and gave a cheer.

"This is what we need, sister mine," he said, rubbing his hands together. "A little beer to refresh us, some tasty food, a cushioned seat, and later a soft bed. We will soon be restored in body and spirit, I am certain of it."

Cat's Tongue opened the front door and pushed Gretel inside before him. For a few fleeting seconds she took in a warm, relaxed ambience, the reviving aroma of a hearty fish stew that set her mouth watering, basic but serviceable furnishings, a lively fire in the hearth, and a fair collection of inn-goers, all male, all of the baser variety, but all, apparently, still in possession of most of their teeth and senses. The instant they noticed the new arrivals, however, the chatter stopped. A heavy silence sat fatly upon the room now, leaving no room for bonhomie or companionable ease. Whether it was their escort that had caused this sudden chill, or she and Hans because they were strangers, or merely her own female presence, she could not yet discern. Pustule led the way to a high-backed wooden settle in the darkest corner of the room. Gretel strode across the floor to the sound of her own footsteps, head high, affecting a manner which suggested that her disastrous hair, weather-beaten skin, and damp, crumpled dress caused her neither distress nor embarrassment. She felt thirty pairs of eyes watching her as she took her place. Hans sat beside her, and the mer-hund slunk beneath the low table. A grunt from Mold indicated that they were to remain seated, while he and his fellows went to the bar.

Gretel quickly assessed their situation. Their circumstances were considerably improved, inasmuch as they were in an inn and not on an empty island. There was a fair chance they would be fed and watered. They were no longer at the mercy of the smugglers, but in company. However, that company was now her main source of concern. The stubborn silence that had greeted their arrival persisted, as stubborn things are wont to do. In a rocking chair next to the fire sat a sea-salted old man sucking on a clay pipe. Gretel chanced a smile in his direction. He removed the pipe, but only to hawk and spit elaborately into a nearby spittoon before replacing it and puffing on menacingly. At the next table sat three young men, all wearing shirts apparently a size too small for them, so that their muscles bulged through the straining fabric. Not one of them spoke, nor so much as nodded a greeting toward the newcomers. Leaning against the bar was an enormous man, so tall his head brushed the ceiling, so beetle-browed as to surely suffer impaired vision. He moved only to lift a frothing tankard of ale to his wide mouth. The barman himself wore an expression both sour and dour. It was hard to imagine help would be forthcoming from any of these taciturn inn-goers.

Pustule reappeared at their table. He slammed down plates and beakers in front of them.

"We have business to attend to," he said, jerking his head in the direction of his brother. "You stay here."

As he turned to leave, Gretel called after him, "And the messenger gull? We will have been missed by now. I must send word to the *Arabella* that we are safe," she said, though she felt anything but.

Pustule grunted and shrugged. "I'll fetch 'n back. You wait here," he repeated. As he and Cat's Tongue went out, Mold took up position on a stool by the door, clearly put there to make sure no one went anywhere they were not supposed to go.

"I say, this bread is not bad. Not bad at all," Hans told her, tucking into the simple fare they had been given.

Gretel found her own appetite compromised by the thought that Pustule had been in contact with the food. However, good sense prevailed, with its winning argument that nobody ever solved a case on an empty stomach. She nibbled a crust and sipped some ale, and soon found herself able to eat properly. Indeed, bread and cheese had never tasted so delicious. As she feasted she glanced warily about her. Still the inhabitants of the hostelry remained watchful and quiet. Were they in cahoots with the smugglers, perhaps? Were they merely biding their time, awaiting the moment when she and Hans were off guard? She decided she must stay awake at all costs. No matter that exhaustion threatened to swamp her. No matter that she had not slept nor so much as rested in comfort for days. No matter that the food she had just eaten and the sweet ale she had just drunk were combining with her fatigue to render her drowsy and slumberous, she must, no matter what, resist the call of sleep.

When Gretel awoke two hours later, it was to a scene so different from the one she closed her eyes upon that for a moment she could make no sense of it. Had she been transported to a better place while she slept? All about her, men were engaged in happy chatter and cheerful drinking. The old man in his rocker rocked merrily, removing his pipe to offer a cheery grin. The colossus at the bar was playing shove-halfpenny with the barman. The three young men were engaged in a good-natured game of Find the Lady with Hans, who was clearly winning, as evidenced by the pile of coins beside him. Gretel sat up stiffly, aware once more of the gritty griminess of her body and apparel both. She would, at that moment, have given a very great deal of her own hard-earned money for a deep, hot bath, clean clothes, and an uninterrupted night in a bed of cool cotton sheets. As none of this was likely to be forthcoming, she returned her mind to their circumstances and the case. The former seemed vastly improved. Surely these good and gentle folk could not be in league with murderous villains? And surely they would not give up their visitors to be done away with? And surely a gull would be found, a message sent, and their return to the *Arabella* assured. While these facts were uplifting, they did little to rescue the situation regarding Gretel's work for Captain Ziegler. It was imperative she return to the mermaid in the time given, and already so much of it had slipped by. The only smuggler who remained was the silent one, so questioning him on the matter of contraband brandy and who might have an interest in it, and why some of it had found its way onto the *Arabella*, seemed an impossibility. That she had taken one of the captain's lifeboats, and no doubt caused a deal of consternation and trouble by going missing, would not improve her standing in her client's eyes. It was time to deliver results, if her reputation were not to be sullied by failure. Equally important was the fact that, were the case not solved, it was unlikely in the extreme that she would be paid. A thought altogether too terrible to dwell upon a second longer.

Hans had just persuaded the table to switch to a different game and was concentrating hard, tongue slightly protruding as he did so. She leaned over to her brother, keeping her voice low as she spoke.

"Hans, what have you learned of this place from your new-found friends, and how is it you came by money to gamble with?"

Without for one moment taking his eyes from the cards he was holding, he explained. "These are decent fellows, Gretel. We have nothing to fear from them. Oh! A running flummery flush, I think you'll find!" he cried, pausing to set down his winning hand with a chuckle. He scooped another palmful of coins toward him. "I traded my lighter for my stake," he told her, inclining his head toward the happy smoker by the fire.

"I intend on buying it back later on. He threw in a pipe, too, look," he said, holding up a worn clay stump of a thing which he then clamped between his teeth. It had a stout bowl, from which malodorous smoke billowed as he puffed. "This is most welcome, don't mind telling you. Not so much as a sniff of a cigar in days."

"Ask them what they know of our gallant rescuers, but do so quietly," she whispered in his ear, holding her breath against the tobacco fumes. She took it upon herself to move a little closer to the elderly man in the rocking chair.

"*Moin moin!*" he said in cheerful greeting.

"Indeed, good evening to you, grandfather," she said, smiling. "It was good of you to assist my brother. I thank you for your kindness."

The old man gave a toothless grin. "'Tis easy to be kind when there's profit to be made in it. Your kin might find his handsome lighter has increased in value somewhat by the time he comes to make me an offer for it."

"I see you are an astute businessman."

"No point getting older if you don't get wiser."

"Quite so. Though I have met many who seem to operate a reverse system."

"Aye, there's plenty of those about."

"The three men who brought us here might well answer such a description," she said, watching his reaction closely.

His expression remained inscrutable as he glanced at Mold, still seated at the door but dozing now. The old man thought for a moment and then said, "There's those as lack wisdom but are still sharp enough to cut unwary travelers."

"Indeed," Gretel replied. "You know them well enough, it seems. Are they natives of this fair island?"

"They are not," he said, pausing to avail himself of the spittoon once again. Happily, his aim was true. "They are from off."

"And yet they frequent this hostelry?"

"There's many from the mainland covet what we islanders have."

Gretel cast her mind wide and far to imagine what this might be.

"Your sandy beaches? Your quaint inns? Your abundance of . . . fresh air, perhaps?"

"Aye, and more besides." He leaned forward in a conspiratorial manner. For a moment Gretel feared he might upend himself into the hearth, but his balance held. She met him halfway, not wanting to lose any useful information to an unfortunate bit of hip snapping. "They are jealous of our freedom. Of our privacy. We islanders live our own lives. We are blessed to live where and as we do, and we want for nought. We ask nothing of others, and we expect to be left in peace. 'Tis how it has always been."

"I imagine, then, a private enterprise, one that would thrive best in seclusion, well, such a business might be suited to these little isles, might it not?"

The old man sat back again slowly, both he and the chair emitting a percussive melody of creaking and popping. He sucked on his pipe again for a while, pointedly using Hans's lighter to set a fresh flame to the tobacco. After a deal of puffing he said, "You're a woman asks a lot of questions, fraulein. You want to be careful. You might get answers you don't like."

"It's a chance I'm willing to take. I have another for you. The men of whom we speak, have you ever seen them in the company of a man named Hoffman?"

Another gummy grin rearranged the smoker's features. His glance dropped to Gretel's bosom. Although their acquaintance was new, this lascivious act seemed out of character, and she was relieved when the gentleman gestured at her somewhat sandy lorgnettes.

"That's a fine set of glasses," he said. "The sort as which shows a person all manner of things a person wants to see."

Gretel frowned. "And the sort of which I am inordinately fond."

"And the sort as which might buy that same person a few answers to a few questions."

"And the sort which I might not want to leave this place without."

"And the sort as which might sit awhile in my possession, maturing in their value nicely for a little time, so that they might fetch a fair price later in the evening."

Gretel gave a heavy sigh. She knew she should be pleased that she had found the old man's price, found a way to obtain from him the facts she required, were he to own them, and yet she felt curiously downhearted. Just for once it would be a pleasant surprise to meet someone, somewhere, sometime, who was willing to do something for someone other than themselves, or at least without it ultimately costing her something. She lifted the lorgnettes from round her neck and handed them to him.

"Hans," she hissed at her brother, "for pity's sake, play well and play fast. You must win enough for me to buy back my glasses."

"What about my lighter?"

"As I said, play well, play fast."

She turned her attention back to the smoker, who was fondling the lorgnettes in a proprietorial manner that seemed designed to irritate her.

"Is your memory refreshed any?" she asked.

He took his time in answering. "Seems to me, I do recall, there was a fellow stood with them at the bar one night . . ."

"Was he of arrogant stance and proud bearing? A man accustomed to issuing commands and having them obeyed without question?"

"That he might have been."

"Had he a smart waistc't, and a pocket watch he was given to consulting frequently?"

"That he might have had."

"For pity's sake, did you hear them call him Hoffman?"

"That I might . . ." The old man, seeing Gretel's darkening expression, had the good sense to stop tormenting her. "Aye. Hoffman. That was the name. They were here together but twice, and neither time for an evening of drinking."

"The connection was business, then."

"They stayed only a short while. They left when it was proper dark. Took a boat out of the harbor."

"To where?"

"That I cannot tell you."

"Cannot or will not? I have nothing more to trade, grandfather."

He shook his head. "They did not let slip the name of their destination."

For a moment Gretel sat in thoughtful silence. She did not feel she was getting much for the pawning of her lorgnettes, but still it was helpful to have her suspicions regarding Hoffman's smuggling enterprise confirmed. Knowing that he was engaged in such an activity explained many things. His wish to be rid of her, lest she discover what he was about and expose him. His need to be rid of Frenchie, given that the bottle he clutched in the grip of death had once contained brandy. Clearly the chef had known of the smuggling. Gretel recalled the superior brandy he had shared with her in his kitchen. Perhaps he had discovered what Hoffman was doing and had demanded a cut of both profits and brandy. Perhaps there had been a disagreement over terms, or the cook had threatened to expose him, and perhaps that had led to his murder. Such speculation was all very well and good, but Gretel was not fond of any theory that must begin with "perhaps." It had a taste of doubt about it that soured the overall flavor of the postulation. Furthermore, what she had learned did nothing to support her original theory that Hoffman could be working in league with Thorsten Sommer to ruin Captain Ziegler's nascent cruise business.

"Tell me one more thing," she asked the old man. "What say you on the matter of mermaids?"

Had Gretel voiced such an inquiry anywhere in her hometown of Gesternstadt, or while visiting, perchance, the sophisticated city of Nuremberg, she would no doubt have been laughed at, long and loud. Here, however, on the little island of Hallig Hoog, cut off from the mainland and indeed the world by the wild seas that surrounded it, existing as it did in its own strange isolation, with its own strange ways and customs, her question was greeted only with mild surprise.

"Mermaids? Ah, 'tis a fair while since I have thought of those winsome creatures. Or at least, it was a fair while, up until a week last Tuesday."

"Oh, how so?"

"The evening was fine, the sea mist had rolled back to let the sun through, so I took my ease upon a bench on the harbor for an hour or so, watching the boats coming and going. So pleasant was the day, and so soothing the rhythm of the tide, time passed without my noticing, and I slipped into a soft and dreamless sleep."

Gretel felt that if he made his answer any more long-winded she might nod off herself, but she resisted saying as much.

"I slept long and deep. 'Twas gone midnight when I was awoken, and the sound that stirred me from my slumbers I shall never forget."

Gretel waited, fighting the urge to drum her fingers on the table. The expectant pause was filled with Hans's gleeful cry of "Full Flummery Flush again! Huzzah!" and still she waited.

At last the smoker judged he had built sufficient dramatic tension into his tale.

"The sound of mermaid song!" he declared. "As sweet and clear as any sound on God's earth, and anywhere else besides. Not since I was a boy in short trousers had I heard that magical singing."

"And recently you have heard it more than once?"

"Most Tuesday and Wednesday nights, and twice last Thursday. Beginning to tire of it a little, to tell you the truth. All a bit samey, after the first half dozen times. Could do with a little more variety, if you ask me."

"It does not frighten you? Some sailors find it intolerable and cannot be pressed or persuaded to remain aboard ship if they think a mermaid is near."

"Ah, sailors." The old man sucked on his pipe. "They have their little ways," he added, as if this made everything clear.

"So islanders tend not to think that mermaids might cause, ooh, let's say madness, or shipwreck, or unexplained disappearances?"

He laughed dryly. "Such nonsense! But that's sailors for you, believe all manner of silliness they do. No." He leaned forward, earnest once more. "If you're looking for the cause of mysterious deaths and such like in these parts, that'll be Ekkenekkepen, of course."

"Ekkenekke . . . ?"

". . . —pen. Aye. Nasty, wicked thing. God of the sea hereabouts, and an evil one at that. Known to swallow up sailors whole. Small boats sometimes, too. Aye, you'd best stay well clear of him."

"Is that so?" Gretel fought the urge to say something cutting. The last thing she needed was fairy stories concerning local mythological creatures. She had quite enough to deal with as it was, what with the sprite and the mermaid.

"It is." The old man nodded vigorously. "Ooh, yes, many's the time things strange and peculiar have turned out to be all the doing of Ekkenekkepen."

"Thank you so very much for the advice," said Gretel, who was starting to feel as if the lunatics might have taken over the asylum while she wasn't looking.

FIFTEEN

Fortunately, Hans's card playing outpaced the old man's storytelling by a swift country mile. Even more fortunately, Hans succeeded in emptying the pockets of all the other card players present and filling his own. This enabled him to buy back both Gretel's lorgnettes and his own lighter, even if it was at a wince-inducing inflationary rate. There was even sufficient money left to pay for a messenger gull. Gretel wrote an urgent note to Captain Ziegler giving their whereabouts and whatabouts and imploring him to send the tender to fetch them at his earliest convenience. Or, preferably, earlier than that. She stipulated clearly that he was not, under any argument, to send Hoffman. Scarcely had their bird flapped out of the low window at the back of the inn than Cat's Tongue and Pustule returned. They were not best pleased to discover their castaways had communicated with the *Arabella*, and hid their ire poorly. Mold, who had only woken when his fellows entered through the door he was guarding, was roundly shouted at by Cat's Tongue, and soundly beaten by Pustule for dereliction of duty.

There had been a difficult moment when Cat's Tongue had insisted that he would be happy to take Gretel and Hans and even the mer-hund back to the *Arabella* themselves. They had invited them to return to their little boat then and there, urging haste, so as to make the most of a favorable tide, and to save Captain Ziegler the trouble of sending his launch out on a wasted journey. Their insistence would have been hard to resist, given that it would most likely have soon progressed from cajoling words to arms being twisted behind backs and persons being frog-marched out of the inn, along the quay, and to, Gretel was certain, a sticky end. As luck would have it, Hans's lengthy gaming had allowed him to form something of a bond with his fellow cardsharps. So much so that they had even forgiven him for taking from each and every one of them their last shiny penny. Indeed, they seemed rather in awe of him. Hans later explained this was in part due to their never having encountered a card player of his particular complexity and guile. Gretel interpreted this as Hallig Hoog being so remote, they only ever played among themselves and were utterly thrown by the arrival of a stranger and his strange ways. Their affection for Hans was indisputably increased by his determination to buy everyone in the inn ale with his winnings. And as there were plenty of winnings, he was able to purchase plenty of ale. The resultant merriment was the perfect defense against Cat's Tongue's attempts to take them from the inn. Each new round of drinks was celebrated by yet another sea shanty or island song, each one increasingly ribald and risqué. If at any point Pustule tried to lay hands on Hans as a prelude to removing him, he was met with howls of displeasure from the by-now-inebriated islanders, who had claimed Hans as one of their own and would not be parted from him.

By the time Captain Ziegler himself arrived to collect his errant passengers, only Gretel, Hans, and Cat's Tongue remained conscious. The rest had succumbed either to fatigue, drink, or a combination of both. The furious smuggler could only stand by and watch as they left. Knowing Hoffman as she did, Gretel did not envy the man the quartermaster's response to his failure to do away with those who now presented a serious threat to their enterprise.

On arriving back on board the *Arabella*, Gretel's dearest wish was a bath and bed, but the captain would hear of no delay. He insisted she accompany him to his quarters immediately. Once there, he resumed his customary dramatic delivery in order to berate her for taking the lifeboat—which was in a shocking state, according to him—and rant anew about the perilous condition of his business and her own lack of results. She waited for him to calm down, sufficiently familiar with the man's character by now to know there was no point in saying a word until his rage had subsided. At last he sat in his chair, plucking his tricorn from his head and hurling it across the room before fixing her with a challenging stare.

"Firstly, captain, I wish to apologize for any damage done to your lifeboat." She experienced a vivid and most unwelcome flash of memory regarding the storm that had near swamped and sunk them, and knew that in truth the captain was lucky to have got the thing back at all. "Secondly, I thank you for your prompt response to my message, and for personally attending to my collection from Hallig Hoog. I am pleased to be able to tell you that, testing, arduous, and indeed dangerous as these past few days have been, the risks and discomforts—most of which have been suffered by myself, I might add—were well worth the suffering. I have gleaned valuable information on two counts."

"You have? God's teeth, woman, have you the name of the fellow who would see my business scuppered? Let's have it!" he cried, aflamed anew at the thought of knowing the identity of his persecutor.

"I ask for your patience," said Gretel, holding up a steadying hand. "In my work, just as there is an order to discovering things, so there is an order to revealing them. That way confusion is minimized, and we are able to clearly see what is what." Captain Ziegler looked less than convinced. She pressed on. "First, my suspicions regarding your quartermaster were accurate."

"He murdered Frenchie?"

"It seems reasonable to suppose that he did, yes."

"The black-hearted scoundrel! And he is about ruining me?"

"That is less certain. It may be a result of his actions, but almost an inadvertent one, for I cannot yet discern a motive."

"Well, is he in cahoots with Sommer or is he not?"

"We must conclude not."

"We must? Damn his eyes. I'd be happier rid of that slippery Norseman."

"I am aware you resent his existence, but is that not, in truth, because he has what it is you crave more than anything in this world?"

"His ships, d'you mean? They are fine enough, but I'd rather have my *Arabella*."

"Your loyalty to your vessel does you credit. No, I was referring to his position. When first ever we spoke of him, you revealed your jealousy of his standing in society—'supping with royalty' was the phrase you used, if memory serves. He is a man respected in these parts, a businessman who is well thought of by everyone, be they crew, paying passengers, dignitaries, royal cruise-goers, or family members. Even the islanders themselves speak well of him, and they, as I have discovered, are resistant to just about everyone until given a reason to like them."

Captain Ziegler looked uncharacteristically subdued. His expression suggested Gretel had hit the nail square on the head and driven it home painfully. He opened his mouth to speak, but she saved him the trouble.

"Before you attempt to explain yourself, I feel it only fair that I confess to knowing of your past."

His eyes narrowed. "How much of it?"

"All of it."

"Ah."

"Yes, indeed, ah."

He sighed wearily and ran a hand through his hair. "I suppose it had to come out. Though damn it all, how far around the world does a man have to sail to outrun his history?"

"The more colorful a past, the faster and farther it travels."

"There's truth in that."

"Tell me, for I am curious, what was it made you turn from the life of a privateer to that of the master of a cruise ship? From what I have learned, you were a successful buccaneer. Famous. Wealthy. What made you yearn for such a quiet life?"

"In my youth I was unmatchable, fraulein. There was none could sail a ship, plot a course, mount an attack, swash or buckle better than I. And yes, I took bounty aplenty. I took lives, too, I'm not proud of that, but it was part of my role. My crew respected me. There were those romantically inclined who enjoyed hearing tales of my exploits." He allowed himself a little smile at this. "But I will not see thirty again. The passing of the years—and such years!—takes its toll. On body and on soul. I was weary, fraulein. Weary of the fight. Of the ruffians whose company I kept. Of the terror on the faces of anyone I met beyond my crew. Weary of being the only man on board could read. Or write. Or talk of anything other than murder and gold and plunder."

"In short, my dear captain, you grew up."

"Let us say a man's needs alter as he alters. I wished for a different life. I knew I could never have it where I was known. I had obtained my pardon, right enough, but if I was to enter society, to move among good folk in the calm waters of peace rather than the turmoil of a life of piracy, I must needs change myself, and change how others saw me. To do that I had to find a new home."

"The name was a good place to start, too. I can't imagine too many gilt-edged invitations being penned to the Snaggle-Toothed Pirate."

"You have it right. So I quit the Caribbean seas and came north, here to this place of pale beauty."

"You liked it?"

He shrugged. "I liked what it could give me. A fresh start. The chance to live calmly. Peaceably. Though 'tis bitter cold three-quarters of the year and has shown me more shades of gray than I ever knew existed."

Gretel nodded. "You are not alone in that experience. But the people, if a little distant at first, they are kind and good, are they not? Your jealousy of Sommer is not born of dislike, in fact, but of admiration and envy. You would be him, were such a thing possible."

"Ha! If ever I stood a slender chance of becoming such, it has vanished along with the crewmembers who have disappeared, both mine and his."

"Your reputation may yet be saved."

"You believe so? I fear not," he said, plucking the stopper from the nearest decanter and pouring two generous measures into crystal tumblers.

"Let the matter of your good name rest with me. In the meantime, we have more urgent concerns."

"We have?"

"If we are to save further men from either fleeing or being done in, yes. Our endeavors must be directed in two places. First, the mermaid."

"She is real?"

"As you or I."

"You've found her, then!"

"Found, met, conversed with, and persuaded of a possible course of action that will, I believe, suit your needs as well as they suit hers."

"Excellent! At last, fraulein, I begin to see a return on my investment. Here's to you!" He saluted her with his glass.

"Yes, my payment is a matter to which I must return shortly. Now, what say you to a short trip to the waters of your youth?"

"Return to the Caribbee? Why would I do such a thing?"

"The mermaid is desirous of a warmer home. I have taken it upon myself to give her an assurance, on your behalf, that she will be conveyed to such a place. For a price, of course."

"She has money?"

"Thanks to whoever it is who pays her to ruin you, she has."

"Ha! I like the roundness of that. There is justice! To use the scoundrel's own coin to stop him. I like that very well! But who is the man?"

"Alas, I do not have his name, not yet. I have my theories, naturally . . ."

"Theories be damned! I must know who is set upon ruining me!"

"And you will, I promise you that. But first things first, and that is to get the mermaid's cooperation."

"If I agree to ferry her south, she'll spill the beans?"

"It will be part of agreed terms, I guarantee. Be under no illusion, you will have difficulty keeping a crew once they know what cargo it is you carry."

"You leave my crew to me. Those who have run back to their mothers at a few notes of singing are well gone. I will face the rest with the proposal. So long as I have sufficient for the voyage, at least, I can be certain more will be willing to join me once it is known I have rid them of the mermaid they so fear. Then I may ply my trade and add to my ship's company and passengers alike with confidence." He thought for a moment and then said, "Tell the fishy maid I will do as she wants, but 'twill be at no small inconvenience and disruption: I will have that gold from her before we sail, and plenty of it."

"You may tell her yourself. In fact, you must, for she will not strike the deal until she has word of it from your own lips. I promised her you would go to her, knowing as I do that you are not troubled by the creatures."

"Tobias Ziegler fears nothing the sea can offer him. That's true enough."

"Excellent. Next we must turn our minds to the matter of the smuggled brandy your quartermaster has been busying himself with."

"What?" roared the captain. "Am I never to break free of skulduggery and nefarious enterprises? How is a man to establish himself as fine and trustworthy if all about him are revealed to be not only murderous cutthroats but devious opportunists to boot?"

"Calm yourself, dear captain. Fortune has favored our cause inasmuch as the isle that the smuggler chose to stow their contraband is the same island on which the mermaid has her current home. Whether he is also her secret benefactor I cannot yet be certain, but I intend on finding out. You and I will return there, seal the deal with the young creature, and so assure you of trouble-free future cruises. We can, at the same time, seek out any further stashes of brandy, claim them, and quite possibly have sight of the mob who either deliver or collect them. Our rescuers took some away with them, but I suspect there will be more. While it is probable Hoffman and his gang will find an alternative location for future transactions, I doubt they will be able to change their plans in a matter of hours, particularly if the brandy is being brought any distance and in secret."

Captain Ziegler sprang to his feet and brandished his sword. "God strike me down as a liar if I don't run that man through before the week is out!"

Gretel wagged a finger at him. "That past of yours is catching you up again, captain," she warned. "You must rein in your natural instinct for violence. Would Thorsten Sommer disport himself thus? I think not."

Returning his sword to its scabbard with a growl, the captain said, "Very well, I will hold my temper. But these are dangerous men we dice with, fraulein. I will not go unarmed or unprepared."

"Nor would I wish you to," she assured him, getting somewhat stiffly to her feet. "Now, if you will excuse me, I will retire to my cabin for what is left of the night."

"We leave at first light?"

"If you agree to send Everard to me with breakfast, hot water, and coconut oil an hour before, I shall be ready," she told him, ignoring the quizzical expression this request elicited. "On the subject of which," she added, an uplifting thought occurring to her, "I believe that as two of our passengers have quit the ship, there must be a berth going begging; is that the case?"

"It is."

"Then, if you have no objection, I shall install my brother in it. We find ourselves somewhat cramped in the present arrangement." When the captain hesitated, appearing to be contemplating some other use for the cabin, Gretel continued, "I must gain fortifying sleep for the arduous adventures that await us, captain. A modicum of comfort is all I ask."

"Very well, as you wish," he said.

"Your kindness is greatly appreciated. And remember now, we must play our cards close to our chest. Do not let Herr Hoffman know that we suspect him. And do not, under any circumstances, let him leave this ship."

On her way across the deck, Gretel glimpsed the sprite. She fleetingly wondered if she should engage it in conversation. Its riddle had revealed its meaning for the most part, but the key element of the identity of the person who was employing the mermaid remained hidden. Did the sprite know who it was? Was it Hoffman? The idea made sense, and yet did not quite ring true for reasons Gretel could not entirely fathom. At that moment, she was too weary to find out. The thought of her small but comfortable bed filled her mind. She would press the sprite on the matter the next day. So distracted was she by the many and various thoughts that were whirling through her mind that Gretel walked smack into the solid frame of none other than the quartermaster.

"Oh! Herr Hoffman. Forgive me, I did not see you there . . ."

Where another might have offered gallant insistence that the fault was his, Hoffman uttered no such platitudes. Instead, he merely glared at her, as if her very existence offended him. Which, all things considered, it most likely did.

Gretel deemed it wisest to keep from sensitive subjects that might lead into tender topics and sore spots, such as islands, and brandy, and smugglers, and so on, and yet the man stood stout and steady before her, considering his own tactics, no doubt. Gretel cast about for some harmless matter on which to converse to calm the moment, and so spoke on the first that came to mind.

"Tell me, Herr Hoffman, have you ever, in your many years aboard ship, encountered a sea sprite?"

He grimaced and then quickly arranged his features in an expression of scorn. But before he could do this entirely, he glanced up into the rigging, as if expecting to see something there. It was a telling gesture. Still, he said only, "There's no such thing as a sea sprite!" and leaned sideways to spit force-fully over the side to his left. The idea had the effect Gretel had hoped for, deflecting his thoughts from ones she would rather he did not think. For all his respectability, the man was at the very least a smuggler, and at worst a murderer. He stepped aside and Gretel, bidding him good night, hurried past.

Fearing that, if she did not rest her aching head on a soft pillow very soon, she would be good for nothing at all, she dropped quickly down the steep stairs toward the longed-for point of collapse. She would even be able to eject Hans and his hound to the new cabin, and so be free of their snores and malodorous habits while she slept.

As so often happened, however, what seemed to be per-fectly reasonable wishes and attainable goals became distant fanciful fantasies because some other freshly born event came to stand between her and her heart's desire. In this case, that event involved Birgit in hysterics, which was obstacle enough for anyone anywhere, but made all the worse by being located in the narrow passage belowdecks.

"My fan!" That Woman cried, her cheeks tearstained, her nose even redder than usual. "My darling ivory-handled fan! Gone! Stolen!" she shrieked. Her two companions did their best to soothe her, but this mostly consisted of their wailing and weeping and dabbing ineffectually at her with lace handkerchiefs.

Dr. Becker, disturbed by the commotion, opened his cabin door.

"Can I be of any assistance?" he asked.

"Oh, doctor!" Birgit fell upon his arm, clearly deciding a physician of ornithology was as close as she was going to get to any sort of medical support. "Help me, please! There is a thief in our midst. A cruel cad who has taken something so very dear to me." Here she began crying and sniffing anew. Gretel was reminded—as if she needed to be!—of the vacuous construction of That Woman's mind, which allowed the silly creature to be so ridiculously concerned about a petty thief when they were in fact sharing a ship with a murderer.

"Come, come now," said Dr. Becker, patting her hand. "Do not distress yourself so. Perhaps the fan is merely misplaced somewhere in your cabin."

"No." Birgit shook her head. "We have searched and searched. It is gone. Quite gone."

Her cronies nodded their agreement. Gretel had to accept that three people searching such a tiny cabin were unlikely to have missed it, were it there.

Dr. Becker was still hopeful of a simple explanation. "Then might it be that you set the fan down somewhere when you were about the ship, taking the air on deck, perchance, or while engaged in a game of quoits?"

"Oh, no, doctor, I would never let it out of my sight in such circumstances. You see, it was a gift from my dear late husband, Algernon. I recall the day he gave it me. Oh . . ." Here her voice cracked to a squeak. More crying followed.

Had there been a way Gretel could pass by this melodrama and access her cabin, she would have done so, but the passageway was stoppered with lachrymose women who must be removed if she was ever to get to her own bed.

"Tell me, Birgit," she asked, "was the fan of high value?"

"To me it was priceless!"

"Quite so, but to another? I merely wish to suggest that a thief is unlikely to risk capture for an item that is of little worth."

"Little worth!"

"Little *monetary* worth."

"How can one put a price on precious memory?" Birgit demanded, her sobs growing louder.

Hans emerged from behind Gretel's trunks at the end of the passage, still fully dressed, but showing signs of having been asleep. "I say, some of us have need of our rest after testing times, don't you know? Might it be possible for the noise out here to be kept to a level allowing others to sleep?" he asked, rubbing his eyes.

"Oh, Hansel!" cried Birgit, dropping Dr. Becker's arm and turning the full force of her mania on Hans. "The sanctity of my boudoir has been violated . . ."

"Oh, for pity's sake," Gretel hissed beneath her breath.

". . . I have been robbed of something dear to me. You see before you a woman bereft!"

Hans, clearly having no idea what she was talking about, and evidently not able to muster the interest needed to find out, merely muttered, "Ah. Sorry to hear that. Well, there it is. Such a pity."

He attempted to turn about and scuttle back to his cabin but Birgit had caught hold of his arm now.

"Hansel, thank heavens you are here."

"Really?"

"It gives me such comfort to know you are near."

"It does?"

Gretel glimpsed an opportunity to bring this nonsense to an end. "In that case, Birgit," she said cheerfully, "you will be pleased to learn that Hans will be even closer to you from this point on."

"I will?" asked Hans, alarmed.

"Will he?" asked Birgit.

"He will. I have secured him his very own cabin. This one here," she explained, pushing open the door opposite Birgit's own.

Hans did not know whether to be pleased or terrified. Conflicting reactions fought within him. His slothful desire for comfort and ease battled against the natural cowardice that would have him as far away from That Woman as was possible. The two elements of his character slogged it out. Sloth won on points. "Good-oh! I'd better get out of your way, then, sister mine," he said, edging past Birgit et al., eager to reach the safety and relative luxury of his new billet.

Happily, Birgit did appear somewhat mollified by the prospect of Hans moving a few yards nearer to her. Her expression relaxed a little and the tears ceased falling. It was then that Hans, bidding them all good night, turned to enter his cabin. It was then that Sonja, the larger and louder of Birgit's traveling companions, spotted the ivory handle of a lady's fan poking out of Hans's back trouser pocket. It was then that Gretel saw her chances of a few hours' sleep receding into the dim and far distance.

"There it is!" screeched Sonja. "Your fan, Birgit. Your fan . . . he has it! Here is your thief!"

SIXTEEN

Birgit gasped.

Dr. Becker uttered a "well, I never."

Hans, twisting around to try to see what it was they were all so excited about, opened his mouth to protest his innocence, and then found that he was, apparently, guilty, so closed it again.

Birgit's comrades-in-arms set up a chorus of noise, chiefly made up of slanders upon Hans's character.

"If you will just give my brother a second to speak for himself," Gretel pleaded, "I am certain there will be a perfectly simple explanation as to why he has Birgit's fan in his . . . possession." Even as she spoke the words, she knew them to be false. First, the only thing simple about the situation was Hans himself. Second, it was obvious—at least to her—that he had no knowledge of the fan's existence, much less how it came to be nestled snugly in his trousers.

Birgit stepped forward, a worrying smile playing across her face. "Sister Gretel is right," she declared, "the explanation is indeed simple."

"It is?" Hans asked nervously.

Birgit placed a hand gently upon his chest. Hans would have stepped backward if he dared, but to do so would have allowed That Woman to follow him into his cabin, and his primeval survival instinct screamed at him on no account to let this happen.

"Oh, Hansel," Birgit cooed, "my sweet, shy, dear prince . . ."

"Prince?" Hans questioned.

Birgit nodded. "How could I have forgotten what a romantic soul dwells within this fine body?"

"It does?" he asked.

Gretel rolled her eyes, horribly aware of the direction Birgit's single-minded reason was taking. "Hans . . ." she cautioned.

Birgit was positively glowing by now, eyes shining, smiling happily. "Why, yes! I have been foolishly overt in my wish to rekindle our friendship when I should have known you better; I should have waited for you to come to me."

"You should?" Hans had lost the ability to converse in anything other than the quizzical interrogative.

"But of course! Oh, how painful it must have been for you, not to be able to voice your feelings. I have been hasty, and in my haste I have hindered your own attempts to woo me."

"Woo you?"

"And you became so desperate, so lovelorn . . ."

"Oh, for heaven's sake," said Gretel.

". . . that you crept into my cabin, searching for some memento, something of mine own that you might keep close to you at all times. I understand, Hansel. Truly I do."

"You . . . ?"

"Hans!" Gretel barked. "Pull yourself together. You no more stole that blasted fan than did I, or Dr. Becker, or the good captain himself."

Shaking his head, Hans pulled the fan from his pocket and held up the somewhat squashed object. "But, Gretel . . . ?"

"The evidence does appear compelling," Dr. Becker put in.

"Nonsense," said Gretel. "Hans has only been back on board the ship a matter of minutes. We have been absent from the *Arabella*, both of us, these past days. My brother has been assisting me in my investigations, and weary work it was, too. We have been without sleep or proper food and our lives endangered. Trust me when I tell you that nothing was further from his mind than romance. Upon our return he went straight to his cabin."

"But to do that, he must first pass our cabin," Birgit pointed out.

"And were not the three of you in it at the time?" Gretel asked.

"Why, yes, but . . ."

"And you would have us believe that Hans sneaked into a space scarce big enough to hold its rightful occupants, let alone also accommodate his own considerable bulk . . ."

"Hey, Gretel, steady on," he protested.

". . . find and take your fan, and leave again, without any one of you noticing?"

"We were asleep," said Birgit.

"Sleeping Beauty herself would be forced into consciousness were Hans to step on her."

However sensible Gretel's argument, Birgit was holding on tight to the idea that Hans was secretly in love with her again and was not going to loosen her grip willingly. "I only *missed* my fan just now; it may have been taken much earlier," she said.

"*Days* earlier?" Gretel countered. "We have been absent from this ship more than forty-eight hours."

"Perhaps he had it with him?"

There comes a point in most debates of such a nature when one of the participating parties entirely uses up their reserves of patience and restraint. Gretel was fast approaching this point. "Fraulein!" She turned the full force of her barely contained rage upon That Woman. "My brother is no thief. He did not take your benighted fan!"

"Then how came it into his pocket?" Birgit demanded.

"I strongly suspect it was the work of a sea sprite."

As one, voices raised, Dr. Becker, Birgit, Sonja, Elsbeth, and even Hans himself intoned, "There's no such thing as a sea sprite!" before engaging in a revolting bout of synchronized spitting, during which Gretel thanked the heavens that she was standing to the right of all involved.

There followed a deal of pointless conjecture and people talking over one another until Gretel simply snatched the fan from Hans and thrust it at Birgit, spun her brother on his heel and shoved him into his new berth, whistled up the mer-hund, which she pushed into the cabin with Hans as guard against later possible visitations from Birgit, hurled several bad-tempered good-nights over her shoulder, and strode to her own billet, slamming the door firmly behind her.

Alone at last, she pulled off her dress, which was ruined by sea water beyond saving, plucked off her equally spoiled shoes, which had rubbed salty blisters onto her poor feet to match the ones on her hands bequeathed her by the oars, and flopped facedown onto her bunk, still wrapped in her damp petticoats, grateful at least not to be struggling out of her corset, which remained tied to the mast of the lifeboat for all to see.

As a feeble dawn struggled to lift the dark of night from the horizon, Gretel made her way back up to the poop deck for her rendezvous with Captain Ziegler. She had slept deeply, the cozy comfort of her cot—which was revealed to her after two nights in a lifeboat—had held her safe and soft, and the calm sea had rocked her through four whole hours of blissful unconsciousness. True to his word, the captain had sent Everard to wake her. The steward had tackled the horror that was her hair valiantly and without comment, even when he found two sea slugs and a miniature hermit crab held prisoners among its tangles. She had allowed him to work in silence, not wanting to waken any of her slumbering neighbors. The fewer witnesses to her departure, the better.

The morning was typical of so many Frisian summer days, which is to say pale, clean, and with a small wind that was relentlessly refreshing. Gretel was glad of the light wool suit she had selected for the occasion. It was the color of mountain heather, flatteringly cut, allowing ease of movement, and of a cloth that was neither too heating nor too flimsy. Her lorgnettes sat fetchingly against the dark, speckled background. She had enjoyed syrupy pancakes in her cabin, and strong coffee, into which Everard had thoughtfully tipped a measure of rum. Although experiencing the light-headedness that so often accompanies insufficient sleep, she felt largely restored. She felt ready. She felt determined. The hour had come to bring her investigations to a satisfactory conclusion. The future of the *Arabella* depended on it. Gretel's reputation depended on it. Her getting paid depended on it.

The captain stepped out of his quarters bearing an equally resolute air. He wore a dark jacket, his sword at his hip, and a pistol holstered across his chest.

"Good morning to you, Fraulein Gretel," he said in a low voice. "Are you prepared for what might lie ahead?"

"As always, captain."

"It may be dangerous. We cannot know what plans the smugglers have, now that their hidey-hole has been discovered."

"We cannot, but we have no choice but to return to that island and return to it with all speed. With luck, we may reach the mermaid without ever encountering the villains."

The captain shook his head. "I confess, I would like very much to encounter them! I should run the devils through!" he insisted.

"The hour will come to deal with them," Gretel promised him, "but this is not it."

"It pains me to be civil to that blackheart Hoffman."

"You have adhered to our plan?"

"I have. I informed him you and I would be absent from the ship for some hours and that he must take command."

"He questioned you on the nature of our excursion, no doubt."

"That he did, though it was a pointless exchange, for I gave him no answers that carried any credence."

"He is aware of your knowledge of his deeds, I don't doubt it. But he will know also you lack proof. He has no choice but to let you go. I only hope he will remain aboard."

The captain was shocked at the suggestion that he might not. "Even a murderer would not abandon command of his ship," he told her.

"Ah," Gretel pointed out, "but the *Arabella* is not his ship, is she?"

They descended to the main deck. A seaman the captain deemed trustworthy assisted Gretel as she climbed into one of the lifeboats. She fought against a creeping sense of deja vu, reminding herself that this time she had none other than the

Snaggle-Toothed Pirate himself to sail the vessel and deliver her safely to her destination. What could possibly go wrong?

Their departure was halted by the arrival of Will, running from the fore of the ship, a large gull perched upon his slender arm.

"Begging your pardon, captain," he panted, "an urgent message. From the *Fair Fortune*."

Captain Ziegler paused, one foot on the edge of the boat, and quickly unfurled the note and recounted the gist of its contents to Gretel. "'Tis from Sommer. He says they are still without a first mate, and their sister ship, the *Pretty Penny*, will not reach them for days yet. It seems some of their passengers are complaining at being holed up in Norstrand harbor."

"I'll wager I know which passenger is complaining the loudest," said Gretel.

"Baroness Schleswig-Holstein wishes to take a berth aboard the *Arabella*!" There was no missing the excitement in the captain's voice. "She is desirous of an authentic sailing experience."

"You are well placed to give her that, captain."

"Sommer says that she will arrive this morning, with her maid, and her pet general as her personal bodyguard. Ha! This is tremendous news indeed!"

Gretel felt the familiar frisson that the mention of Ferdinand—even disparaging—evoked. It was certainly a pleasant turn of events that he and she were to share the same ship. It added an extra incentive to bring matters to a close with the mermaid as swiftly as possible. In addition, the general might prove a useful sword arm when things with Hoffman and his cronies came to a head, which they surely and imminently must.

Captain Ziegler turned from the lifeboat and strode about the deck. "At last, this is the manner of passenger I have long dreamed of."

"The baroness? A person more likely to inhabit nightmares than sweet dreams, I would have thought."

"Ah, but where she treads, others will follow. Do you not see? A titled lady, an aristocrat of some renown. Why, perhaps her regal cousins will hear of her happy time aboard the *Arabella* and book their passage this very season. Royal patronage, fraulein! That is what awaits us."

Gretel glanced about her at the lackluster fittings and features, the absence of glamor or luxury, the single sailor next to the boat who, while not actually scurvy as far as she could tell, offered rather too much authenticity with his food-stained shirt and bristly chin. She tried very hard to imagine King Julian, Queen Beatrix, and their fastidious princesses sitting among the tarry ropes and patched deck chairs. It was not an easy image to conjure.

"All that is required of us"—the captain was lit up with enthusiasm—"is that we please the baroness. I ask you, fraulein, how hard can that be?"

Deeming it inadvisable to crush the man's dreams just as they were about to embark on a difficult mission, Gretel merely smiled gently in reply. "Indeed," she said, "how hard."

There followed a delay during which Captain Ziegler hurried off to inform Hoffman of the new passengers. He was to greet them, apologize for the captain's temporary absence, and settle them into their quarters. The downside of this was that Hans would be ejected from his newly claimed cabin. Gretel was downcast at the prospect of sharing her own small space with him and his hound again, so she suggested he be given a hammock in the kitchen, and a bed be made up for the merhund outside the galley door. Braun, the sailor assisting them with launching the lifeboat, was dispatched to inform the sous chef to set these things in motion. Ferdinand would share the captain's quarters, which seemed a fitting place for a military man. The helpful aspect of this new development was that it would assure them of Hoffman's whereabouts. His visible presence would be essential now, and had he any intention of stealing away to follow the captain and Gretel, such an action would be nigh impossible while the baroness demanded he dance attendance upon her.

While Gretel sat in the lifeboat, still in its position on board the *Arabella*, she detected a nearby presence in the shadows.

"Why don't you step out and show yourself," she said. "I would very much like to talk with you again."

For a second or two, nothing, and then the sprite flitted from its hiding place and alighted on a rope a little above and in front of Gretel.

"You look funny," it told her, "sitting in a boat on a boat." The creature gave a giggle, treating Gretel to another glimpse of its disturbing teeth.

"I am on the point of departure," she told it, "but then, you already know that. You know so many things."

"I listen. I hear people's planning and scheming."

"Quite so. You knew Herr Hoffman was involved in smuggling, didn't you?"

"Oh, that's been going on quite some time. Poor Captain Ziegler shouldn't be so trusting. Hoffman is really a very nasty person."

Gretel was aware that the sprite liked to play games, but time was short. The captain would return soon and her chance to press the little creature for answers would be lost. "I enjoyed your second riddle," she told it. "I think I worked most of it out. 'Look close at hand' and 'the special drink'—you put that brandy bottle in Frenchie's hand after he was murdered, didn't you? A clue for whoever found him."

"Well, I knew it would be you, eventually. I was a bit cross when they moved him to that other ship, but they bundled him up and didn't bother taking the bottle away."

Gretel smiled to herself, eager to have the sprite confirm her suspicions, but choosing her words with care. She knew the little creature's love of game playing: to state things boldly would only provoke it into being obtuse again.

"Frenchie knew about the smuggling too, didn't he?" she asked it.

"Yes, but he didn't do any of it himself. He found out, and made them give him some of the brandy. At least, that was all to begin with."

"He began blackmailing Hoffman."

The sprite frowned. "Bo'sun Brandt is not so bad. He loves money, that's all. He'd sell his own grandmother if he had one. But don't think he wanted to hurt anyone. Not really. He would have given Frenchie what he wanted."

"He was working with Hoffman?"

"He didn't want to kill the poor cook."

"You saw what happened that night, didn't you?" Gretel had had a suspicion, but hadn't been sure. Now she was certain. "You saw who cut Frenchie's throat."

"Horrid Hoffman! I wish he'd never come to this ship."

"Well, this is most unusual, I must say. A witness to a murder who clearly saw what happened, but who can never expose the murderer, because . . ."

". . . because there is no such thing as a sea sprite," it said, and Gretel could swear, even in the dim early light, that she could see tears in its almond-shaped eyes. The creature looked suddenly the loneliest of things. What would it be like, to spend one's existence watching the lives of others but never be involved, never be acknowledged, never so much as be believed in?

"Tell me, " Gretel asked, "what made you choose to talk to me? I'm very glad that you did, but I don't know why I was chosen."

The sea sprite gave a little shrug. "I watched and listened. You see things plainly. Facts. No nonsense. And you're not

afraid, not like half these daft sailors trembling at the sound
of a mermaid. I knew you would listen to me."

"You have been helpful in solving the case."

"Have I?"

"Oh, yes. Your riddles made me think and gave me clues."

"But I can't stand up in front of a judge and tell him what I
saw Hoffman do."

"No, you cannot. But there are one or two other things you
could do to help me."

The sprite dipped its head a little, shyly. "Would it help
Captain Ziegler?"

"Yes. Yes, it would."

"All right, what do you want me to do?"

"Keep an eye on Hoffman and Brandt while we are off the ship.
I want to know everything they've been up to when I get back."

"Oh, that's easy. What else?"

"Well, my brother's time on this ship would be a good deal
happier if you ceased meddling in his love life and stirring
Birgit into a delirium over him."

The sprite laughed. "But they are such fun to tease!"

"More importantly, please tell me, if you know it, and I think
you do, the name of the person who is paying the mermaid
to sing."

The sprite laughed at this. "Haven't you guessed yet, silly?
I'll give you another riddle, shall I?"

"If that's all that is on offer."

The sprite thought for a moment and then recited in a little
singsong voice, "Look sharp for the sharp-eyed man. Look
again for the sharp flaw in another's plan."

"Is that it? Wait, come back!"

But at the sound of approaching footsteps, the small purple
being skipped away and was instantly lost among the rigging
above.

"Right!" said the captain as he stepped into the boat. "All is arranged. Hoffman is ensnared by the very position he covets. He will act as master of this ship while I am away from it; he cannot do otherwise. And while I am absent, I will see an end to this mermaid business and finish his smuggling enterprise at one and the same time. Upon my return, I will then find a way to see he is exposed for the murderous rogue he truly is. Will we have our proof, fraulein? What say you?"

"I say that we will, captain. One way or another, we will."

"Then lower us away, Sailor Braun! Lower away and let us be on course at once!"

SEVENTEEN

I t was impossible for Gretel not to compare her earlier voyage in a lifeboat with the one she was now embarked upon. Her memory of those hours of hardship and danger were still fresh and vivid in her mind, not least of all Hans's suggestion that they might have to start eating each other to survive. This time, she felt only a building excitement as Braun and the captain rowed skillfully away from the *Arabella* and toward the mermaid's home. Captain Ziegler had ascertained the location of the island from locals at the inn on Hellig Hoog the previous night. He assured Gretel it was no distance at all. She remembered saying those very words to Hans, and felt a pang of guilt at having put him through such a testing and risky experience. Still, she reasoned, such happenings strengthened character, and would surely make him all the more appreciative of the comforts of home when they returned there.

The day was warm but not unpleasantly so, and in any case, Gretel had equipped herself with a parasol to keep the strongest rays of the sun off her face. She could not help but be aware that she presented an alluring picture, seated in the little boat wearing her fresh clothes, her hair wrestled into submission by Everard. She found herself peeping through her lorgnettes from beneath the *broiderie anglaise* parasol in a way that Birgit would have approved of, and quickly stopped doing it. There was a time and a place for such coquettish nonsense, and this was neither. Besides, charismatic as the captain was, he was not Ferdinand. The thought that the Uber General was even now making his way to the *Arabella* made her feel happy. It was typical of the way things were that she should, at that very same moment, be heading in the opposite direction, but no matter. By the day's end they would be on the ship together, which was an added incentive to getting the task at hand done and dusted as swiftly and effortlessly as possible.

Much to her surprise, it took less than an hour to reach the rocky shore of the island. It was galling to realize how long she and Hans had drifted and struggled in all directions, suffering heinously uncomfortable nights and days, when they were such a short distance from their intended destination. Sailor Braun jumped into the sea spume and pulled the boat into the shallows. Captain Ziegler gallantly offered to carry Gretel to dry sand, but she declined, citing such a thing not being fitting for a detective, a professional woman, blurring the lines of the client/detective relationship, and so on. In truth, she would rather not risk possible embarrassment and humiliation should her not insubstantial weight prove too much for the captain to stagger beneath. A vision of them both collapsing in an undignified muddle of flailing limbs in the water made her wince. Better to get wet feet.

"Braun," Captain Ziegler instructed his man, "stay here. Pull the boat up into the dunes and cover it as best you can. Keep yourself hidden but with a view of the water, so that you are able to observe anyone landing on this shoreline. Now, fraulein, lead on to the mermaid's lair, if you please."

The path was rocky but the going considerably easier on this occasion, coming as it did after some sleep and food, and being tackled with the most sensible shoes Gretel had packed. The sun flashed brightly off the sea. Gulls of many kinds swooped and cried overhead. The surf lapped the sand or splashed upon the rocks in a most appealing manner. Were Gretel the sort of person who found nature endlessly enthralling, as many were and did, she might have been distracted by all this oceanic charm. But she was not. While she could appreciate a pretty seascape and scarlet sunset with the best of them, she was at heart an urban woman. She had already had her fill of sea air and sand between her toes, and was now entirely focused on the task given her, so that she might return to more civilized pleasures as soon as possible.

When they reached the mermaid's cave, they found it empty. If Captain Ziegler was impressed that Gretel was able to take him directly to the place, he did not say as much. The empty cave, however charmingly decorated and furnished, however dazzling the crystal within, lacked a mermaid. And it was the mermaid the captain was interested in.

"I'm sure she will appear presently," Gretel said, with more confidence than she felt. What if the creature had gone off on some long swim somewhere or other? Or to visit another mermaid on a far-distant shore? Might she not return until dark? Or at all? She sought to quell her own doubts as much as those of the captain when she said, "We have simply to make ourselves comfortable and settle to waiting. When she returns, it will be through this rather attractive pool." She indicated the circle of water set among the sparkling rocks and pearly shells. Captain Ziegler strode over to stand next to her, and for a moment they both stood and stared into the gently undulating blue-grayness.

It was while they were occupied thus that their assailants crept up behind them. Later, when Gretel had time to think about it, she would deduce that the fellows must have been hiding in the shadowy recesses of the cave, awaiting their moment to pounce. And pounce they did. The first Gretel knew of their presence was a speedy scuffle of footsteps, and then rough hessian against her face as a large sack was forced over her head. Judging by the muffled oaths uttered to her left, Captain Ziegler had also been caught entirely off guard and was being similarly ensnared. Gretel shouted out, more from alarm than anger. The sack was sufficiently capacious to come down to her middle, and as soon as it was in place her attackers wound rough rope around it, tying her arms to her sides and rendering her bagged, trussed, and helpless as a farmyard fowl on its way to market.

"Take your hands off me!" she insisted, as she was man-handled, stumbling, across the uneven floor. But the villain gave no reply. She could hear the captain raging and bellowing, the sacking masking his exact words, but sentiments nonetheless clear. The pair of them were marched a short distance and then shoved into a nook farther inside the cave, on a slope. She could hear waves entering the cave via another pool—this one was not peaceful and low, but obviously affected by the tides. She was forced to sit, whereupon her feet were also bound. Once sitting, the sack over Gretel's head moved slightly, so that, as chance would have it, her left eye came level to a small patch worn threadbare. There was just enough light to enable her to see through. The first thing she saw was Pustule's heavenly visage. The sight of it so close up made her gasp, but she quickly recovered herself. They were in a tight enough spot without her letting her captors know that she had discovered their identity. Her mind raced. The smugglers had evidently been expecting them. But how? Had the mermaid told them? Had Hoffman guessed their plans and sent a gull? It really mattered not. What did matter was what the ruffians planned to do next, and how she might stop them doing it. Particularly if they planned on doing it to her. At that precise moment, she was being secured to a rock by yet more rope, as was the captain.

She squinted through her prickly window. She could make out Mold and Cat's Tongue as they stooped to fasten the captain's feet. Mold took his sword and pistol from him, deaf to his victim's vehement protestations. Cat's Tongue felt the need to cut a piece of rope in two, and so removed the dagger from its sheath. Gretel gave a small shout, which fortunately the men took no notice of, well able as they were to ignore cries of distress. What had caused her to exclaim, however, was not fear or despair, but amazement, for she saw that Cat's Tongue did not have a dagger at all. What he did have was a large, bone-handled knife with a silver end to it, and a curiously curved blade. Frenchie's knife. It could be no other. The very murder weapon itself, and now a link between the smugglers and the cook's death. The puzzle was, how had it come into Cat's Tongue's possession? He had not been on the *Arabella* the night Frenchie met his end, if ever. Gretel's thoughts scampered this way and that, exploring promising avenues that quickly revealed themselves to be cul de sacs. Surely Hoffman would have thrown the thing overboard; it would have been the wisest and safest thing to do. But here was the knife. The sprite said that Bo'sun Brandt had been present at the killing. Had he been charged with disposing of the weapon, perhaps, but seen value in the thing, as was his nature, and gone against his master's wishes? He might have sold it to his fellow smuggler. It seemed the most likely explanation. Gretel cared not for the detail, but knew, as certainly as she knew her own shoe size, that she must obtain that knife. Here at last was the proof she needed to condemn Hoffman.

As she and the captain fell to silence, the men, being of limited intellectual capacity, began to fill that void with their own increasingly audible mutterings. So it was that Gretel learned her intended fate. The men were waiting for the tide to come in, so that they could take delivery of more brandy from a vessel evidently larger than their own boat. Once they had their cargo safely stored away in another cave, they would return to deal with their prisoners. They would let the rising water in this cave do its work, then transport the bodies back to their own lifeboat, which they would hole before setting it out on the sea once more. If the wreckage was found, it would suggest it had been snagged upon rocks, and its occupants, were they ever to float to notice, would bear no scars other than where the fish might have feasted upon them, as is often the case with those unfortunate souls who drown at sea.

At last their captors satisfied themselves that their catch was secure and headed off to make their rendezvous. For a moment neither Gretel nor the captain spoke, so that all that could be heard was the echo of the smugglers' dwindling footsteps and the teasing roll and splash of the waves entering the nearest part of the cave. At last Gretel ventured to voice her thoughts.

"It would seem that matters have not gone entirely to plan."

"God's truth, woman, you have that right! What folly have you led me to?"

"Me?"

"Aye, 'tis plain we were expected."

"By the mermaid, yes, but . . ."

"But we found no mermaid, only a watery death, if those rogues have their way. How is it that they knew we were to come here? Someone told them of our plans."

"Well, it wasn't me. Really, how could you think I'd put my own person at risk of such a fate, let alone that of my client? Credit me with wishing to preserve my own neck, even if you think me ready to give up yours!" The ropes were starting to chafe at her wrists and ankles, and she was in no mood to be tactful.

"It was you who brought me here," the captain insisted on pointing out again. "You who persuaded me to take this course of action."

"And you who kept brandishing your weapons and strutting about before we left in a manner suggesting we could be assailed by a small army and still come off the better party in the encounter."

"I was taken by surprise!"

"And where is it written that your enemies must give notice of their intention to attack? You cannot entirely blame me for our predicament when you have so singularly failed to protect us."

"Should a detective need to be protected?"

"My work is of the mind, not the sword. For pity's sake, I was safer with Hans!"

"Blast you for a woman! Have you nothing more to offer than complaints?" he growled.

He had a point. There was little to be gained by argument, and time was against them. Even now Gretel could feel the cool water touching the soles of her shoes. They had an hour, maybe two at most before the sea level would rise to claim them. They had better not waste it in fruitless conjecture and disagreement.

"Very well," she said, more calmly than she felt, "I accept that I am in part to blame for the predicament in which we now find ourselves. We must now work together if we are to escape our fate. I'm certain those villains would like nothing better than for us to turn on each other."

The captain harrumphed in a way that suggested grudging agreement. He struggled against his bonds. "The knots are tight and the rope new," he told her. "I cannot break free."

Gretel wriggled her feet and was able to kick off one shoe. This enabled her to remove her foot from the rope that tied her to the rock. "Look," she cried, "I am untethered."

"How can I look?"

"Oh, yes, of course, forgive me. I have a small hole in my sack and can see through it."

"Is there any sight of the scoundrels who bound us?"

"Alas, there is not. Still, I have freed myself from the rock to which I was tied, but, argh . . ." She cursed as, in her attempt to get up, she pitched forward and landed hard upon the rough floor of the cave. Her legs were still tied and the knees and her hands still bound, her arms pinned tight to her side. She tried again, this time kneeling and trying to shuffle forward, but again she lost her balance, catching on her head a glancing blow as she toppled sideways, the rough sacking providing ineffectual protection. "It's no use," she said. "I can make no purposeful progress like this. I might well knock myself senseless."

"Ha! At least you will know what to do to escape a slow drowning." Captain Ziegler was surprisingly quick to give up hope. Gretel was on the point of attempting to raise his morale when she heard a sound.

"Listen," she hissed in an excited whisper. "Someone is coming."

Footsteps ruled out the mermaid, so that it seemed at least one of their attackers was returning. Gretel wondered if they had decided to put them to the sword instead. She lay tense and still, peering through her unhelpfully ragged eyehole. A figure came into view. A man, moving quickly and quietly. He approached the captain, hesitated, and then lifted the sack from his head.

"By all that floats!" exclaimed Captain Ziegler, at the same moment Gretel recognized their visitor.

"Dr. Becker!" she cried. "Dr. Becker, how came you here?"

"By a small boat, much like your own," he explained gently, removing Gretel's hood.

She gasped air and shook her head, spitting hessian fibers as she did so. She was irritated at the thought of what the wretched sacking must have done to her hair and thought briefly of how exasperated Everard would be to see his efforts yet again ruined.

The captain was incensed. "You followed us! I was certain our departure went unseen. I had not reckoned with such an early riser as yourself. But, no matter. It is our good fortune that you are here."

"I am only too glad to be of assistance. I saw the ruffians responsible on the cliff path."

"Did they see you?" Gretel asked.

"I am certain they did not. I was able to duck into a crevice in the rocks and remain hidden. They were too engaged in discussing their plans to notice me."

"And you were intent on your own," Gretel suggested. The words of the sprite's riddle were coming back to her and, at last, making sense. *The sharp-eyed man*—surely there was no eyesight sharper in the region than Dr. Becker's with his ever-present binoculars.

Dr. Becker smiled ruefully. "I confess, fraulein, my mind is ever on one matter, and that is what brought me here, as I think you know."

The captain finished untying his bonds and stood up, striding about the cave to stretch his cramped legs. "You took up a dangerous course in following us, Dr. Becker. We are, as you have witnessed, dealing with murderous rogues."

Gretel allowed her fellow passenger to assist her to her feet. The scrapes and bruises from her falls upon the rocks were beginning to smart unpleasantly, but there was no time to concern herself with such trifles. "I think you will find, captain, that the good doctor's interests lie with someone, indeed, something, other than ourselves. Is that not correct, Dr. Becker?"

"Your powers of deduction are impressive, Fraulein Gretel," he replied.

"Alas, such powers, if powers they be, have come a little late in the day for convenience."

"Better late than never," he said.

"Had you not come here upon your mission," she replied, "there might have been no 'later,' either for myself or the captain."

"Mission?" Captain Ziegler was confused.

At that moment, a sound from the main part of the cave disturbed their conversation. The trio moved toward the little pool and stood watching as the mermaid emerged from the silky waters. Gretel was struck anew by the creature's allure. No matter that she had seen her before, it was impossible not to gaze in awe at the beautiful face, curvaceous upper body, and iridescent blue-green shimmer of her tail. The mermaid lifted herself gracefully from the pool and sat on the mossy edge, arranging herself in the most decorous manner.

"Well!" she purred. "Three visitors all at once. How lucky I am. I do hope you have not been waiting long. It can be chilly in here at times."

The captain had been momentarily rendered speechless by the vision before him. For all his insistence that he had no fear of mermaids, he was certainly overawed by the presence of this one. Gretel fancied there raged within him the confusion any man must endure when faced with a vision of loveliness even more beautiful than was fabled, undeniably erotic, and yet somehow sexless at the same time. It was yet another instance, as far as Gretel was concerned, that demonstrated how fortunate she was to be a woman.

"Good morning to you," she said to the mermaid.

"Fraulein! I am so happy you were able to return."

"Did I not promise that I would?"

Dr. Becker stepped forward. "Good morning," he said.

"Oh!" the mermaid exclaimed. "I know that voice! You are my shadowy benefactor. At last I see your face."

"Benefactor?" The captain had rediscovered his voice. "What goes on here?"

"Allow me to enlighten you, captain," said Gretel. "This charming creature is the source of the singing that has so disturbed your crew and your business. And this"—here she indicated Dr. Becker with a sweep of her arm—"is the man who has been paying her—and paying her handsomely, I might say—to sing."

"This! Dr. Becker!?" The captain's face darkened with fury. His hand went instinctively to his scabbard, forgetting that his sword had been taken from him. "Hell's teeth, man! It was *you* who sought to see me ruined?"

"My wish was never to do you any damage, captain, I assure you."

"What? My crew disappearing, my clients following, and my reputation likely to go the same way, and yet you think you do me no harm?"

"It was my intention only ever to see you go elsewhere. To leave these waters and offer your cruises somewhere other."

"He did not single you out for this treatment," Gretel told him. "The mermaid was to sing for one and all ships, not only the *Arabella*. Is that not the case, Dr. Becker?"

"It is. My desire was to see no more cruisers here. There was nothing personal in my actions . . ."

"Damn you for a fool, man!" roared the captain. "There is nothing more personal to a ship's master than his ship, do you not know that?"

Gretel stepped between the two men, not entirely trusting the captain's command of his temper.

"Dr. Becker is not a scoundrel, captain. He is, in fact, a man of passion like yourself, the difference being that while your passion is for your ship, his is for birds."

"Birds?" The mermaid was at a loss. "What has my singing to do with birds?" she asked. "I am a creature of the sea. Fowl pay me no heed whatsoever, and I confess I find gulls most raucous and tiresome things."

"Birds?" Captain Ziegler shook his head. "You talk in riddles, fraulein. Everyone knows the doctor is enamored of the things, spends his days looking at 'em. But what in Neptune's name does that have to do with me and my ship?"

"If I might be permitted to explain . . . ?" Dr. Becker asked.

"Get on with it, man!" was the captain's reply.

"I have made a lifetime study of the sea and coastal birds in this region, and I have discovered that the little Frisian Islands that dot these waters are crucial to their continued well-being. It is upon these islands that the birds make their nests and rear their young."

The mermaid gave a yawn. "I cannot see why one would care," she said, "as there are so very many of the shrill things. And they travel so far. Why cannot they go elsewhere if needs be? Who would notice?"

"Forgive me, fraulein," the doctor continued, "but there are many different varieties and species of bird. You are correct when you say that common gulls are plentiful, and indeed they are able to make their homes in many different places. The problem lies with the rarer birds, those of a nature more shy and delicate. Their numbers are few and they often raise only one chick in a year. Should they be disturbed, should they fail to produce young, well, the decline in their numbers would certainly be swift and could very well be dire."

The captain was struggling to find it in himself to understand. "We take our own food aboard, doctor. We do not stoop to trapping gulls and the like to feed crew or passengers. We have no interest in your damn birds."

"Happily, no, I grant that your detrimental impact upon these fragile species is not deliberate. They would, in any case, prove unpalatable, I believe. No, the problem lies with your very presence, or rather, that of your ship and its passengers. If the parent birds are disturbed during the breeding season, they may abandon their eggs or even leave their chick before it is fledged and able to fend for itself."

Gretel put in a thought. "The excursions to the islands . . . they must be particularly bothersome for the birds, I should imagine. All manner of people tramping and squealing and taking their noisy leisure. Enough to disturb tame and fed farmyard fowl, let alone shy birds unaccustomed to having humans in their midst."

"You have seen the dilemma precisely, fraulein," Dr. Becker told her. "And what is more, upon one of the islands, Amrum, there dwells a very rare bird indeed. The pigeon-toed yellow-necked speckled wader. Such a delightful bird! So elegant, so timid, so graceful in flight and deft in its wading habits. There is not its equal . . ." He pulled himself back from his rapturous reverie. "The fact is that only three breeding pairs remain. Three! Should their clutches come to naught this season, that would be the end of them."

"No more pigeon-toed yellow-bellied . . . ?" Gretel asked.

"Yellow-necked speckled waders," the doctor corrected her. "No more. Gone forever. I simply could not stand by and see that happen. I saw it as my duty to act."

"So you paid the mermaid to sing"—the captain shook his head—"for a few birds."

Now it was Dr. Becker's turn to become angry. The man was quite transformed.

"Have you no soul, captain? Have you no heart? Do you not see that such fragile beings, such delicate examples of what is pure and innocent in this world, are to be cherished and protected? Is not a society judged upon how it treats its weakest members?" he demanded.

Gretel knew that there was one word in the doctor's argument that might sway the captain: society. Did he not aspire to elevate himself, after all? Was that not his goal in all that he did, to rise above his brutal origins, to slough off his rough past and become a brighter, cleaner, better person? If he wished to join society, whatever that might be taken to mean, must he not then strive to make sure it was something worth the joining? Even if he cared not one sailor's spit for the wretched birds.

It was, however, difficult for him to reconcile the needs of a few feathered beings with the danger to his crew or the threat to his business. "Surely, Dr. Becker," he said more levelly, "you will grant that a man's life cannot be forfeit to that of a bird? Men have vanished. My cook was murdered . . ."

"Not by the doctor," Gretel reminded him, "nor anyone acting in his name."

"But the men who disappeared . . ." the captain insisted.

"Likely either fled because they were overcome by their superstitious fear of the mermaid," she pointed out, "or else were paid to go."

"By whom? This savior of birds?"

"Not he."

"How can you be certain? He seems ready to spend his money when it suits his purposes."

Here the mermaid found the conversation of interest once more. "He pays me well, that's true. And he's due to pay me again, unless you can persuade me otherwise."

"The captain has agreed to your terms," Gretel assured her. "His presence here should reassure you of that."

The mermaid smiled prettily, reaching out to touch the captain's cheek with a long, cool finger. "Will you take me to the lovely warm waters of the Caribbean, then, captain? Will you convey me safely away from this cold, dreary place?"

"Aye, I will."

"And will you stay there?" asked Dr. Becker hopefully.

"I will not! I have my reasons for choosing to make these seas my home. I intend on returning to take up my cruises the minute I have delivered my cargo."

"Cargo!" The mermaid bridled, snatching back her hand. "I would not be called such—"

Dr. Becker became agitated once again. "Sir, if you insist on returning to these islands, I will have no choice but to do my utmost to prevent you. I give you fair warning."

"Do you threaten me, doctor?!" Captain Ziegler stood tall and strong in front of the older man, who at once looked even more flimsy than usual.

"Gentlemen, please." Gretel raised her hands. "This is not the moment to fall to squabbling. May I remind you, captain, that even now Cat's Tongue and his cohort are on their way to scuttle our boat? Are we not people of logic and reason? It cannot be beyond us to find a solution that is satisfactory to all, but for now, we must work together, else we shall be at the mercy of those villains, and with no boat in which to return to the *Arabella*."

Both men deflated a little. The mermaid, bored with the whole business, took to combing her lustrous hair with a shell. "As long as I am given safe passage, as agreed, I am content."

"But," Dr. Becker stuttered, "what of *our* agreement?"

"I agreed to sing for gold because it was what I needed to leave this dismal place. Dear Captain Ziegler has agreed to take me, so I have no further need of you, doctor. I am sorry if that does not suit, but there it is," she told him with a shrug.

"Dr. Becker." Gretel put a hand on his arm. "I ask you to trust me when I tell you that we will find a solution. One that does not entail ruining Captain Ziegler."

"But one that will protect my birds?"

"It will."

"Including the pigeon-toed yellow-necked speckled waders?"

"Especially . . . those."

"I have your word?"

"You have it."

He took a breath and nodded steadily. "The word of Gretel of Gesternstadt is enough for me."

"Excellent!" She strode toward the entrance of the cave. "Come, gentlemen, there is no time to lose. Fraulein," she said, turning briefly to address the mermaid, "as soon as our business is concluded, we will return to collect you."

"Must I wait more?" she whined.

"Not beyond two more days and nights, I promise. And so does the captain, don't you, captain?"

"You have my promise, fraulein, but now we must take our leave," he said with a flamboyant bow.

So saying, the three of them hastened from the cave, the mermaid, mollified, bidding them *adieu* and blowing them charming kisses as they went.

As they made their way along the narrow path, the captain gave a shout.

"Ship ahoy!" he exclaimed, pointing at the horizon.

Dr. Becker raised his glasses to his eyes. Gretel peered through her lorgnettes.

"A rough vessel, apparently heading toward us," she said.

"And sitting low in the water," observed Captain Ziegler. "She's loaded up with something, and I'll wager it is brandy."

"That's one bet even Hans would turn down. Come along, we must get to the lifeboat before it is too late."

Dr. Becker piped up, "There is always my boat."

"Hell's teeth!" exclaimed the captain. "I should make more money hiring out my tenders and launches than I do cruising! And yet you are no sailor; how is it you are able to find your way at sea unassisted?"

"My many years of studying the birds of these islands have given me a familiarity with both the seas hereabouts and the craft necessary to travel about them."

Gretel urged them to hasten, saying, "We cannot be certain your boat will not have been discovered by our attackers. Their own, they succeeded in hiding before we arrived. We must assume they know these isles even better than you do, Dr. Becker. Let us make all haste!"

They scrambled on. As they approached the stretch of shore where they had left the boat with Sailor Braun, they were relieved to spy it still sitting among the dunes, apparently undisturbed. On arriving at the spot, they found poor Braun trussed as they had been. Dr. Becker employed his small pocketknife to free him from his ropes.

"How long ago did the villains leave you?" the captain asked, keeping his voice low and looking about him as he spoke.

"They've been gone an hour or more, cap'n," Braun told them. "They went upshore. One of them was wearing your sword, Cap'n Ziegler, sir. I feared the worst."

"You underestimate me," he replied, then, catching Gretel's eye, added, "you underestimate *us*."

"Let us not dawdle," Gretel chivvied the others along. "We must be gone from here before they return."

The captain growled. "But I should like to see to them, God damn me for a liar if I would not."

"May I remind you, captain, that we are all of us unarmed? The odds are stacked against us. For all we know, they may bring further assistance from the approaching ship. We cannot risk facing them now, but must leave this place and return to the *Arabella*."

"But what of our proof, fraulein? We may have set terms with the mermaid, and I believe you have a notion of how an agreement might be made with our doctor of birds, but where is the means by which I might give Hoffman his comeuppance?"

Gretel was about to speak eloquently on the wisdom of quitting while one was ahead, and of how they must count themselves fortunate that Dr. Becker had arrived to release them from their predicament, when a shout from the dunes alerted them, too late, to the return of the smugglers. In seconds they were upon them. Pustule charged, fists raised. Mold brandished not only his own but the captain's pistol. Cat's Tongue drew the captain's sword. There were roars, there were profanities, there were oaths and vulgar vocatives. Among it all, Gretel heard Captain Ziegler swearing that he would not be felled by one of his own weapons. Braun, an exemplar of his name, waded into the fray with nothing more than his muscles, which were easily a match for the unarmed Pustule, whom he knocked to the ground with a single blow and then held tight around the throat to prevent any further trouble from that direction. Cat's Tongue swung the sword awkwardly at the captain, who nimbly sidestepped his inexpert thrusts. Mold leveled one of the pistols at Dr. Becker and Gretel. She found the sun, dropping low behind their assailant, hard to face, making her raise her arm to shield her eyes as she attempted to see what Mold was about to do. As luck, and anatomy, would have it, the raising of her arm caused the raising of her bosom and therefore the raising of her lorgnettes, which tilted back due to the sloping nature of their resting place. As it did so, that same dazzling sun caught the lenses so that a flare rebounded directly into Mold's eyes. He was blinded and confused. Gretel saw her moment and charged, meeting his chest with her shoulder and the full force of her full figure behind it. Mold dropped both guns, one going off as it hit the ground, the shot finding the sword arm of Cat's Tongue, who let out a shriek and let go of the blade, which the captain snatched up.

In a matter of seconds it was over, and the six were frozen in a tableau of halted violence. Captain Ziegler loomed above a kneeling, sobbing Cat's Tongue, the point of his reclaimed sword hovering inches from the ruffian's heart. Braun had wrestled Mold into complete submission and now held him firm by twisting his arms behind his back. Pustule lay where he fell with Gretel sitting upon his chest, utterly unable to move. Dr. Becker had retrieved the pistols.

"Damn you for curs and halfwit villains!" the captain bellowed. "Take me on, would you? I'll not suffer a single blow more from the likes of you!" he declared, raising his sword.

"Captain Ziegler, no!" Gretel shouted.

"I plan to run the devil through, fraulein. No use trying to stop me!"

"But who is it that you are?" she demanded of him. "Will you act as the Snaggle-Toothed Pirate? Or are you truly become the man you claim to be, Captain Tobias Ziegler of the good ship *Arabella*?"

There was a tense pause, filled with hope on Gretel's part, horror on the doctor's part, silent rage on the captain's part, and a steaming stream of urine on Cat's Tongue's part. Reluctantly, slowly, the captain took a step back and lowered his sword. Gretel smiled a *well done!* at him. Cat's Tongue fainted from relief and loss of blood.

Gretel found the business of binding the rogues who had so recently bound her rather satisfying, enjoying the opportunity to let them see how rough rope chafed and rubbed, how knots dug into tender places, and how extremities were alternately throbbing or benumbed. Before Cat's Tongue came to what little senses he possessed, she removed Frenchie's knife from him and tucked it into her skirt pocket. She then tore off a strip of petticoat with which to wrap his wound and stanch the flow of blood, which was in fact not a threat to his life. She made a note to add a hefty amount to Captain Ziegler's bill to cover the cost of the proportion of her wardrobe that had been sacrificed during her investigations into the case. It was decided that Dr. Becker would take his boat, with Braun to assist him, and ferry Pustule and Mold to the island of Sylt, where there was a kingsman's station, which would no doubt be happy to receive them and mete out justice in due course. Cat's Tongue they would take back with them to the ship, Gretel having explained to the captain about his having been in possession of Frenchie's knife. The last they saw of the larger vessel involved in the smuggling, it was turned about and making all speed in the direction opposed to the island, likely having heard pistol fire, seen an altercation on the shore, and decided on discretion being the better part of valor.

As they tied Cat's Tongue to the oarlocks in the lifeboat, Gretel put the situation to him bluntly.

"You are in no small amount of trouble, there's no dressing it up. You are a smuggler and a would-be murderer. Your future, in short, does not look bright. Or long."

Here Cat's Tongue fell to weeping.

"However," Gretel went on, allowing the word to come loaded with hope and possibility, both of which, she knew, would have a profound effect on the man, "there is yet a way you might, to some extent, redeem yourself, and possibly even avoid the scaffold."

"What? What is it you want me to do? I'll do anything, just tell me," he begged.

"Give me Hoffman," she said. "Tell me all that he is and all that he has done, spare not a single detail, speak up and speak quickly, and it will go easier for you, I promise."

And before the captain had maneuvered the little boat beyond the breakwater, an eager Cat's Tongue was singing louder and clearer than the mermaid herself.

EIGHTEEN

As they came alongside the *Arabella*, Gretel could make out the distinctive silhouette of Hans at the rail. It was by now past the hour for cooking lunch, and he stood in his chef's apron, an unlit cigar in his mouth.

"I say, sister mine, you've caught one of our old acquaintances," he noted as she came aboard.

"We have. His fellow villains are even now being found a cozy bed in the jailhouse on the island of Sylt. Tell me"—she glanced about her—"has the baroness arrived?"

"She most certainly has. She and her party are in the dining room finishing their meal. Difficult woman to please, I don't mind telling you. I served up the very finest of Frenchie's recipes, did him proud, if I say so myself, and still her ladyship kept a face as sour as a Greek lemon."

"It is, to my knowledge, the only face she has." Gretel hesitated, then, lowering her voice, asked, "And the Uber General? He . . . ?"

"Is here, too, yes, and asking after you."

"Oh?" Gretel's feigned nonchalance was unconvincing.

"Yes, though I think he mainly wants your protection from That Woman's traveling companions. They have set their caps at the poor man." Hans shook his head slowly. "A woman so fixed on her prey is a frightening thing to see. I came up here for a soothing cigar"—he gestured with the unsmoked one in his hand—"but my lighter is lost, gone from my waistcoat pocket where it has always been. No sign of the thing."

The captain called to Gretel. "Shall we summon Hoffman directly?" he asked. "Where is the scoundrel?"

Hans confirmed he was below with the visitors, playing the part of host adequately.

"If you could just give me a few minutes, captain. There is something I must attend to first. Hold our guest out of sight for now."

"This cannot keep long, fraulein."

"I know it. But we have only one chance to snare the quartermaster. There is another step to be taken before we reveal our knowledge and our charming witness."

"Very well. I will await your word in my cabin, but be quick, I urge you." Captain Ziegler summoned a sailor and together they marched Cat's Tongue toward the poop deck.

Gretel turned to her brother. "I believe I know where you will find your lighter."

"You do?"

"It will be somewhere in plain view in Birgit's cabin."

"What?" Hans was appalled. "But I have not been within arm's length of the woman all day. How could she have taken it from me?"

"She did not. Another did, on her behalf, and will have placed it where she can easily find it."

"Another? Who?"

"You need not concern yourself with that now. Do I need to tell you to what conclusions Birgit will fling herself if she finds it?"

Hans gulped.

"You must fetch it back, and quickly."

"But, to enter the lair of the gorgon . . ."

"Don't be so wet, Hans," she said, pushing him gently toward the stairs. "She will be in the dining room with her friends, by the sound of it. Go now, go on."

She watched him disappear and then switched her attention to the rigging. Shielding her eyes against the sun, she searched for the sea sprite. Sure enough, it was not far off, but watching from its high hiding place.

"Won't you come down?" Gretel called to it. "I'd very much like to speak with you."

As she watched, the little creature descended in a small purple blur though the ropes, masts, and sails. It came to rest on the mainbrace, its tiny wings fluttering with excitement.

"Well," it said, "you have missed the most unusual arrivals. A baroness, no less, very cross and scratchy, and your lovely general with her. He's almost as handsome as the captain." It grinned.

"From what I've heard, some of the passengers certainly seem to think so."

"Ha-ha! Those silly, silly women will not leave him alone. You'd better run to his rescue!"

"I am certain he is in no real danger and fully able to secure his own safety. Besides, I wish a word or two with you first."

"Did you work out my riddle? It was really so very simple, and everyone keeps saying how very clever you are. The cleverest person aboard, they say."

"That is because they have not met you," Gretel told it. "I found your puzzle to be most amusing. Sharpest of sharp eyes indeed! Very good."

"And the sharp flaw, did you find that, too?"

"Ah, Frenchie's knife. That is precisely what I wanted to talk to you about. I have a favor to ask, if you are willing."

The sea sprite put its head a little on one side, considering. "I might be. I might not. Is there fun to be had?"

"A certain amount, yes, I can promise you that. More importantly"—Gretel leaned a little closer, shutting her mind to the sharp teeth the sprite was baring in a mischievous smile—"you would be helping Captain Ziegler."

At this the sprite squealed with delight, clapping its little velvety hands. "Then of course I shall assist. Tell me, quickly, what is it you wish me to do?"

❖

The dining room was packed, despite the majority of the diners having finished their meals. People sat about sipping port or brandy, lingering as long as they could to remain in the company of minor royalty. They laughed loudly at the baroness's attempts at wit, and applauded just about anything that came out of her mouth. Such sycophancy never ceased to amaze Gretel. Is wasn't as if the baroness were young, beautiful, stylish, or even pleasant company. On the contrary, she was dreary to look at and equally dreary to talk to, the only spice to flavor her conversation being the bitter pepper of a put-down or the tartness of a sharp remark. But still the common man, and woman, it had to be said, hung on her every word, desperate for her favor. They were likely to be disappointed. Baroness Schleswig-Holstein's natural demeanor was one of grudging tolerance of humanity. She did not bestow her approval or thanks lightly. And from what Gretel could deduce as she entered the dining room, the baroness had found little aboard the *Arabella* to lift her innate tendency to gloom. To her left sat Herr Hoffman, grim-faced and silent as ever. To her right, Ferdinand, handsome, but at a loss, no doubt, as to his purpose beyond the baroness's safety. Her lady-in-waiting was attempting to elicit some tiny crumb of good humor from her mistress.

"Such delicious food, baroness," the pale, tired-looking girl tried. "The lobster bisque was particularly tasty, do you not think so?"

"It tasted of lobster," the baroness observed, "as lobster bisques are apt to do. The quality was high, I grant you."

"And the wine?" Ferdinand joined in. "A very passable claret, I thought."

"Yes, I could find no fault in it. I can find no fault in anything," she said flatly, whipping out a fan, which she proceeded to work as much for something to do as to create a cooling draft.

Watching from the entrance to the room, Gretel saw at once what the problem was. Hans had, as always, excelled himself in the kitchen. The food that had been served, and the wine with it, had been of an excellent standard. Everard, standing close to the baroness's table, had clearly been on hand to provide smooth and swift service. The sea was calm. The air pleasant. The assembled diners deferential and well behaved. In short, there was nothing new for the royal guest here, nothing remotely different or unexpected. She had come looking for an authentic sailing experience; a little rough glamor, some romantic rustications, perhaps even a smidgen of danger. Instead, all she had found—due to the diligent and strenuous efforts of everyone involved—was a scaled-down imitation of what she had been accustomed to getting every day of her long life. Where was the adventure in that?

Gretel touched the shoulder of Will the cabin boy as he scampered past the doorway.

"Will, be so good as to take a message to the captain, would you?"

"Of course, fraulein."

"Tell him I am ready. Ask that he bring our newest guest here at once."

"Yes, fraulein," he said and ran off to do her bidding.

Gretel hurried over to the center table. She saw that Elsbeth and Sonja had taken seats as close to Ferdinand as was possible. She also saw that Birgit was not with them and experienced a fleeting moment of worry for Hans.

Ferdinand looked genuinely pleased to see her.

"Fraulein Gretel," he said, getting quickly to his feet to offer her a low bow. Herr Hoffman could barely summon the manners to lift his posterior from his seat as she approached. "You are returned in good time. Your task went well, I trust?"

"Well enough," she replied, ducking a little curtsy as she spoke to his mistress. "Baroness, I do hope you have been made properly welcome aboard the *Arabella*." She was about to compose a short but pretty speech singing the praises of the ship and its crew, but a commotion behind her made her pause. Turning, she saw the mer-hund, rope trailing, come charging into the room, weaving its way at breakneck speed between the tables, rubbing its damp fur on diners as it passed. It barreled into Gretel, knocking her to the floor, where it pinned her, the better to wash her face with its rough and smelly tongue.

"Argh," she gasped, "get off me, you ridiculous animal."

So delighted was the hound at having found her, it took both Ferdinand and Everard to haul him off so that she might get to her feet.

"Good heavens," said the baroness, "whatever sort of creature is that?"

"That, baroness," Gretel told her, "is a mer-hund."

"A mer-hund, you say? Well, what is it doing on this ship? And why is it so obviously enamored of you?"

A titter ran around the room, the baroness's idolaters eager to show their adoration. Ordinarily, Gretel would happily have stamped on that impudent laughter and ground it into the rug beneath her oh-so-sensible-and-I-wish-I-was-wearing-something-more-attractive shoes. Ordinarily. On this occasion, however, her pride was of minor importance. She brushed herself down.

"My brother purchased the mer-hund to assist me in my work, for the breed has been developed over generations to hunt the elusive and mysterious mermaid."

"Mermaid?" The baroness was unconvinced. "Pshaw! A thing conjured to entertain children and frighten sailors. None such has ever been found."

"But, baroness, surely you cannot have forgotten the song you heard from the deck of the *Fair Fortune* on the night of the ball?"

"Merely a trick, a folly designed to divert the guests from the horrible discovery of a dead person. A discovery you made yourself, as I recall."

Gretel ignored the gibe, determined to keep the conversation on track. "The reason the mer-hund is so keen to be close to me today is that he can detect the scent of the mermaid with whom I conversed earlier today."

"You conversed with one?" The baroness was beginning to enjoy the whimsy.

"Did you now?" put in Hoffman.

"I did, on an island not far from here."

"And was she as beautiful and deadly as legend would have us believe?" Baroness Schleswig-Holstein wished to know.

"Every bit. But fear not," Gretel addressed the room, making a point of taking in any crewmembers present, "she is leaving these waters presently, desirous of making her home somewhere a little warmer. We will not hear her singing again."

"Oh." Now the royal guest was disappointed. "For a moment I was rather intrigued, and think I should like to have seen her for myself." She gave a sigh. "But no matter."

Gretel could see her attention beginning to wander, and so was relieved when the captain entered the dining room, Cat's Tongue, his hands still tied, dragged in behind him by two burly sailors. At the sight of him, Hoffman came out of his seat as if it were on fire. He quickly recovered his composure, but not without noticing Gretel's small smile. Captain Ziegler adeptly greeted his honored guest, sweeping his tricorn from his head for a wide, extravagant bow, apologizing for his absence upon her arrival.

"I had serious business to attend to, my lady," he told her. "Business that dealt with a threat to my crew."

"I understand that a captain's first responsibility is to his ship," the baroness assured him. "Indeed, any woman wishing to win the heart of a man of the sea must accept she will always take second place to his vessel. Is that not so, Captain Ziegler?" she asked.

"That, baroness, would depend entirely upon the caliber of the lady in question," he told her, straightening up and catching her eye as he treated her to a devastating, snaggle-toothed smile.

Gretel was amazed to see the older woman's cheeks tinged with pink. The captain certainly had a talent for unsettling females. It was one he could, she decided, gainfully employ. She would speak with him on the matter later.

The baroness recovered sufficiently to notice the prisoner. "Who is this . . . person?" she inquired.

Gretel kept her eye on the quartermaster as she replied, "This, baroness, is a ruthless and nefarious smuggler!"

All present gasped.

"A smuggler, you say?" The baroness leaned forward for a better look. "And what was he attempting to smuggle?"

"Brandy," Gretel explained. "Of a particularly high quality and expensive nature. He and his partners in crime took deliveries of crates of the liquor, and stowed them away on a tiny island, which was also, it transpired, the home of the mermaid."

"Oh? And was the mermaid a smuggler too?"

The baroness's question was as ridiculous as it was pointless, but her loyal company laughed uproariously. When the hilarity had subsided, Gretel continued.

"She was not. Though she did unwittingly assist the smugglers in their work."

"How so?"

"The smugglers reckoned on the fear most sailors have of these legendary creatures. They would stay well away from a place from which mermaid singing was heard to come."

Now Ferdinand spoke up. "But they had not reckoned with Gretel of Gesternstadt and her thorough investigations."

"They had not," she agreed. "Which is why Hans and I were able to find the villains and discover their plans. Captain Ziegler saw it as his duty to return with me to the island to tackle the criminals and catch them in the act of their illicit business." This might not have been to the letter of the what and the why and the how of things, but, Gretel felt confident, it was in the spirit of it. No point cluttering up a tale with unnecessary detail.

"Was it dangerous?" The baroness's question was directed at Captain Ziegler.

"Danger must be no bar to acting when that action is the correct course to take," he told her, nimbly climbing up another step in her regard for him.

"But you were not harmed, captain?" she asked a little breathlessly. "Your body not wounded, perhaps?"

Gretel decided enough was enough. It was time to bring things to their conclusion. She did not allow time for the captain to respond, but took the floor again herself.

"The facts are these," she declared. "Captain Ziegler has suffered damage to his business and the ship's cook lost his life, all for the greed and single-minded wickedness of these smugglers. Frenchie was not of their number, but he discovered what they were about and demanded payment for his silence. When his terms became too rich for their liking, the smugglers silenced him forever. And the murderer stands before you now."

At this, Cat's Tongue set up loud and forceful protestations. "'Twas not I! I never set foot on the *Arabella* before today. I am no murderer!"

Gretel frowned at him. "You've Dr. Becker to thank for the truth of that, or have you forgotten a certain cave, with certain persons shackled within it, awaiting a certain watery death?"

"But here you are," he pointed out. "I never killed no one!" he insisted.

"But you know who did, do you not? You know who killed Frenchie," Gretel insisted.

"'Twas him!" Cat's Tongue raised his bound and bandaged hands to gesture at Hoffman. "He's the one as did him in. He's your murderer!"

Now the audience was properly astounded. Here was a shabby villain, dragged into the room tied and bloodstained, accusing none other than the ship's quartermaster—a man who wore his respectability like a suit of armor—of murder. There were shouts of "liar" and "scoundrel" and "well, I never, surely not."

Gretel held up a hand for silence. "Well, Herr Hoffman, what have you to say?"

"I say this is calumny! Slander!"

"I speak the truth!" Cat's Tongue cried.

"Silence, rogue!" Hoffman strode forward, chest puffed out, staring the whimpering ruffian down. "Hold your tongue and your lies." Now he turned to Gretel. "You would have all here believe the word of a common criminal, a man of no standing, of no consequence, over me? Is not the word of a respected, honest quartermaster, whom Captain Ziegler saw fit to leave in charge of his ship, his crew, his honored guests, to carry weight and be trusted?"

"You can hide your true nature behind your mask of respectability no longer, Herr Hoffman. The game is up. Your associate here has given us chapter and verse."

Rattled into forgetting himself, Hoffman snarled at Gretel. "But he gave you no proof, though, did he, eh? Where is your proof, Detective Gretel of Gesternstadt?"

There were times when Gretel truly loved her job. Times when, after days or even weeks of diligent work, after dangerous encounters, hardships endured, and lengthy investigations, things came together in the most pleasing and satisfying manner. Times when her adversaries showed themselves to be less than her equal by meekly stepping into the neat and clever trap she had prepared for them. Times such as these. Times such as now.

"So you deny all charges, Herr Hoffman?"

"I do!"

"You are innocent of all that has been said of you here?"

"I am!"

"You have nothing to hide?"

"I have not!"

"In which case you will have no objection to our searching your cabin?"

The quartermaster hesitated. Fear flickered across his stony face, but so very quickly, and so very minutely, that is was likely only Gretel saw it. Saw it, and congratulated herself upon it, for it revealed that Hoffman now understood what she herself had always known: that he could not, in the end, outsmart her. That she would, ultimately, get her man.

The main players descended to the lower deck and the cabins, Hoffman all the while protesting his innocence and declaring that not a single incriminating thing would they find in his quarters. Indeed, he led the way, Gretel having given him the opportunity to do so with a gracious nod and sweep of her arm. She followed on his heels, Captain Ziegler behind her, eagerly pursued by the baroness, who was evidently thrilled by the entertainment, and who was, naturally, accompanied by the general. Hoffman was berthed on the same deck as the passengers, his billet being two doors down from Birgit's. Upon arrival, he threw open the door in a defiant gesture, which was somewhat lessened by the narrowness of that door and the mean proportions of the room onto which it gave.

"Search all you want," he instructed, "for you will find nothing untoward here."

"Uber General, would you kindly assist me? I would value your presence as an independent witness."

Ferdinand stepped forward. "I am pleased to be of service, fraulein," he said, squeezing into the cabin with her. Now that both were inside there was, in fact, no room for anyone to look for anything.

"On second thought," said Gretel, "I would be grateful if you would conduct the search yourself, as space is limited, and I would not have it said that we have been anything but fair and scrupulous." She inched her way back out into the passage and took her position with the others, who all stood with necks craned for a better view.

Ferdinand looked about him. The cabin, as anyone who knew Hoffman would expect, was spick and span and tidy as could be, the cot made up tightly, and nothing out of place. So it was that the brandy bottle on the little writing desk was plain for all to see. The general held it up.

"Might this be of interest?" he asked.

"'Tis brandy," Hoffman growled. "What of it? Cannot a man have a drink in his own cabin?" He spoke confidently enough, but Gretel knew he was shaken by the appearance of the brandy in his room.

Captain Ziegler took the bottle, wrenched out the stopper, and downed a swig.

"God's truth!"

"Is it terrible?" asked the baroness.

"It is sublime!"

Gretel nodded. "So you are certain, captain, that this is not the brandy you serve aboard the *Arabella*?"

"Ha! Such luxury would be the ruin of me. We favor honest fare here. I give my passengers the same brandy I drink myself, and I tell you, this is not it!"

Hoffman scowled. "Which proves only that you are a cheapskate with an ignorance of fine living, sir!"

The captain might well have punched his quartermaster squarely on the nose for this remark, were it not for what Ferdinand held up for inspection next.

For it was a knife.

A bone-handled knife with a silver top to it.

And a curiously curved blade.

There was an intake of breath before everyone began speaking at once. Hoffman's language descended into oaths and curses, mostly directed at Gretel. Ferdinand appealed for calm and placed himself firmly in front of Gretel to fend off the worst of Hoffman's threats. The captain declared the case proven and damned Hoffman for the murderous blackguard he clearly was. The baroness egged them all on with refined but forceful declarations that she had never witnessed such scenes, and demanded that the quartermaster be clapped in irons, or tied to the mizzenmast, or made to walk the plank, or keelhauled.

It was Gretel who cut through the noise with her own call for quiet.

"Let Herr Hoffman speak," she said. "Let him tell us how he came by this very particular and distinctive knife."

"It is not mine. I have never seen it before!"

"But here it is, among your things, in your very cabin," Gretel pointed out.

"So what if it is? In any event, it could be any knife. Not necessarily the one that belonged to that cook you were so fond of."

At that moment a door opened in the passageway. Such was the nearness and up-closeness of everything on the sleeping deck that it was impossible for the interruption to go unnoticed. It was Birgit's door that opened, and it was Hans who emerged through it. A severely ruffled, disheveled Hans, pink-faced and collar askew. He was clutching his precious lighter as if his life depended on his holding on to it, and his eyes had a dazed and faraway look to them. His cheeks bore marks of rouge in blurry kisses, and his hair appeared to have weathered some sort of storm. Even at such a heightened moment, his appearance attracted puzzled stares.

"Hans . . . ?" Gretel struggled to form an appropriate question. "Are you quite well? You look as if you have suffered an assault."

"Indeed I have. But fear not, sister mine, it will be the last. There comes a time when a man has to speak plainly, even at the expense of another's feelings. I can be no woman's plaything. I have my own life to lead, my own responsibilities. I explained as much and Frau Lange and I have reached an understanding." From the cabin behind him there came the sounds of soft sobbing. Hans drew himself up, appeared about to say more on the subject, and then noticed what Ferdinand had still in his hand. "I say!" he exclaimed. "You've found Frenchie's knife!"

Hoffman looked fit to spit with fury.

"You put it there!" he screamed at Gretel.

"I? But I have been off this ship, Herr Hoffman, and have had no access to your cabin, which in any case I imagine you keep locked."

"It was that thing!" he raged. "You are in league with it. This is the work of your tame sea sprite!"

"Come, come, Herr Hoffman," said Gretel, smiling, "everybody knows that there is no such thing as a sea sprite."

NINETEEN

I t was only two days later, as Gretel sat in her cabin while Everard worked his magic on her hair, that she felt fully able to relax and congratulate herself on a job well done. Hoffman had wriggled and squirmed, of course, but the game was up. With Cat's Tongue, and indeed Pustule, keen as mustard to testify against him in the hope of saving their own necks, Hoffman's unreliable alibi in the shape of Bo'sun Brandt—who was also arrested—and the damning evidence of Frenchie's knife in his cabin, the quartermaster could not escape justice.

Everard held up the looking glass. "Now then, madam, what do you think?" he asked, showing her the elegant and pleasingly complex hairdo he had created for her.

Gretel smiled. "I think that if there is one souvenir I should like to take home with me from these silvery Frisian waters, it is you, Everard. I shall miss your skills. Here." She took a small roll of notes from beneath her corset and handed them to him. "You have more than earned this."

"Why, madam! This is too much!"

"Nonsense. You have made this ship tolerable. I have been well paid. I am happy to share a little of my good fortune with you. I hope you will put it to good use."

Everard stared at the money. "Indeed I shall! I have been harboring a notion to leave this ship and try my luck as a master of coiffure in one of the larger cities. Now I have sufficient funds for my journey!"

"Splendid idea. Where will you choose?"

"I thought Paris."

"Oh! An excellent plan. Let me know when you are established there and I promise one day I shall visit. You can maintain my locks and wigs in the most fashionable of styles while I take in the delights of the city."

Everard gripped his hairbrush excitedly. "It will be a dream come true, madam. Though I shall be sorry to leave the *Arabella*. This curious little ship has come to feel like home. And who would ever have thought it? Captain Ziegler going into partnership with none other than Thorsten Sommer? I do declare, nothing could have surprised me more."

"I confess, had you suggested such an alliance a few short weeks ago, I would have thought you quite mad. It seemed the captain had such a loathing of his rival. But I came to see that his attitude stemmed from his own frustrated desires, and that the two need not be at odds. The arrangement they have come to will benefit them both. Herr Sommer will continue to run his luxury cruises, and Captain Ziegler will offer an optional package of days aboard the *Arabella* for those desirous of the Authentic Sailing Experience, as it is to be called. The baroness will spread the word of her own exhilarating and singular experience."

"Oh, my goodness, my gracious, madam, let us hope such cruises do not always involve anyone as sour and dour as Herr Hoffman."

"His presence will not be missed."

"What I do not understand," Everard mused, gazing at the ceiling, gesturing with the hairbrush to underline his point, "is why Hoffman had it in for Herr Sommer. I mean to say, I understand he wished to make money with his smuggling, but putting poor Frenchie's body on the *Fair Fortune* . . . it was as if he sought to ruin the man."

"Hoffman saw an opportunity to turn the cook's death to his advantage. Another man might have panicked—a man dies at his hand on board a small ship—but not Hoffman. His chief reason for putting the body on that ship was to distance it from himself, and throw me off the scent, no doubt. The fact that the discovery of a murder victim on the *Fair Fortune* might damage Sommer's business was a bonus. It must have been what made him choose that course rather than tipping the body into the sea. It transpires that Hoffman used to work as first mate to Herr Sommer. He had his heart—wherever he kept the stony thing—set upon captaincy proper, and saw the Sommer fleet as the way to get it. But Herr Sommer must have seen something rotten at the man's core and found a reason to dismiss him."

"Ooh, that cannot have sat well with our quartermaster."

"It did not. His plan was to earn enough money from smuggling to purchase his own ship one day. If, when that day came, there were no rival cruise ships operating in the area, so much the better for him."

Gretel got to her feet, patting lightly at her hair. "I shall go up on deck now. I believe we are about to make port."

Everard bobbed a bow. "I wish you good-bye and safe journey home, madam," he told her.

Outside, the day was pretty in the pale and whispery sort of way that the region did so well. Most of the passengers were on deck to see the *Arabella* come into the harbor at Bremerhaven. The crew worked hard to bring her safely to her moorings, apparently happy to do so under Captain Ziegler's flamboyant instructions rather than being barked at by Herr Hoffman. The *Fair Fortune* had docked but moments earlier, so that the quayside was filled with a small but well-dressed crowd who cheered and threw streamers and rice in a rather delightful way. In fact, Gretel was finding most things delightful. This was her moment; a case solved, a client happy, a payment—plus healthy bonus—received; hers was a triumphant return.

She found Hans making a meal of managing the luggage.

"Dash it all, Gretel," he puffed, "I swear these things have got heavier during the voyage. You didn't sneak off to do any shopping, perchance?"

"Alas, Hans, I had no need of thatching shears, wooden clogs, fish embalmed in salt, or cheese from which all flavor has been thoughtfully removed to save us the trouble of tasting it. No, the trunks are not heavier, but it is possible that you are."

"What? Do you think so?" He patted his belly as if pleased with the idea. "Well, all that time spent in the kitchen . . . a chef has to test and taste, you know. Wouldn't do otherwise. Test and taste, that's the work of a good cook."

Gretel noticed Birgit standing a little way off and making no attempt to approach. She looked subdued, and yet she still wore the wistful countenance of a person in love.

"Whatever did you say to That Woman to convince her you were neither interested nor available?"

"Ah, yes." Hans seemed reluctant to explain further. His expression was all too familiar to Gretel. It was the one she saw when he had spent the housekeeping at the inn, or finished the last slice of gateau, or washed his lederhosen with her Moroccan cotton petticoats, turning them all brown. It was the expression that said *you're not going to like this.*

"Let's have it," she insisted.

"Well, she was so very persistent, so very excitable, she simply would not listen when I told her I did not share her amorous feelings, and such. I had to find a way to convince her, to make her see that I would not, no never, not ever be hers."

"So . . ."

Hans cleared his throat. "So I told her that, however capable you might appear, you couldn't do without me. I told her that you were *mostly* perfectly fine and normal and able to do your work really quite well, given your regrettable condition . . ."

"Which is?"

"A . . . feebleness of the mind. A weakness of the nerves. A delicacy of the emotional constitution that means you simply cannot be left alone, cannot be abandoned to the mercy of your own fragile mind and irregular but debilitating febrile imaginings." Hans took a tiny step back.

Gretel ground her teeth. "Let me get this straight, Hans. You found yourself incapable of being man enough to tell That Woman to go away and leave you alone, so instead you made out that your responsibilities and obligations tied you to me forever because I am, on a part-time basis, a feeble-minded lunatic?"

"Um . . . yes."

To her own surprise, and very much to Hans's astonishment, Gretel found herself laughing loudly. Loudly enough to draw pitying glances from Birgit and her companions. "Ha! Well, Hans, I must congratulate you. You are your sister's brother after all, and I am impressed by your cunning. Now go and fetch the rest of the luggage. I still have a valise in my cabin, and I am, apparently, too flimsy of brain to find it myself."

It was then that she noticed the noble party disembarking from the *Fair Fortune*. She moved forward to the ship's rail for a better view. Baroness Schleswig-Holstein was descending the beribboned gangway, accompanied by her small but stylish entourage, waving and smiling as if she were someone considerably more important than a mere baroness. Two steps behind her, in his smartest uniform, the one with the burgundy cape with the gold lining that Gretel found so devilishly attractive, walked Uber General Ferdinand von Ferdinand. Her heart skipped lightly at the sight of him.

"Silly woman," she told herself.

Ferdinand, as if sensing he was being watched, paused and turned. Seeing her, he smiled. Gretel's heart twirled about in a fuzzy little spin. He raised his hand as if to salute or wave, but then changed his mind and instead blew her a silent kiss. Gretel's heart performed two backflips and a double somersault.

"Silly woman," she told herself again, as she forced herself to merely smile in acknowledgment, however much she might have felt like responding more exuberantly. There would be a time and a place, and this was not it. The baroness could not keep him indefinitely. Soon he would return to his post at King Julian's side at the Summer Schloss, where he would be only a short gallop from Gesternstadt.

"Fraulein Gretel!" Captain Ziegler's voice brought her quickly back to her present reality. "The good doctor here is about to leave us and wished to bid you farewell before departing."

"Dr. Becker." She nodded at him. "I trust you are satisfied with the alterations to the *Arabella*'s sailing routes?"

"I am indeed, fraulein. The captain has been most accommodating, particularly when one considers all the trouble I caused him."

"We will not mention that again," the captain assured him, slapping the older man so heartily on the back that he stumbled forward. "We have studied the charts together and I have given Dr. Becker my word that we will sail nowhere near the islands the birds use during the breeding season."

"I have supplied Captain Ziegler with the information he needs regarding their habits."

"Particularly those of the pigeon-toed yellow necked speckled wader, I presume," said Gretel.

"Aye!" laughed the captain. "He has supplied me with drawings of that mysterious fowl to boot, just to be sure I don't bag a brace for my supper, ain't that so, Doctor?"

The doctor, by now accustomed to the captain's little ways, was not in the least alarmed. He told Gretel, "We have a new plan, fraulein. On certain cruises I am to sail aboard the *Arabella* as an ornithological consultant."

Captain Ziegler looked especially pleased with himself. "A plan of my own invention. Seems those folk with a passion for birds will pay good money to see 'em. The doctor will be their tour guide, with evening talks on the matter, so insatiable is their appetite for details of the feathery things."

"You are turning into quite the entrepreneur, captain. I applaud your business acumen."

At this the captain turned quite pink with pride.

Dr. Becker took his leave, carrying only one small case, his ever-present binoculars still around his neck.

"So, captain, when do you set sail for the Caribbean?" Gretel asked.

"Four days' time. The mermaid would have had it sooner, but we must take on more supplies and several new crewmembers."

"Ah, yes, your number has been somewhat depleted."

"Most are replaced easily, though some will not sail with our special . . . passenger," he said, remembering not to refer to the sea creature as cargo. "I confess we shall feel the lack of your brother the most. His skills in the kitchen were much appreciated."

"He tells me you sought to persuade him to stay on."

"I hesitated to part you from your family, fraulein, but, well, I am a man of business now."

"Thankfully, he declined, so your conscience need not be troubled further."

"He said a life at sea would not suit him."

"I suspect he would pine for his own kitchen. And his own inn."

The captain shook his head. "Newer and better versions of both can be found: it is the companionship of a beloved sister that is irreplaceable."

Now it was Gretel's turn to blush.

Captain Ziegler begged her to excuse him as there were many matters demanding his attention. He left her with his customarily low bow, his tricorn sweeping the deck as he backed away.

"I bid you *adieu*, fraulein," he called after her. "I shall call on you for your assistance, should I ever again encounter an unsolvable puzzle."

"I have yet to find such a thing, captain," she assured him. His dashing grin was filled with genuine fondness, she felt, but in truth her warmth toward him was due largely to the generous payment, with the sizeable bonus, that he had so willingly handed over to her.

At that moment, Hans appeared, trailing the mer-hund on its lead.

"He doesn't want to move," he told her. "He knows I'm leaving him and he's sulking." Hans knelt down beside the panting animal and ruffled its fur as he spoke to it. "You can't come home with us. There isn't any sea. You wouldn't like it."

"You are doing the right thing, Hans. Mer-hunds are bred for the ocean. He would find Bavaria altogether too dry."

"But he might pine when I go. He might not eat."

Gretel knew her brother was talking about himself as much as his hound, although she was fairly certain his appetite would recover at the first sight of a little weisswurst with grainy mustard.

"He will be treated exceptionally well," she reminded him. "He is to be one of the star attractions for the passengers—a genuine mer-hund."

The animal hung its head low and looked moribund and pathetic and very un-starlike.

"But he might be lonely," Hans said.

"Ah, I've thought of that." Gretel glanced about her. There was no one close by, as their fellow cruise-goers were busy with their luggage and travel arrangements, and the crew was employed in the business of unloading the ship. She peered up into the rigging. "Hello?" she called in a stage whisper. "Hello, are you going to come down?"

"Who the devil are you talking to?" asked Hans, getting stiffly to his feet. He and the mer-hund followed the direction of her gaze. Hans could see nothing, but the hound's ears stuck out and he began to wag his tail a little. And then, suddenly, there it was. The sea sprite flitted effortless down and settled on a pile of rope beside them.

"Well, I'll be!" exclaimed Hans. "Look at that!"

"Good morning to you," Gretel said. "This, as you know, is my brother, Hans, and this is his mer-hund . . ." But already she could see that the sprite's attention was elsewhere, as it reached out a tiny purple hand to Hans's pet. The hound sniffed at it gently. The sea sprite touched the big black nose and hopped down to examine the great shaggy webbed paws before springing lightly up to hover next to its head, the better to look it in the eye. The mer-hund wagged more enthusiastically.

"The thing is," said Gretel, seizing the moment, "we have to leave him behind. Captain Ziegler is happy to have him on board. He thinks the passengers will like him. I can't see it myself, but there we are. Anyway, Hans is worried that the animal might be lonely. Thinks he needs a special someone. I was wondering . . ." But she needed wonder no more. The sprite leaned forward and, showing surprising strength for its size, tugged at the collar and rope until the hound was free of them.

"He doesn't need these," it said, shoving them at Hans. Standing beside the animal, the sprite came barely up to its shoulder, but as it leaned into the hound's furriness it was plain to see that the two were a good match, both misfits and misunderstood, both creatures bound to the sea, both in need of a friend. The sprite started to flit off, the mer-hund happily padding after it. Gretel was pleased to see such a satisfactory solution found, but she was aware of a strangled sob from her brother. To her surprise, the sea sprite stopped, turned, and called back to Hans, "Don't worry. I'll look after him." And then the curious pair moved on and were soon lost to view among the sails and rigging and bollards and such like that littered the deck.

❉

A week of steady and testing travel south, and at last they were in sight of the tiny town of Gesternstadt. Gretel experienced, as she always did on returning, a mixture of relief—for here was home, hearth, rest, safety—and disappointment, that she should live her life in so provincial and insignificant a place.

Hans's reaction was simpler.

"We are home, sister mine! We are home, hurrah! Best bit of going away, I always say, the coming back. Don't you think?"

They were set down from the stagecoach outside their little house, which had changed not one jot in their absence. Hans insisted she help him inside with the luggage, so that it was another tiring half hour before she sat on her beloved daybed, a pile of mail and parcels on her lap. Hans fetched a bottle of schnapps and the biscuit barrel. Most of the letters were bills, chiefly from dressmakers and tailors, or notes of little interest. What was intriguing was a heavy square parcel, carefully wrapped and packaged. Gretel shook it gently but could discern no clue as to its contents, save for a faint and not particularly pleasant odor.

"What have you there, Gretel?"

"I shan't know until I open it," she told him.

She undid the string and cautiously peeled off the brown wrapping paper.

"Hell's teeth!" she exclaimed, reeling backward.

"I say! Gretel, what a stink!"

Holding her breath, she opened the box. Inside there were a note and a jar. She read the brief lines.

"Who is it from?" Hans wanted to know.

"A widow. The wife of a sorcerer who has recently met a violent and untimely end."

"Murder, you mean!"

"It would seem so. It says here that the kingsmen are baffled and clues are scant. The grieving widow asks that I make all haste to find her husband's killer and bring him to justice."

"Another case! Well, you are in demand. Plenty of business coming your way now. Can't complain at that, can you?"

Gretel felt that she would like to complain very much. She had just spent a long, tedious, bottom-numbing journey, dreaming of days lounging on her comfy daybed and nestling into her silk bolsters, imagining being fed restorative and reviving snacks by Hans. She had hoped for a little respite, a little peace and quiet, a little tranquility and pampering. All the same, it was gratifying to find her services in such demand. And the tone of desperation in the note suggested a client on the edge, and in her experience, such clients could easily be persuaded that the only way to be pulled back from the brink of the abyss was to invest in Gretel's expertise. Heavily.

Gingerly, she lifted the jar from the box and held it up to the light. It contained a cloudy yellow liquid, in which floated something small, shriveled, and pink.

Hans recoiled at the sight of it. "Great heavens, sister mine, what is that?"

Gretel glanced at the letter again and then back at the contents of the jar, her eyebrows raised. "This is just about all we have to work with. The only clue left to us. This, brother dear, is the sorcerer's appendix."

※

And so, as one case closes, another springs open . . .